LOVE YOU MADLY

Alex George worked as a lawyer for eight years before becoming a full-time writer. He lives in London with his wife and son. This is his third novel. For more information visit his website at **www.alexgeorge.co.uk**.

ALSO BY ALEX GEORGE

Working it Out
Before Your Very Eyes

ALEX GEORGE

LOVE YOU MADLY

HarperCollins*Publishers*

HarperCollins*Publishers*
77–85 Fulham Palace Road,
Hammersmith, London w6 8jb

www.**fire**and**water**.com

A Paperback Original 2002
1 3 5 7 9 8 6 4 2

A catalogue record for this book
is available from the British Library

ISBN 0 00 711795 7

Typeset in Perpetua by Palimpsest Book Production Limited,
Polmont, Stirlingshire

Printed and bound in Great Britain by
Clays Ltd, St Ives plc

www.loveyoumadly.net

For Hallam

O, beware, my lord, of jealousy!
It is the green-eyed monster, which doth mock
The meat it feeds on.

William Shakespeare,
Othello, Act III, Scene 3

As the rubber-clad temptress bent down to pick up her whip, Ivo opened his eyes, startled like a grazing fawn at the sound of distant gunfire. He felt a pang of irrepressible longing. He would do anything to stop the ten inch heels of her patent leather boots treading on anyone but him. Suddenly Ivo felt a constriction in his throat. Was this jealousy he was feeling? Or merely a tightening of the noose?

Matthew Moore,
Licked

Ladies and gentlemen, we *do* love you madly.

Duke Ellington

PART ONE

I gaze at the solitary stalagmite of calcified chewing gum six inches in front of my face and wonder whether this was such a good idea.

The column of gum sprouts incongruously out of the carpet, a tiny grey phallus. Nearby lie two chocolate-covered raisins, an old Fruit Pastille, and a sprinkling of spilled popcorn. The carpet rubs against my cheek as I contemplate this eclectic menu.

When the lights finally go down, I gingerly pull myself up from my hiding place on the floor, and sink silently into my seat. A stark, sombre chord echoes through the cinema, and the dirty wooden sign materialises on the screen, barely legible in the half-light: *No Trespassing*. The ghostly silhouette of Xanadu emerges from the fog as the music rises to a strident crescendo. Then those famous lips fill the screen and whisper their anguished elegy to a lost childhood. *Rosebud*.

As the film's opening images crash on to the screen, instead of the usual shiver of delightful anticipation, I feel nothing but cold, gnawing anxiety.

Upturned empty seats stretch out on either side of me,

easy escape routes in both directions. The auditorium is almost deserted. I watch the solitary figure ten rows ahead of me. My wife's arm stretches into the carton between her knees as she rhythmically shovels handfuls of yellow popcorn into her mouth. I gaze at her flickering silhouette.

What is she doing here?

I was introduced to the delights of *Citizen Kane* on my first date with Anna, while we were still at university. She didn't suspect then that we would eventually marry and do all that happy-ever-after stuff. (Me, I knew. I'd already known for months.) Anna was a big film buff back then, and she told me, half serious, that she couldn't go out with anyone who didn't love Orson Welles. I nervously confessed that I'd never seen any of his films. Shocked, she insisted on taking me to see *Citizen Kane*, which was showing in a small repertory cinema in north Oxford. I agreed, blinking in disbelief: this girl had even spared me the anguish of asking her out, that ritual dance with the spectre of impending humiliation.

After the film, I lavished extravagant praise on its radical camera angles, the playful chronology, the myriad techniques which Welles had borrowed from his earlier experiments in radio. This spontaneous and instinctive criticism was delivered in a breathless, hurried monologue, and poached verbatim from a film guide that I had anxiously studied that afternoon in Blackwells. It didn't fool Anna for a moment, of course, but something about the nervy *chutzpah* of my performance persuaded her to accept my dry-mouthed invitation to dinner later that week.

Once she had decided that I was going to be worth the

effort, Anna launched me on a crash-course in film history. She dragged me to countless screenings of old films, all fabulously obscure and exotically subtitled. I went along in a haze of ecstatic bewilderment. We could have been watching paint dry, for all I cared; I just wanted to be with her.

Still, I paid attention. After a few months, I was able to spot abstruse cinematic references at fifty paces, with one eye on the screen and one hand down Anna's knickers. I could distinguish Kurosawa from Kubrick, Peckinpah from Polanski. But I still loved *Citizen Kane* the most. Its story of a vain, lonely man in search of love pinned me back in my seat every time. And, of course, it was the flame that first welded our lives together.

I watch Anna as she impassively guzzles popcorn, her face tilted towards the screen like a flower to the sun. By now I thought I would be shadowing her through the infernal misery of an Oxford Street Saturday afternoon. But when she left the flat, rather than turning towards the Tube station, she strode purposefully in the direction of Haverstock Hill. She arrived in front of the cinema exactly ten minutes before the film was due to begin, and stepped inside without a moment's hesitation. It was all too neat to be a coincidence, too convenient to be excused as a sudden change of plan. Besides, Anna is hardly the impulsive type. Which means that her story about the shopping trip was a considered, deliberate lie.

Suspicion and fear cloud my thoughts.

This was a mistake. I should not be here. Forgive me my trespass.

But what's done is done: the past slams shut behind us.

After an hour I slip quietly out of the cinema. As I walk back towards Camden in the winter sunshine, I try and assimilate what I have seen. Questions ricochet around my head. Why is Anna not shopping? What possible reason could she have to lie to me?

Back in the flat, my worries continue to smash into each other, causing a multiple pile-up at the front of my brain. I collapse on to the sofa, thinking black thoughts.

Today, of all days.

Anna arrives home at half past six. She kisses me on the cheek, and lights a cigarette.

I have changed into my smartest suit. Two days of carefully-monitored stubble lurks on my chin, roguishly subversive. Anna takes a step backwards and gazes at me critically, before letting out a low whistle of appreciation.

'Phwoar, bloody hell,' she squawks in her best Cockney.

'How was the shopping?' I ask stiffly.

There is a terrible pause as Anna crosses the sitting room. She calmly flicks her ash into the ashtray on the window sill and turns back towards me. 'Awful,' she says.

I stare at her. 'Awful? Awful how?'

Anna shrugs. 'Couldn't find anything I liked. That's all.' She gestures around her. 'Hence the lack of bulging bags.' She exhales a thin column of smoke, not looking at me.

There is no mention of *Citizen Kane*, no last-gasp confession. My wife is lying to me. 'Oh,' I say, stunned. 'I'm sorry.'

She waves a dismissive hand. 'It happens. No disaster. But I'm afraid I'll have to wear something old tonight.'

'You'll look wonderful anyway,' I reply, meaning it.

Anna smiles and kisses me on the cheek. 'Ah, Matthew, always the gallant husband. Bless you.' She grinds her cigarette out in the ashtray. 'Are you looking forward to the party?'

I *was*, I want to say.

'Yes, I think so. I'm a bit nervous.'

'Don't be. You deserve to enjoy it. It's not every day you get to celebrate the publication of your first book.'

I look at her, my heart cracking. 'I suppose not.'

'So what have you been up to this afternoon?' asks Anna as she walks into the bedroom, pulling off her top as she goes.

'Oh.' I stare at the floor. 'Nothing much.'

She takes a dress out of the wardrobe and holds it up to her body. 'What do you think? Will this do? Suitably literary for you?'

I look at my wife with anxious longing. 'It's perfect.'

Anna grins, pleased. She puts the dress on the bed and sits down at her dressing table in her underwear, as unselfconscious as a child. She leans towards the mirror, scrutinising her face. I always enjoy watching Anna put on her make-up. She becomes wholly engrossed in these minute manoeuvres – an eyelash curled, a lip discreetly contoured. There is a touching innocence to these focused moments. As she prepares her mask, her defences momentarily come down.

I am still paralysed by Anna's deception. 'Where did you go on your shopping expedition, then?' I ask.

'Oxford Street, mainly,' she murmurs through one side of her mouth. 'The shops were full of terribly dull autumn stuff. And *unbelievable* crowds. Truly staggering, the number of people. Very few of whom were English.' She rummages in her make-up tray and extracts a small but lethal-looking multi-pronged device. 'I had to give directions to a Japanese couple who were looking for the South Bank Centre. Christ knows how they got quite so lost.' I stare at her. She's even gone to the trouble of inventing a small story for added effect. This embellishment, this arch adornment of the lie, torments me. God, I think, it's so easy for her. She lies so *well*.

Anna swivels to face me and pouts. 'What do you think?' she asks. 'Am I gorgeous?'

Is she gorgeous? Anna still renders me speechless on occasion. Gorgeous doesn't do her justice. She's exquisite. She's stunning. Thirteen years in, she still makes my heart do back flips.

'You'll do,' I say.

She smiles. 'Actually,' she announces, 'I have a special treat for you.' She leans forward and pulls open the top drawer of her dresser. 'Look what I've got.' Between her thumb and forefinger she is brandishing a fat, tightly wrapped joint, crowned by a deft twist of Rizla paper. She waves the cigarette at me. 'Shall we?'

Anna seems utterly unencumbered by her lies. Well, fine. If it's not going to bother her, I won't let it bother me. Not tonight, at any rate. I try a small grin. 'Why not?'

I follow her out of the bedroom.

Tonight is the launch party to celebrate the publication of my novel, *Licked*.

I have sweated blood over that book. It has taken me three and a half years to write. *Licked* is part paean, part eulogy, part threnody. It celebrates and mourns the passing of youth's innocence. It unsparingly charts the descent into the emotional detritus of tarnished middle-age. Using as a central leitmotif my own schoolboy experiences of stamp collecting, the novel's principal character, Ivo, chooses to retreat into the rarefied, musty world of philately rather than confront the harsh brutalities of life. His stamps, which he cares for like precious, exotic butterflies, are a wonderfully profound metaphor for love. Or, rather, Love. They are beyond price, yet worthless; beautiful, yet useless. The book is funny, sad, gentle, acerbic, enriching, and devastating.

Now, after years of wandering through bookshops, glancing longingly at what I have come to regard as *my* bit of shelf space between Nancy Mitford and Iris Murdoch, *Licked* is about to be published. It has taken me, in total, twelve years and five unpublished novels, but I am finally going to be able to call myself a *writer*. Henceforth I shall be Matthew Moore, purveyor of literary pearls.

I have dreamt of tonight's party, my introduction to London's literary scene, on every day of those last twelve years. Those dreams have sustained me as I ploughed my lonely furrow through the dark times, when I was annihilated by creative exhaustion, when the well of inspiration ran dry. This evening represents the triumphant culmination of all of those years of solitary work, the apotheosis of more than a decade of determined grind.

So why did Anna have to start lying to me *today*?

Twenty minutes later, the doorbell rings. I open the door and Sean, my literary agent, sweeps into the flat, waving a bottle of champagne at me as he goes.

'So,' he shouts as he walks past me into the kitchen, 'the big day has finally dawned.' He puts the bottle of champagne down on the table. 'I thought we should start the evening off with a bang. Begin as you mean to go on. Get off on the right foot. It's time for you to turn over a new leaf, Matthew. This is the beginning of a new dawn for you. All your Christmases have come at once.' Sean turns to look at me with a messianic intensity. 'It's time for you to step up to the plate, walk into the spotlight, knock their socks off. Are you ready to be the toast of the town?'

I lean against the kitchen wall, dazed by the linguistic roadkill that Sean employs instead of conversation. I can feel my spirit being crushed beneath the weight of all those mangled metaphors. 'Hi, Sean,' I say.

Sean flaps a flamboyant hand at me in greeting and carries on. 'Are you ready to take the bull by the horns, Matthew? Prepared to grasp the thistle in both hands? Are you set to take the plunge?' He looks around him. 'Where are your glasses?'

'I'll get them for you.' I open a cupboard and pull out three champagne flutes.

Anna walks into the kitchen. 'Hi, Sean,' she says.

'Hello, *gorgeous*,' says Sean. 'You look like a million dollars.' There is a brief pause as Sean opens the champagne and pours us each a glass. 'A toast, then,' he says solemnly. He raises his glass towards me. 'To Matthew, and his exciting career. Here's to literary superstardom. And, of course, to *Licked* itself – the steamiest, sexiest novel about stamp collecting ever written. Cheers.'

We drink. I let the bubbles pop against the back of my throat. 'Thanks, Sean,' I say.

Sean tilts his head to one side and gazes at me. 'I mean it,' he says. 'Soon everyone will be talking about you. The word will spread like wildfire. Your ears will be burning.' He smiles as he drinks his champagne. 'Everyone will want a piece of you. They'll be after you ten to the dozen, as quick as a flash, faster than the speed of light.'

'Well, I hope so,' I say. Sean is one of the most successful literary agents in the country. His client list reads like a *Who's Who* of famous and successful authors. I've never been quite sure why he agreed to represent me. Perhaps I am a speculative play for future greatness. Perhaps I am a tax loss. I haven't dared to ask.

Our earlier joint was, in retrospect, a mistake. It has relaxed Anna: she giggles as she chases it down with champagne. I, on the other hand, have become edgy. The fringes of my consciousness have become tinged with a hyper-real buzz. I know the relentless nudge of paranoia is not far behind.

Fired up by Sean's infectious enthusiasm, my excitement at the approaching party grows. I know that I'm fortunate to be having a launch party at all. Neville Spencer, my publisher, doesn't believe in them. Launch parties, he told me, are despicable, shallow affairs, an endless self-congratulatory gravy train of free booze and cliquey back-slapping. Exactly, I replied, that's why I want one. After hours of squabbling, Neville finally conceded, with considerable bad grace, and promised to look after everything. I just have to turn up. The venue he has chosen is in Shoreditch (sufficiently modish, I feel), and is called *Il Cavallo Bianco*, which sounds perfect. As I quaff the champagne, I wonder who has been invited. Industry big-shots, journalists, perhaps a celebrity or two. I have been practising my lines, trying to perfect the sort of self-deprecating modesty that every author on the verge of greatness should aspire to.

Anna looks perfect in her dress, a dramatic, dark red thing, very Daphne du Maurier. She is wearing a shawl over her shoulders to protect against the November chill. We quickly finish the bottle of champagne and go outside to look for a taxi. Half an hour later, we arrive at the address Neville has given me.

'Some mistake, surely,' says Sean.

I check my piece of paper with the address on it. 'This is right, I'm sure.'

We are standing in front of a dirty, modern pub, within gobbing distance of the concrete outposts of a vast, graffiti-strewn housing estate. A streak of neon flickers in the grimy window and tattered pennants hang limply over the door. A blackboard on the pavement announces 'EXOTIC DANCEING LUNCHTIMES'.

'What did Neville say the name of the place was?' asks Anna.

'*Il Cavallo Bianco*.' I look around me. 'It must be near here somewhere.'

Anna nudges me in the ribs. 'This is it,' she says. She points to the mock gold letters on the pub's frontage. 'The

White Horse,' she says. 'Or *Il Cavallo Bianco*, if you happen to be Italian.'

'Oh, bollocks,' I mutter.

'I think Neville's been having a little joke with you,' observes Anna.

There is a pause. 'Well,' I say, gesturing towards the front door. 'Shall we?'

Inside the pub, Neville and his wife Patricia are standing by the bar, drinking half pints of lager. Together, they make a peculiar sight. Patricia is extremely tall. Neville, on the other hand, is very short.

Fed up with the crass commercialism of the British publishing industry, six years ago Neville Spencer established his own publishing house, Wellington Press – named in honour of the Iron Duke's famous riposte to a blackmailer to publish and be damned. Coincidentally, Wellington's exhortation is also a cogent description of Neville's business practice. Everybody hates him. He is fractious, aggressive, and truculent. His antagonistic, curve ball approach to the business of selling books has publishing wallahs throughout London shuddering over their gins and tonics.

Neville, though, is unique in the publishing industry, because he's actually interested in *books*. Sales figures and business plans, by contrast, are anathema to him. The suggestion that one should even *try* and make money out of selling books produces torrents of foul-mouthed invective. Over the years Neville has developed his own skewed criteria for measuring success. He is, basically, an incorrigible snob. He believes that there is an inverse correlation between a book's popularity and its artistic significance. For him, obscurity is the thing. He relishes the esoteric, he celebrates the arcane. He wallows exultantly in the failure of his books to sell a single copy.

Of course, I relish the fact that I'm being published by a small, cutting-edge publishing house. It gives me instant cachet, immediate, ready-to-wear literary spurs. But there are times when I wish that Wellington Press wasn't *quite* so cutting edge. It would be nice, for example, if Neville was at least on nodding terms with the concept of a marketing budget. As it is, his idiosyncratic approach doesn't help me earn much of a living. There would be no chance of earning out my advance if it wasn't so very, very small.

Neville and Patricia appear to be the only people in the pub. Quite how Neville has managed to find such an unprepossessing place for a party is beyond me. It has all the cosy warmth and charm of a vandalised Portakabin. The room is harshly lit by naked bulbs dangling from the puke-coloured ceiling. In one corner is a small raised platform with coloured lights dotted around its periphery, presumably the venue for the lunchtime strippers. Two battered speakers are bracketed high up on the wall; cobwebs dangle from them like discarded underwear. Immediately in front of the stage is a carpet of cigarette ends, a legacy from this afternoon's crowd. It seems that the punters like to get up close for a good view.

We approach the bar. 'Hi, Neville,' I say. '*Il Cavallo Bianco*, eh? Very funny.'

Neville smiles thinly. 'Yes, well. You have to let me have my little laugh.'

'Indeed,' I say, wondering why Neville's little laughs always have to be at my expense. 'So, what, have you booked this place out for the evening?'

'You're joking,' he says. 'No need. It's always empty. Even on a Saturday.'

'Ah.' My spirits sink a little lower. I turn to survey the rest of the pub, and see that in fact we are not quite alone. In one corner, two skinheads are slumped over a table. A scrawny dog lies asleep on the floor next to them. 'Clever old you,' I say.

'You know Patricia, don't you?' says Neville.

Indeed I do.

Patricia Spencer is the reason why Neville can afford to indulge in his financially suicidal publishing venture. She is one of the bestselling novelists in the country, and vastly rich. Under the sobriquet of Candida Divine, she churns out nineteenth-century sagas of deprived childhoods in Northern industrial towns. Her novels all have the same poor-girl-conquers-impossible-odds-to-fulfil-her-hith-erto-mocked-childhood-ambition-and-then-finds-True-Love-only-to-have-it-cruelly-snatched-away-two-chapters-from-the-end plot. Her stories have an astronomically high mortality rate: the characters are ruthlessly killed off to boost the Kleenex count. It's drivel. And what the millions of readers who avidly devour her books don't know is that Candida Divine, whose ear for regional accents has been heralded as 'ringingly authentic' by the *Daily Telegraph*, arrived in Britain from Jamaica when she was five years old.

Patricia Spencer makes Grace Jones look like an under-nourished pussycat. She towers over most men, myself included. Her pneumatic body is all sleek muscles and well-toned limbs. She has a long, swan-like neck. Her head is shaven. She has big white teeth, which she flashes occa-sionally from within her large, luxurious brown lips. She possesses an untouchable, ineffable elegance, and moves with impossible grace.

She's the most terrifying woman I've ever met.

Obviously, I fancy the pants off her.

'Hi, Patricia,' I say, standing on tiptoe to kiss her cheek. She has an exotic, feral scent. I inhale deeply while I'm up there.

'Matt. And Anna. How nice.' Patricia looks down at us and smiles. I stand there and grin stupidly.

Sean walks up to Neville and pumps his hand with gusto. Neville's distaste is obvious to everyone, except Sean. In Neville's opinion, agents are the equivalent of amoeba in the literary food chain. Parasitic amoeba, at that. Not that Sean is at the *bottom* of the food chain, though. No: that place is reserved for me. As an author, I'm little more than a necessary inconvenience to the whole process of publishing books, an unavoidable irritant, like the maiden aunt who must be invited to family get-togethers but who always drinks too much sherry and ends up complaining about her haemorrhoids. That's me. I am that pissed, pile-plagued spinster.

'I suppose you all want a drink,' says Neville sourly.

'That would be great,' I say. Anna and Sean nod.

'Well, there's the bar,' replies Neville, pointing.

'Right,' I laugh.

I wait.

'I'll have a pint, if you're buying,' says Neville.

With a disbelieving sigh, I extract my wallet. As I distribute the drinks a few minutes later, I ask, 'So Neville, who else is coming to this bash, then? Journalists? Booksellers? Any celebs?'

Neville snorts. 'Do me a fucking favour,' he says. 'That lot? *Parasites.*'

'Who *have* you invited?' asks Sean.

'Well, all of you, obviously.' Neville calmly takes a sip of his drink.

'That's it?' I say, dismayed.

'That's it.'

'Oh.' I pause. 'Did you bring some books along?'

Neville looks at me oddly. 'Now why would I want to do that?'

I hesitate. 'It's just that, I don't know, a book launch without any actual *books* seems a bit peculiar.'

'Well, I'm *very* sorry, Matthew,' says Neville sardonically. 'No books.'

There is an awkward pause.

'This is certainly less run-of-the-mill than most book launches I've been to,' remarks Sean doubtfully. 'I love it, though. It's gritty. It's real. It has a certain *je ne sais quoi*.'

'It's a disaster, is what it is,' I retort.

'A working launch,' suggests Anna.

'Ha ha,' I say, unamused.

'We're all out to launch,' says Anna.

'All right, sweetheart,' I say.

Anna points at Patricia, then at herself. 'We're ladies who launch.'

Now Sean decides to join in.

'There's no such thing as a free launch,' he says, looking *very* pleased with himself.

'For fuck's sake,' I mutter.

'Anyway, cheers,' says Neville ill-naturedly. 'Here's to *Licked*.'

'Hear, hear,' agrees Sean. 'Congratulations on publication.'

'Thanks very much,' I mumble.

'Yes, well,' says Neville.

We lapse into silence.

'So, yeah, anyway,' says Sean. 'I just *love* the book.'

I look at him. He hasn't read a word of it, I know. 'Really,' I say.

To my surprise, Neville agrees. 'Me too,' he declares. 'It's like, what, Anaïs Nin meets Stanley Gibbons.'

I look at him quizzically. 'You think?'

'Definitely.' Neville takes a swig of beer. 'Nobody else has published anything like it. Whatever else it may be, it's different.'

'Thanks,' I say uncertainly.

'And November's a *great* time to be published,' enthuses Sean. 'The book will be in the shops well in time for Christmas.'

At the thought of Christmas and its attendant retail excesses, Neville shudders visibly. We stand about chatting in a desultory way. Anna listens to the rest of us talk, languidly smoking. In the absence of anything better to do, we all begin drinking too much.

'Excuse me a moment,' says Anna after a while. 'I'm off for a pee.' As she leaves, I turn my attention to Patricia, who is telling us of the squabbles between three Hollywood starlets, who each want to play the lead in the forthcoming film adaptation of one of her books. The story is met with amusement by Sean and Neville, but I am so overcome with bitterness that I can barely muster a smile. Waves of bilious jealousy froth within me. Hollywood? I don't even have any bloody *books* at my book launch.

Some time later, Anna has still not returned. My mind drifts as I begin to wonder what could possibly be taking her so long. Suddenly this afternoon's worries crowd back in on me again. Why did Anna lie to me about her shopping trip? What is she trying to *hide*? Before long I can no longer ignore the relentless prod of my suspicions. With a mumbled excuse I break off from the group and go in search of her, fearful that I might be missing something – what, I do not know.

I go to the back of the pub. In front of the women's toilets, I hover uncertainly, wondering what to do next. I can't very well just barge in. The thought of Anna's clandestine trip to the cinema this afternoon needles me insistently. I am paralysed by indecision. My spirits, astonishingly, contrive to dip even lower than they already were.

'Hello,' says Patricia into my ear.

I spin round. 'Patricia,' I gasp.

Patricia eyes me with interest. 'What are you doing out here?' she asks, pointing at the door to the ladies' lavatory. She smiles. I stare at her big teeth.

'Ah.' My mind goes blank. 'Actually, I'm glad you're here. I wanted to ask you a question.'

She folds her arms across her chest. 'Be my guest.'

I stare at her, unable to formulate a thought. Then, inspiration strikes. 'It's about your name. That is, your pen name. Your pseudonym. Your, um, nom de plume.'

'What about it?'

'Well, I've always wondered. Of all the thousands of names you could have chosen, why did you go for Candida?' I swallow. 'Was there, you know, a *reason* for naming yourself after a fungal infection?' I attempt a look of serious enquiry.

Patricia draws herself up to her full height and looks down at me through her melting dark eyes.

'I *beg* your pardon?' she says.

To my relief, the door to the toilet opens and Anna comes out. 'Look, don't worry,' I say hastily. 'Wasn't important.'

Anna sees me and smiles. '*Hi*.'

'Anna,' I breathe. 'There you are.'

'I think I'll just –' says Patricia, frowning. She turns and pushes open the door to the lavatory.

I wave weakly at her disappearing back.

'What are you doing out here?' asks Anna, slipping her arm through mine and giving me a squeeze.

'I, er, oh, just chatting with Patricia.'

'Well, come on,' says Anna. 'Let's get back to the party. We're missing all the fun.'

'OK,' I say, my nerves electric.

The rest of the evening passes without further incident. There are no big scenes, no dramas of note. Anna and I finally fall into a cab at about eleven o'clock. As I sit next to her, watching her laugh, I feel myself torn in two. I don't want this moment to end. I want to stay within the cocoon of this taxi and keep the outside world at bay. This is all right; this will do just fine. But the journey will end, this moment of sanctuary will pass, and then I will have to square up to my wife's lies.

Anna chats on, unaware of my anxiety, pulling on a cigarette. Her shawl slips as she talks, revealing a bare shoulder, vulnerable in its nakedness. I hold her hand, and watch her talk.

Anna and I have been married for five years. We lived together in glorious, highly enjoyable sin for six years before that, and dated each other for two years before *that*. A grand total of thirteen years, so far. We have gently graduated from each stage of togetherness to the next, merging our lives in new levels of delicious interconnectedness. There were the obvious things – our paperbacks mingling together on the bookshelf, the joint bank account – but the real intertwining took place in a more private sphere: the reassuring warmth of our collective history, a mutual repository of memories; each other's favourite jokes fondly tolerated; the solace of shared values; the bliss of unreserved intimacy.

After we left university, we got a place together in London. While Anna spent her days at law school, I did the housework and worked on the first of my five abysmal, unpublished novels. We had only just enough money to survive, but we were young, and in love. We didn't need much, except each other.

While I remained at home, still seeking the elusive formula for that critically-acclaimed-yet-phenomenally-successful first novel, Anna began her job in a large City

23

law firm. Ten years on, she's still there. She specialises in non-contentious corporate work, which consists of an apparently never-ending list of gnomic acronyms – M and A, HBOs, IPOs, and the rest. It baffles me how someone as sharp, funny, and quick-witted as Anna could have chosen to do something so excruciatingly boring. She's very good at her job, though, and has gradually climbed up (or down, depending on your opinion of lawyers) the slippery pole of her profession, determinedly working her way towards promotion to fat-cat partnership. Sometimes she even appears to *enjoy* it. And, in the final analysis, if she's happy, then I'm happy. After all, she's the one who's been putting bread on the table for all these years, and so it would be churlish of me to object to her career on aesthetic grounds.

My wife is the consummate professional, all snappy suits and ferocious work ethic. Together, we make a great team. That corporate pizzazz of hers is a perfect counterpoint to my flighty artistic temperament. She keeps my feet on the ground; I keep her eyes fixed on the stars. Anna's colleagues are all married to other lawyers, and my creative, bohemian lifestyle makes us an exotic pair in comparison. At dinner parties I am expected to *épater les bourgeois* and taunt these affluent contemporaries of mine – a task that I relish, due to my staggering inferiority complex about the size of their incomes and their obvious sense of professional fulfilment.

Anna has never complained about being the sole income provider in our household. In fact she loves it that I'm a writer. She has been unfailingly supportive and generous. It was Anna who picked me up each time the onslaught of publishers' letters came barrelling through the letterbox, rejecting my latest novel and smashing my confidence. It was Anna who cajoled me back to my typewriter, persuading me to try again. Without her, I would have given up years ago. She is my spine, my support system, as reliable as a mother's heartbeat.

Of course, we've had our moments. We're human, after all. We fight, like everyone else. My refusal to face up to some of life's more earthly realities frustrates her sometimes. And there have been occasions when she over-analyses things, which can act as a brake on spontaneity. But we do all right. We're each other's biggest fans. I am her hero. She is my life.

Now, I know that I'm one of the lucky ones. After all these years, I am still madly in love with my wife. I have adored her, worshipped her, idolised her, ever since we met. Since I first laid eyes on her, in fact. She is the only woman I have ever loved. She makes me breathless, giddy with the possibilities of life. Not everyone gets dealt the full hand, the love that changes your life for ever. But lucky, lucky me – I got the whole shooting match, the full kit and caboodle. I have felt the ecstasy of indescribable ardour, the delirium of true, deep romance.

But.

Just lately, something is not quite right.

It began with nothing more than a niggle, which I did my best to ignore. While I was looking the other way, though, the niggle quietly worked through my emotional defences, mutating as it did so into fully-fledged disquiet, and then took up residence, implacably unbudging, at the forefront of my brain, holding every idea hostage, souring every felicitous thought.

Here's the thing: Anna has changed.

It's nothing big. She hasn't grown horns. Indeed, the accumulated evidence is flimsy at best, perhaps nothing more than circumstantial. But I've become so attuned to her behavioural nuances that even the smallest deviation from the norm is grotesquely distorted through the prism of my expectations. Perhaps I am deluding myself. Maybe I'm seeing ghosts where there are merely shadows. Well, yes. Perhaps. But if you mistake a shadow for a ghost, you're still spooked. Anyway, my doubts are immune to logic; they mock reasoned analysis. They're simply there, wreaking their own poisonous brand of havoc.

So, to the naming of parts. Dissecting my paranoia item by item:

In conversation Anna used to latch on to an issue and rip into it mercilessly, analysing and arguing with her flawless, legally-trained logic. For her, intellectual stimulation was a matter of rigorous exercise rather than capricious whimsy. Every opinion, every assertion, had to be backed up and justified with rational and cogent arguments. No intellectual floppiness was tolerated. Talking to Anna was like cerebral boot camp.

But recently there has been an unmistakable change: Anna's head now seems to be lodged firmly in the clouds. She meanders carelessly from topic to topic, leaving matters unresolved, issues open. She often drifts off into wordless reverie halfway through a sentence, as if she has been distracted by a more diverting train of thought. After years of her unflagging intellectual rigour, this new approach is unnerving. It's as if a convoy of hippies has accidentally wandered into her brain and set up a commune there.

Next, we have perhaps the most frightening words in the English language: Gym Membership.

For Anna, sport and physical exercise have always been a boring irrelevance, a fatuous waste of time. She has never understood why I cherish my Arsenal season ticket so much. (I once made the mistake of asking her to the pub to watch an away game on the big screen. She didn't talk to me for two days afterwards, furious that I had ignored her completely for an hour and a half. I tried to explain: you go to watch, not to chat.) There's a neurone missing up there somewhere, a faulty connection: the excitement, the passion, the despair and the elation all just pass her by. And although I love football, I would never dream of playing myself. Dedicated and indolent smokers, Anna and I were united in our scornful rejection of any activity (except for the obvious) which required any physical exertion.

Suddenly, though, Anna has started going to the gym.

She arrived home one evening with a carrier bag from Lillywhites full of leotards and dazzlingly white trainers with soles as thick as telephone directories. She had decided, she announced, to treat her body with a bit more respect. She was spending too much time sitting behind her desk, letting her body go. I protested that her body hadn't gone anywhere – and indeed it hasn't. But her mind was already made up. Now she goes to a swanky gym near her office three times a week. She arrives home completely wiped out, but strangely elated, speaking in riddles about endorphins. I always thought that endorphins were small, grizzled creatures in *The Lord of the Rings*. I listen to her talk, and wonder what has prompted this madness.

The final piece to this rather hazy jigsaw is the abrupt change in Anna's musical taste. Or, to be more specific, the sudden advent of Anna's musical taste. She has never been particularly interested in listening to music. Instead, she listens to pop. And not just pop, but bad pop. Since the heyday of Take That she has had an unfathomable fondness for boy bands. You know the type. There are usually four or five pretty-looking boys, whose only apparent talent is the ability to walk moodily along a windswept beach. For some reason only one of them can ever actually sing, so he does all the work while the others prance about behind him in carefully choreographed ataxy. I have pointed out to Anna on numerous occasions that these manufactured bands are monstrously cynical exercises in the exploitation of the burgeoning libidos of prepubescent girls, and that someone of her age and intelligence should know better. Still, she can't resist the lure of Tower Records on Camden High Street every Saturday afternoon, where she will eagerly buy the latest offering of undiluted schmaltz from Ronny, Donny, and Johnny. And Brian. (There's always one called Brian.)

Well, all that has suddenly changed. Anna's Westlife CD has been consigned to the dusty racks of the unloved, and has been replaced by something which is actually (hard though this may be to imagine) far scarier.

It's bye-bye boys; hello Ravel.

Now, Ravel: 'Boléro', right? Torville and Dean. Dudley Moore and Bo Derek. Naff, pseudo-Spanish gimmickry. Well, yes. But this isn't 'Boléro'. This is something altogether different. Anna has brought home a recording of Ravel's piano trio. And it's beautiful, beguiling music — rich, compelling, and frightening beyond belief. Anna listens with a rapt, faraway look in her eyes which I do not recognise. As I watch her immerse herself in the music, new barriers silently erect themselves between us. I find

28

myself yearning for the bland awfulness of Anna's fabricated pop stars and their lovely teeth.

Regarded objectively, I'm aware that all of this may not seem like much, but the accumulation of these tiny changes has slowly been crowding in on me, messing with my head. All I really want is some reassurance. I need to know that none of this portends a more significant, more sinister change.

That's why, last week, I began to examine the contents of Anna's suit pockets.

My searches have revealed little so far: a receipt for a new pair of tights, a plastic toothpick, a chewed biro top. This bland innocuity whips me up into ever increasing spirals of anxiety, so I've also started to conduct jittery forays into Anna's handbag while she's in the bath. Her contented splashes almost make my heart stop as I delve into the bag's scented darkness, clumsily scattering peppermints and tampons in my quest for clues.

The lack of meaningful results from my surreptitious prying made me realise with an unpleasant jolt how little I know about what Anna actually does all day. Vast swathes of her life are hidden from view behind the grey façade of her office near Moorgate. Consequently I spent last Friday hovering on the street near where she works, waiting to see what would happen. Nothing did, of course. Anna didn't even leave the office for lunch. She eventually emerged, looking tired and drawn, at seven o'clock in the evening, and went straight home.

It was the frustration of that unenlightening experiment that prompted me to follow Anna on her purported shopping expedition on Saturday afternoon. Out in public, I reasoned, I would be able to observe her without interruption. There was nothing sinister about it, nothing untoward. I'm no deranged obsessive. (Anyway, I doubt whether it's technically possible to stalk your own wife.) I just wanted to observe Anna with her guard down. I wanted to see how she behaved without me around. That was all.

Of course, I wish I hadn't done it now. All of my worries have been compounded by Anna's purposeful stride towards the matinée showing of *Citizen Kane*, and her cool, deliberate lies.

Why did I not stay at home?

I am trapped, helplessly pinioned on the skewers of my own distrust. Worse, I don't even know what it is I should be worrying about: my emotional radar isn't sufficiently well-equipped to interpret all these alien signals. There's a little green dot flashing angrily on my screen, telling me that there's *something out there*, but I can't tell what it is.

Sometimes I wonder whether I want to know.

On Monday morning, when I wake up, I am alone in the bed.

I roll over and look at the alarm clock. It is just after nine o'clock. I stare at the ceiling for a few moments, then reluctantly pull back the duvet and stagger into the kitchen. On the table is a note.

Have a good Monday, darling. Hope the writing goes well. Please will you get some (lavender!) loo roll when you go shopping today? We're nearly out.

A

On weekdays Anna is always long gone by the time I wake up. Instead of a goodbye kiss every morning I receive one of these notes, which contain the occasional unsolicited endearment and (more regularly) gentle reminders of the chores that I, the doyen of house-husbandry, am expected to do each day.

Also on the kitchen table is an envelope with a lurid Australian stamp. It is a card from my parents – late as always – wishing me luck for the launch party. My mother has written a brief message inside the card, *Sorry we can't be with you on your special day*. I snort at this. They're not sorry in the slightest.

My parents had been living a quietly middle-aged life in the shallows of Hertfordshire until one Saturday evening four years ago, when their lives changed forever. My mother called me as soon as she had recovered her power of speech after she had watched her numbers roll out of the National Lottery machine. Six balls nestling alongside each other in a narrow Perspex tube: their passport away from Home Counties drudgery. They had to share their jackpot with four other winners, but still pocketed well over one and a half million quid. There was much celebration, not least by me. Two of the numbers that my mother always picked were based on my birthday, so I felt that I had a legitimate claim to some of the proceeds. Anyway, all parents would distribute at least a share of such a huge windfall to their nearest and dearest, wouldn't they?

Apparently not.

Within a week, my mother and father had put their house in Potters Bar on the market and had decided to move to Australia. I wasn't given a penny of their new-found fortune. It was explained to me that nowadays one and a half million pounds wasn't really *that* much, and that they couldn't afford to start giving handouts to all and sundry. I pointed out that, as their only child, it was arguably disingenuous to describe me as 'all and sundry', but my complaints fell on determinedly deaf ears.

My parents' new ambition is to annexe the world through their camera lens. They spend more time travelling than they do in their brand-new, architect-designed beach house just outside Perth. The only place they refuse to visit is England – too boring, apparently, my continued presence here notwithstanding. Whatever happened to growing old gracefully? They really shouldn't be having so much fun at their age, especially not as they're whittling away my inheritance in the process.

At least Mum and Dad have acknowledged that my novel has been published, which is more than can be said for my parents-in-law. There is nothing that Anna's father likes to do more than enumerate, at length, my many failings – particularly when I am within earshot. My greatest transgression is that I do not have a Proper Job. A Proper Job, in this context, is one that commands a basic annual salary in the middling six-figure range (that's excluding twice-yearly bonuses large enough to buy a Porsche or two) and requires a wardrobe full of pinstripe suits. My father-in-law thinks I'm little more than a parasite, greedily feeding off the fruits of his daughter's industry. He obviously has no idea how much effort goes into writing a novel. I had rather hoped that the publication of *Licked* would allay his misgivings, but both he and Anna's obnoxious mother have ignored it completely. There have been no polite enquiries, no words of congratulations, nothing but the icy silence of sour indifference.

Sometimes, I have to admit, I share Anna's parents' loathing of my job. There are occasions when I wish I had become an accountant instead, but my fate was writ large in the constellations, indelibly inscribed in the heavens by a celestial hand greater than my own. Ultimately, I was powerless to resist the sweet song of my Muse. I was put on this earth to write; and so write I must.

I began making up stories as a child. I would slave over these heavily derivative tales (one was called, 'The Tiger, the Wizard, and the Chest of Drawers') and would then solemnly recite them in front of my parents, who always applauded kindly (and doubtless with relief) when I finished. And this was the key: I loved being the centre of attention. That clapping was for *me*. The hubristic lure of approbation was what got me in the end. I was powerless to resist my all-consuming egotism.

But it's not all my fault. I also blame Ernest Hemingway. It was reading *A Moveable Feast*, his account of his life in Paris during the twenties, that made me think that being a writer would be an enjoyable way to earn a living. Hemingway, the lying bastard, made the writer's existence sound too alluring to resist. He cavorted around Paris with his glamorous chums, knocking out literary masterpieces in between drinking binges in the glittering bars of the Left Bank. I was captivated by his stories of ordering oysters and a bottle of white wine to celebrate the completion of a story. I wanted a slice of that carefree, bohemian existence.

(I did get a job, once. It was after my third unpublished effort, *Peeling the Grape*, had been met with the by then familiar chorus of indifference and hostility from thirty-five of the country's largest publishers. Crushed, I decided to give my self-esteem a break and resolved to abandon fiction completely. I had done my best; it was time to submit to the inevitable. Literature's loss was to be the advertising industry's gain. I sent my rather sparse CV – embellished with one or two half-truths and three or four outright whoppers – to a few advertising agencies. To my surprise, I managed to blag my way into a copywriting job in a small agency in Fitzrovia. It wasn't nearly as glamorous as I had anticipated; there was none of the coke-snorting excess amongst the creatives that I had always imagined. Instead people nervously sat at their desks, desperately trying to think of ways to persuade people to buy things that they didn't want. The atmosphere of paranoid terror quickly seeped into me by some sort of awful corporate osmosis. I began to lie awake at night, terrified that my creative juices would abandon me. In fact, released from the demanding, unforgiving shackles of writing fiction, my creativity blossomed. It was just a pity that the narrow-minded account executives couldn't see past the ends of their noses, which were buried in the lucrative feeding trough of bland conventionality. They weren't interested in my radical ideas. Personally, I thought that my use of some of Elizabeth Barrett Browning's *Sonnets from the Portuguese*, cleverly altered to praise a diabolical brand of versatile low-fat cream cheese ('How do I eat thee? Let me count the ways', etc.), was breathtakingly innovative. When I refused to come up with alternative ideas, they sacked me on the spot. I went back to my typewriter, weeping with relief. The experiment had lasted three and a half weeks.)

The irony is that now I sometimes think that I would love an ordinary, boring job again. All this freedom is getting me down. Hours, days, and weeks stretch ahead of me, oppressive in their emptiness. The ordered structure of a nine-to-five existence would give me a solid framework for my life, a means of regulating the chaos. I would dearly love to be told where to put my pencil-sharpener; I yearn for a militantly officious boss. As it is, the only taskmaster I have is me, and I am a workshy dilettante at the best of times. I have the worst of both worlds. I don't get any work done, and have nobody but myself to blame.

Another long day looms.

I go into the sitting room, and turn on the record player. The needle lands softly on the rotating vinyl, and after a moment —

Bam! The pitch-perfect trumpets punch out the jumped-up tune, the saxophones gliding smoothly beneath them. This is 'Cotton Tail', ladies and gentlemen, performed by the Duke Ellington Orchestra, the greatest jazz band in the world. Here comes the warm tenor sax of Ben Webster, rocking gently through his solo, prancing over the band's tightly syncopated chords. Duke's piano gets a few rollicking bars, and then the seamless sax section takes up the charge, followed by the swinging trumpets, spiralling ever higher.

I shut my eyes. This is the spiritual equivalent of brushing my teeth. The music leaves my soul refreshed and protected against decay. I sit on the floor, next to the speakers, and wallow in the rich symphony of jazzed horn lines which spill into the room.

Edward Kennedy Ellington, the Duke, that grand old aristocrat of jazz, was one of the music's true pioneers. From his beginnings as a dapper and debonair band leader in 1920s Harlem, he became the friend of royalty and presidents, loved and admired the world over. He toured tirelessly throughout his career, spreading his own brand of syncopated happiness, dazzling audiences everywhere with his exciting rhythms, his unforgettable tunes, and his suave showmanship. He loved us madly – and his gift to the world was his music. Now jazz, of course, is meant to be the quintessence of cool. It's about tortured genius, complex chord structures, jarring time-signatures. It's about squalling saxophone solos, smoky subterranean joints, and sultry, mysterious women. Duke was as hip as they came, but this isn't just music to smoke to. It's music to dance to, as well. I have pulled Anna around this room many times, laughing and twirling to the band's upbeat tempos.

As the music plays on, I survey the spines of my record collection. I own yards of Ellington records, neatly arranged on their shelves. I have LPs, EPs, battered 78s, reissues, and foreign imports, from the pristine and unplayed to the almost unplayable. I love them all dearly. They are the proud result of fifteen years' trawling through the dusty racks of second-hand record shops, hours spent hunched over acres of old cardboard. I still spend days arranging and rearranging my records. I love the endless cycle of processing and regulation: marshalling my Duke Ellington collection allows me to impose my own brand of order in at least one small corner of this otherwise uncontrollable world.

I own almost every note that Duke ever recorded, but there's one performance that I still dream about. Here's the story. Billy Strayhorn, Ellington's enigmatic collaborator and co-songwriter, dies on 31 May 1967 – finally claimed by cancer. Duke is devastated. He's lost his crutch, his right-hand man, his creative pivot. Three months after his death, the Ellington Orchestra assembles in RCA Victor Studio 'A' in Manhattan to record a tribute album of Strayhorn compositions. At the end of the second day of the session, while the rest of the band are packing up and getting ready to go home, Duke sits at the piano and, unaccompanied, plays a tender Strayhorn tune, 'Lotus Blossom'. It is Duke's personal tribute to a man he loved deeply.

That much we all know. It's after this that the myth begins:

As the studio empties, Duke remains at the piano, staring at the keys, alone with his memories. He's an old man, now. Still dapper, still elegant, but tired after a lifetime of hard graft and sacrifice. Ellington turns and faces his loss – and starts to play the blues. Tune after tune, the piano cries a sad song of loss and heartache. The wistful, tender lyricism of this final, intimate salute is unbearably poignant. He plays seven or eight laments, quietly closes the piano lid, and shuffles home.

Unknown to Duke, one man has remained in the engineering booth throughout, and has quietly switched on the tape to capture the impromptu performance. The engineer, a young Italian called Alessandro Ponti, has a string of gambling debts to his name that he is unable to pay. He spirits away the illicit tape, his eye on a quick profit and an end to his financial troubles. Some test acetate pressings are produced before Ponti loses his nerve and decides to destroy the master tape. But by that time the acetate pressings are already in circulation, and *they are still out there somewhere*.

That, at any rate, is the story.

Since then, the fate of those lost recordings has inspired decades of obsessive speculation and wishful rumours. For Ellington enthusiasts, those acetate pressings are our Loch Ness Monster, our Holy Grail. Nobody even knows if they really exist or not. I still cannot resist scouring the second-hand record racks in the hope that one of the pressings will magically appear at my fingertips.

I climb into the shower, whistling a medley of Ellington tunes. A few minutes later, as I am drying myself (by way of indolent rub, rather than the efficient, chafingly vigorous towel-work that Anna favours) I notice three virgin rolls of lavender loo paper in the wicker basket next to the toilet. This is what Anna calls 'nearly out'? I cannot think of any disaster – global, domestic, or intestinal – that could possibly put our present reserves of toilet paper under immediate threat, but Anna suffers from that exclusively female psychosis whereby she gets twitchy if we have less than a quarter of a mile of readily available bog roll.

By the time I have washed and dressed, it is almost ten o'clock. With a knot in my stomach, I put on my coat and walk to our local bookshop.

As I stand in the doorway of the shop, I take a couple of deep breaths. I want to be poised, calm, so that I will remember this moment. I've been into this bookshop hundreds of times, but this morning is different. *Licked* is officially published today. My role has changed. I'm no longer just another browser. From now on I shall be part of the *stock*. I shall be a commodity. I shall be a browsee.

Inside, there are only one or two customers nosing about. Behind the main desk stand two scruffy individuals in shapeless jumpers. I wander up to the New Releases table. *Licked* isn't there. I inspect the Bestsellers table. Finally I walk over to my bit of shelf between Nancy and Iris. Then I go over to the desk.

'Do you have a novel by Matthew Moore?' I ask. 'It's called *Licked*.'

One of the assistants pulls a face. 'Matthew Moore? Doesn't ring a bell.'

I smile thinly at him. 'I think it's quite new.'

The man turns to his colleague. 'Declan. You ever heard of a Matthew Moore?'

The other man wrinkles his nose. 'Nah.'

I put my hands deep in my pockets. 'Could you check?'

'Hold on.' The first assistant taps at the computer keyboard on the desk, and peers at the screen. 'Let me see. Here we are. Moore, M. *Licked*. Wellington Press.'

'That's it,' I say eagerly.

'It's actually published today,' the man tells me.

'Oh,' I say. '*Right*.'

There is a pause.

'So have you got any?' I ask.

'No.'

'Oh.' Deflation beckons. 'Have you got some on order?'

The man peers at his screen again. 'No.'

'Are you going to order some?'

'No.'

I think. 'Can *I* order one?'

'I suppose so,' says the man reluctantly.

'Right,' I say. 'I'll do that, then.'

'Who are Wellington Press, anyway?' asks the man. 'I've never heard of them.'

'Me neither,' agrees Declan, yawning.

Neville, I reflect ruefully, would be delighted.

'It's just that I heard that this book was absolutely brilliant,' I say.

The first man looks doubtful. 'What's your name?' he asks.

I stare at him, dumbstruck. I can't admit who I really am. It would be too embarrassing. And lying would be too desperate, too sad. 'Look, don't worry,' I mumble. 'I'll see if I can find it somewhere else.'

The assistant shrugs. 'Suit yourself,' he says.

I walk away from the till with the saunter of a man without a care in the world, the saunter of someone who isn't bothered whether this stupid bookshop has any copies of *Licked* by Moore, M., or not. I stroll nonchalantly back towards the front of the shop, whistling to myself, until I stop short, the tune dying on my lips.

In front of me is not a stack, not a pile, but rather a *mountain* of books. They have been built up in a pyramid, about six feet high and four or five feet across at the base. The book which has been used to construct this monstrous edifice is called *Virgin on Mergin'*, the latest effort by another of Sean's clients, Bernadette Brannigan. This is the most recent novel in her long-running *Virgin* series, which began with the now infamous pile of tripe, *Virgin on the Ridiculous*. I pick up a book and read the blurb on the back cover. *Virgin on Mergin'* tells the story of the gormless heroine, Poppy Flipflop, and her attempts to find a husband. To my disbelief there are quotes from several literary luminaries on the back cover. Julian Barnes describes the book as 'Devastatingly Original'. A. S. Byatt calls Brannigan 'the most astute chronicler of female social angst since Jane Austen'. I am convinced that these encomiums have been fabricated without the knowledge or consent of their alleged authors. As if A. S. Byatt would ever *dream* of reading such dross.

The book is atrociously written, with pedestrian jokes, terrible puns, mildly raunchy sex scenes, and painfully obvious payoffs. It is undemanding pap. It is, frankly, shit. I know, because I've read it. Actually, I've read all of Bernadette Brannigan's books, and they're all exactly the same. That, of course, is why she is the most popular writer in Britain.

I stomp home, utterly deflated.

*   *   *

After the anticlimax of my trip to the bookshop, a cloud of gloom settles over me. I lie on the sofa, staring at the ceiling. Sometimes the flat feels like a prison. We live in Camden, in a small street off Kentish Town Road. It's as good a place as any to live in London, except perhaps on weekends, when millions of bargain-hunters invade the area in search of tatty afghan coats and PVC boots at the weekend markets. Our one-bedroom flat is in the basement of a converted terraced house. There's a small garden, conveniently swathed in concrete. I live here; this is my home; but my name isn't on the property deeds. We were advised that it might be best if the mortgage were taken out solely in Anna's name. Building society managers, we were told, were a conservative lot. They might be reluctant to lend money to a writer with no meaningful income. Solicitors were a much safer bet. I was, in other words, a liability.

So, here I am, in my home which is not actually mine. I feel remote, deracinated. It is hard for me to share Anna's enthusiasm for the place. When we venture out to the antique stalls of Camden Lock, she leads the charge. I do my best to muster some interest, trying to make an emotional investment, if not a financial one.

I clamber off the sofa and find Anna's recording of the Ravel piano trio. I prise open the case. The compact disc, catching the winter sunlight and rainbowing promises into the room, glints like the polished blade of a killer's knife. I put it into the machine and press play.

I listen as the violin paints its simple melody, elegant arcs of beauty hanging in the air. The cello weeps a rich, mournful echo. Each day I listen to this music, secretly, on my own. I have been beguiled, seduced. But even as I am hypnotised by the piece's sorrowful beauty, a small voice in the back of my mind is whispering: what happened to those cheeky chappies in Westlife? Where is Anna's Backstreet Boys CD now?

When the fourth movement of the piece draws to its electrifying conclusion, I stand up and open my saxophone case. I need to chase away the ghost of Ravel's music, which lingers long after the notes themselves have died. I have a Weltklang tenor saxophone, a 1950s model. The bell of the horn is chipped in a hundred places. The bottom keys were broken off long ago when Ron accidentally trod on them after a gig, but I don't mind. It's mine, and I love it.

I begin my daily practice by playing some arpeggios in diminished fourths. Some I knock off easily; others I struggle with, going over them again and again, until I am satisfied or too bored to carry on. Gradually my mood lifts, as I concentrate on the patterns of notes. Gavin has written some new music for the rehearsal tomorrow. The tune is called 'Urban Machinations — the Plight of the Zeitgeist'. I play it through a few times. It's a gentle waltz, really quite pretty.

The tune reminds me of another waltz, the old Rodgers and Hammerstein tune 'My Favourite Things' — not the saccharine-heavy rendition by Julie Andrews in *The Sound of Music*, but John Coltrane's interpretation, tinged with eastern mysticism and steeped in lyrical beauty. I have the music somewhere. I put down my saxophone and go into our bedroom. There I open one of the cupboards, humming quietly, looking for my folder of sheet music.

As I search, I find an old diving mask and snorkel gathering dust in a cardboard box. I pull them out and examine them. I remember these. When I was a young boy I wanted to be a scuba diver. Every night I took this mask and snorkel into the bath, and spent hours lying face down in the water, my face just submerged, staring at the plug. In my head I was exploring ship wrecks, inspecting coral, swimming through schools of exotic fish. In the end, though, my asthma thwarted me. I was told that I would never be able to dive with an aqualung, as my lungs weren't strong enough. The mask, and my dreams, were abandoned.

I replace the mask and snorkel in the box and continue my search. When I find the folder of music, I take it back into the sitting room and spend an hour flicking through the yellowing sheets, playing old tunes.

My practice finished, I can procrastinate no longer. Cautiously I slide into the chair in front of my typewriter. (Proper writers use typewriters, by the way. No word processors for us. The soundtrack of creative genius is the clatter-clatter of crashing keys, not the soulless hum of the laptop.) I stare at my Olivetti for ten minutes, and then with my right index finger I wipe a layer of dust off the space key.

For this is my terrible secret: I am suffering from writer's block – a heavy-duty, career-crippling dose of it, as unmoveable as the Alps. It weighs me down like an unforgiving yoke, pulverising my spirit. The longer I sit in front of my typewriter, the harder it is to begin. I am caught in a hellish downward spiral of petrified inactivity.

To complicate matters further, I have been less than forthright with Anna about my problem. She believes that my next novel is nearing completion. In fact, so far I have written only one sentence.

Here it is:

> The moustachioed peasant rested his not inconsiderable weight on the swarthily crooked ash walking stick that he carried with him everywhere he went – Illic had never seen him without it somewhere on his corpulent body – and gazed up towards the towering clouds that were amassing ominously overhead in the sky above the terrain upon which they stood, side by side, and emitted a raspy breath before intoning in that authoritative voice that the boy loved and admired almost as much as the old man himself, 'All I am saying, Illic my boy, is that we should give peace a chance.'

I've spent hundreds of hours crafting and reworking this, but it's still very much a work in progress. For example, I'm having second thoughts about the 'swarthily crooked' walking stick. The image is almost too rich, too complex. I read my solitary sentence again. Is it, I wonder, too demanding, too *majestic*, for an opening paragraph?

This will be a rites-of-passage novel which uses, as a structural device, song titles of the Plastic Ono Band to establish the chronology of the narrative. It's all rather complicated, and is lodged firmly in my head. The difficulty is getting it from my head on to a sheet of paper. At the moment it refuses to budge. Instead it just sits there, driving me mad with frustration and guilt.

After a few minutes I abandon my typewriter and prowl around the flat. A sea of champagne corks floats in a bowl on the coffee table. I pick up a cork and examine it. Around its neck Anna has written in black biro, 'A's BIRTHDAY. M, A, THERESA + AL'. This is one of Anna's intransigent habits: every time we drink champagne, she keeps the cork and inscribes on it the details of the event and who was there to help us drink it. This bowl is an alcoholic documentary of our time together. If I delve deeply enough, I will find corks commemorating our engagement, the flat purchase, Anna's qualification as a solicitor. These corks have always bewildered me. I have never been able to invest inanimate objects with particular emotive significance, but Anna loves to rummage through the bowl, sighing with memories. Her birthday was five months ago; I remember nothing about it. I certainly don't remember drinking champagne with my sister-in-law Theresa and her idiotic husband Alistair. This bowl, so full of memories for Anna, is quite empty for me.

I walk into the bedroom and start sifting through the laundry basket. It's Monday, so it's whites. As I work, I ponder the fate of my novel. Given Neville's aversion to advertising or marketing, perhaps it's not surprising that the staff in the bookshop hadn't heard of me. I put down the bundle of dirty clothes on the bed and open the top drawer of Anna's dresser. I am confronted by her collection of exotic silk underwear. Beneath these alluring items lie prosaic white cotton stand-bys, and one or two more elaborate pieces, frilly things with lace panels and interesting quick-release gussets. I begin to dig, but I am not looking for saucy lingerie: this is where Anna hid the joint that we smoked on Saturday evening, before the launch party. I am hoping that she had more than one stashed away: I am suddenly craving a calming hit of marijuana. I'm not in the habit of smoking pot in the middle of the day, but after my book's abject non-appearance in the bookshop, I need cheering up.

As I delve, my fingers fall on some   of Camden
the smooth silk. I pull out a small, sk   step thr
front are printed the words 'TIFFAN   the
type. Curious, I open the bag and tip
On to my open palm fall two silver cuffl
is simple: heavily-wrought silver knots
a gleaming argent arc. They are elega   ssy, and
beautiful.

I sit down on the bed, my search for drugs forgotten.

After half an hour I carefully put the Tiffany bag back where
I found it.

They were unquestionably men's cufflinks. But they
couldn't be for me. Anna knows I'd never wear them; I
own one shirt and one tie which I put on, grudgingly, once
a year, for the mandatory appearance at church with Anna's
family on Christmas Day.

But if they're not for me, then who are they for?

And why has Anna gone to the effort of hiding them?

Suddenly the flat seems unbearably small. The walls close
in around me. My discovery of the cufflinks brings all my
worries about Anna back, redoubled. Claustrophobia
crowds in. Pulling on my coat, I hurry out of the flat.
Drawing in cold lungfuls of icy November air, I walk
quickly through Camden, hoping to escape my anxieties.
The streets are quiet, unrecognisable from the edgy chaos
of the weekend and its quick, carnival atmosphere.

I turn left past Chalk Farm station and walk over the
bridge which spans the railway lines, towards Primrose
Hill. On Regents Park Road, the atmosphere of domestic
refinement is in stark contrast to the litter-strewn sprawl

High Street. Leaves dance in the quiet road. I ... through the gate at the bottom of Primrose Hill. In ... distance two figures, their collars turned up against the wind, walk their dogs. I begin to climb the steep path up the hill. At the summit, the wind whistles past my ears. I almost feel as if I've escaped London's grimy clutches. I look southwards across Regent's Park and towards the grey, silent city beyond.

What is happening with Anna?

I allow the wind to sweep through me, clearing my head. Up here I am free, shucked from my life. Finally I walk back down the hill, through the long grass towards the swooping aviary of London Zoo. At Prince Albert Road I turn left and trudge back towards Camden, my mind a grateful blank. On the way home I go into the supermarket. After finding everything I need for supper, I wander over to the Household Goods aisle for a spot of thoroughly modern angst.

There comes a time in everyone's life when the grim realisation dawns that the party is over – that it's finally time to grow up. This usually happens when people take out their first mortgage, make their first pension contribution, or change their first nappy. Of course, I haven't done any of those things. For me, the death knell of my carefree youth, the herald of sombre responsibility, was when I started having to buy lavender toilet paper.

Until our bathroom was redecorated I never worried about what colour of loo roll I pulled off the shelf; I chose whatever pastel hue took my fancy. But all that has changed now. Now it's any colour I like, as long as it's lavender. Lavender, Anna tells me firmly, is the only colour that works. I have reservations about this rigidly monochromatic approach. Does it really matter whether we use colour co-ordinated paper? Would it really spoil the overall aesthetic effect if we had Buttercup Yellow, just for once? It's a bathroom, after all, not an art gallery. But Anna is unmoveable on this issue. Lavender it must be. I pull a pack of four rolls off the shelf and deposit them in my basket with a heavy heart.

I walk home with my shopping. Tonight, as usual, I will be cooking chicken. I am great at chicken. I am a *maître de poulet*, a fowl supremo. I can grill it, roast it, poach it, steam it, pan-fry it, blanche it, deep-fry it, curry it, stew it, parboil it, barbecue it, griddle it, marinade it, or stuff it. Unfortunately, it's the *only* thing I can cook. Tonight, I am preparing pan-fried chicken breasts in a cream, garlic and cider sauce. I put the shopping away and consult the recipe book, even though I won't be cooking for hours yet.

Lunch is baked beans on toast, and then I settle down in front of the television for my usual afternoon diet of wooden game-shows and repeats of old soap operas on UK Gold. My brain goes numb, which is how I like it nowadays. I resolutely ignore my typewriter on the table behind me. It sits in silent reproach as I stare, eyes glazed, at the television screen. My fingers never stray far from the remote control, as I flash across the networks, praising the day they laid the cable in our street. I try and follow six or seven programmes simultaneously, in an attempt to distract my brain from Anna and the cuff-links hidden in her underwear drawer. It doesn't work. I cannot get the sight of the heavy lumps of silver out of my mind.

After all the recent changes in Anna's behaviour, especially after her furtive trip to the cinema, I no longer know what to think.

By the early evening news, I have wound myself into a tight ball of anxiety. I realise that I am going to have to ask Anna about the cufflinks if I am to avoid the descent into fretful madness. I run through various possible opening gambits, trying to decide how to broach the subject. I need something nonchalant, urbane, and relaxed. Every formulation I concoct is nervy, self-pitying, and paranoid.

Finally, at about eight o'clock, I hear the front door open. I feel my heart stretch and skip a beat in anticipation.

'It's me,' calls Anna from the hall.

I get up to greet her. She is hanging up her coat. 'Hello you,' she says. I kiss her on the cheek. We walk into the kitchen. Anna sits down at the table and lights a cigarette.

'So,' she says. 'Come on. Tell me everything. What was it like?'

'What was what like?'

'Don't be a tease, Matthew. Seeing your book on the shelves. All that stuff. Did you see anyone buy a copy?'

I sigh. 'Actually, they didn't have any.'

Anna looks at me. 'None?'

'None.'

'Oh.'

'They told me that they'd never heard of me, they hadn't ordered any copies, and they weren't going to. It wasn't exactly the most electrifying start to my career.'

'Oh, sweetheart. I'm sorry.' Anna takes a long drag of her cigarette. 'Have you told Neville?'

I shake my head. 'He'll probably be delighted.'

'Well, don't worry. It's only one bookshop, after all. There are plenty more out there.'

'Hmm,' I reply doubtfully.

'How was the rest of your day?' she asks. 'What progress on the next masterpiece?'

I think guiltily of my solitary paragraph. 'Actually, it's hard going at the moment. I'm struggling with some of the characters.'

Anna grins. 'Are they not doing what they're told? *Naughty* characters.'

I shift uncomfortably. 'Something like that. The main character, right, Illic —'

'*Illic?*' snorts Anna. 'What sort of name is that?'

I pause. 'It's Eastern European.'

'Eastern European?' Anna looks at me strangely. 'What do you know about Eastern Europe?'

'Enough,' I stammer. Actually, I know nothing about Eastern Europe. But everyone accepts that nowadays serious fiction tends to be about Eastern Europeans. The only authors who still write about English characters are people like Bernadette Brannigan, because neither she nor her readers have the wit or imagination to understand how parochial and mundane it all is. In Eastern Europe, on the other hand, you have the lingering spectre of Communism, lots of war, unpronounceable names, and grittily authentic characters who have not been spiritually disembowelled by the capitalist excesses of Western civilisation. It's the perfect setting if you want to say anything *relevant*.

There is a pause. 'So, go on then,' prompts Anna. 'About this guy Illic. Tell me more.'

'Oh. Well, it's difficult to explain. He's a very complex character.' As he would be, coming from Eastern Europe.

'But at the moment he's, er, subverting the author-character dialectic.'

Anna pulls a face. 'Sounds serious.'

'Oh, I'll soon knock him into shape.' There is a pause. I look at my wife anxiously. I decide to wait until after supper before I ask her about the cufflinks. 'Hungry?' I ask.

'Ravenous. What are we having?'

'Well, just for a change, I thought I might have a go at chicken.'

Anna gasps. 'Chicken? Surely not.'

'I'll get started, then.' I stand up.

Anna remains where she is, looking at the ashtray in front of her. 'Matthew,' she says after a moment, 'I have some news.'

I am crouching in front of the open fridge, a blue polystyrene tray of chicken breasts in my hand. Slowly I stand and turn to face her.

'News?' I say uncertainly.

'We need to talk,' she says.

'Talk?'

'Something's happened, Matthew. I'm leaving.'

I have misheard her. Surely.

'What did you say?' I breathe.

Anna sighs. 'I have to go. I have no choice. I'm sorry.'

So this is it. A scythe of gut-wrenching nausea rips through me. I knew something was wrong, but I wasn't expecting *this*. Anna is leaving me. Just like that. My head is filled with shrill panic. I realise that she is still speaking.

'. . . until about the end of the week. Mind you, it could be worse.'

I stare at her.

Anna looks at me quizzically. 'Is that OK? I know it's not ideal, but I thought maybe you could do with some time to yourself. You can crack on with the book.'

I shake my head. 'Sorry,' I say. 'Run it by me again.' I put the tray of chicken breasts down on the kitchen table. My over-anxious thumb-print is clearly indented against the cool flesh of the meat.

Anna sighs. 'Do you *ever* listen to me, Matthew? I have to go to Paris. On business. That pharmaceutical client I told you about.'

Paris. Business. I nod blindly. The edict has been handed

down, gubernatorial discretion exercised. Clemency has been granted! I am escaping the noose, skipping away from the electric chair!

'I have to leave tomorrow,' continues Anna. 'The deal should be done by the end of the week. Although you never know with the French.'

Ah, yes, the French.

Inevitably, the very mention of our garlic-chomping cousins from across the Channel sends me into a spin. The genesis of my neurosis was one Frenchman in particular, but as the years have passed my antipathy has spread to the whole lot of them.

I should explain.

A statistic that one hears from time to time on true-crime television shows is that in eighty per cent of all murder cases, the murderer and the victim know each other.

I sometimes wonder how police statisticians will categorise my crime, when I exact my longed-for revenge on Jean-Philippe Durand. Will they say we knew each other? I, the assassin, know the victim intimately. Too well. He has haunted my dreams for years. Conversely, when I step out of the shadows, my stiletto blade poised to be driven into his heart, he will look at me blankly. Which is a pity, really, because I won't have time to explain to him exactly *why* it is that he must die.

Allow me to spool back fourteen years, or thereabouts:

October time. I had recently arrived at one of Oxford University's less prestigious colleges, looking forward to an indolent three years of studying English. When I realised just how cheap the beer in the college bar was, I resolved to bluff my way through the entire syllabus. Within days of my arrival, unshakeable slothfulness had settled comfortably upon me like a high tog duvet. I spent the days eroding my paltry student grant twenty pence at a time, trying to beat the high score on the college pinball machine. I spent the evenings drinking with my friend Ian. We had met on the first day of term. Recognising in each other a shared depravity, we dispensed with the cautious friendliness that typified most new encounters in those first days of term. We didn't bother with the usual preliminary small talk, timidly splashing around in the shallow end of the conversational swimming pool. Instead we dived right in to the heavy, do-or-die stuff, and it turned out that we both thought that 'Too Drunk to Fuck' by the Dead Kennedys was the best song ever. Suddenly we were best friends.

(Actually, I lied about the Dead Kennedys. At the time my favourite record was 'Such Sweet Thunder', Duke Ellington's Shakespeare-inspired jazz suite, but I knew that there were occasions when honesty had to be sacrificed for expediency.)

The inevitable descent into puerile loutishness followed. We spent most evenings in the college bar, drinking ourselves stupid. We liked to sit near the door so that we could ogle at all the women who came in. After the barren hinterlands of Hertfordshire, I looked on, agog. The self-confidence, pulchritude and sheer *numbers* of the females on display left me breathless. One evening Ian and I were sitting in our usual spot when the door opened and a girl walked in.

Whatever it is that triggers the delicious chemical imbalance in our brains that makes us stupid with infatuation, it happened to me just then. Just like that, without warning. I fell in love on the spot. Literally. All of the other girls were instantly eclipsed, fading into lifeless daguerreotypes. In contrast, this girl shone in glorious, crisply focused Technicolor. As I stared at her, I could feel the fissure cracking deep within me as her face carved itself indelibly on to my consciousness. From then on I was branded, a marked man.

The girl wasn't wearing any make-up. She didn't need to: her face was radiant, even in the smoky penumbra of the subterranean bar. Looking at her, it was as if someone had opened a window and let the sunshine in.

She was wearing a pair of fantastically tight jeans and a pink twin-set affair which seemed impossibly classy amidst the surrounding sea of Next jumpers and Hard Rock Café T-shirts. She had, patently, the body of a goddess. Her hair was blonde and straight, cut to just below her shoulder. Her black boots emerged alluringly from the bottom of her jeans in an unspeakably erotic way. They tapered from her elegant ankles to mean-looking points. Those boots were foxy. They just *looked* like trouble.

My mouth hanging open, I watched the girl walk towards the bar until she disappeared into the scrum of bodies. Stunned, I turned to Ian. His mouth was hanging open, too.

'Holy fucking shit,' I said.

There was a brief debate about tactics.

'Here's what we'll do,' said Ian, taking a coin out of his pocket. 'Heads you go, tails I go.'

I gulped. Surely I wasn't going to stake all of my future happiness on the toss of a coin? 'OK,' I said after a moment. If it was tails, I reasoned, I would go anyway.

Ian spun the coin and caught it on the back of his left hand, covering it with his right. He slowly lifted his fingers, hiding the coin from my view. I saw his face fall. 'Best of three?' he said tentatively, but I was already out of my chair, striding after her.

Now, I wouldn't want you to think that I was some sort of silver-tongued ladies' man. Quite the opposite, in fact: usually in such circumstances I would be an awkwardly stammering wreck. But this was an unusual situation.

I found the girl standing by the bar. And miracle of miracles, she was alone. I stood next to her, deliberately looking the other way. With fumbling fingers I lit a cigarette. Slowly I counted to five, and then pretended to notice her for the first time. I cocked a cool eyebrow.

'Hi,' I murmured, exhaling meaningfully through my nose. Unfortunately I was recovering from a bad cold, and the smoke shot out of my one functioning nostril in a single, lopsided plume.

'Hello,' said the girl neutrally.

'I'm Matt,' I said.

She looked at me appraisingly. 'I'm Anna.'

'Well, *hello*, Anna.' I stuck my hand out towards her, pleased with how well this was going. She shook my hand with an amused glint in her eye, which I judiciously decided to ignore. I gestured towards the bar. 'Can I get you a drink?'

'No thanks,' she answered. 'I'm not staying. Just waiting for someone.'

She *did* try to warn me, you see, but I sailed resolutely

on past the bank of flashing hazard lights, heroically oblivious. Waiting for someone? Pah!

'So tell me, Anna,' I said, 'what are you studying?' I leaned back against the bar, neatly sticking my elbow into a puddle of spilt beer.

'Law,' she replied flatly, cocking her head to one side as she lit a cigarette. (Anna has always been a fantastic smoker. She smokes in an effortlessly glamorous way, as if it's still the Sixties. I, on the other hand, just puff away artlessly, with no panache, no *drama*.)

'Law? Really?' I hoped that the crippling intellectual and sexual intimidation that I was now experiencing was not manifesting itself too obviously. 'Wow,' I said anxiously.

There was a pause. 'What about you?' she asked.

'Me?' I shrugged nonchalantly. 'English, actually.'

Anna nodded, apparently not surprised.

I felt my armpits prickle with sweat. I looked down at my cigarette, and tried to compose my thoughts. 'So anyway –'

'Hello.' Suddenly, the most beautiful man I had ever seen was standing next to us. Dark, curly hair fell over his eyes in a messily random way that I cattily estimated must have taken him at least thirty minutes to get just right. He could have balanced a small sherry glass on each of his cheekbones, which jutted out from a texturally flawless face. He had dark green eyes, and his chiselled jaw-line was more gracefully contoured than the leg of a Rodin nude. He smiled at me, revealing absolutely perfect teeth.

This was bad; but then things got unspeakably worse.

'Hi sweetie,' said Anna – and then she kissed him. My fantasy world imploded messily.

'Having fun?' said the man in heavily accented English.

'This is — I'm sorry, I've completely forgotten your name.'

Anna hadn't just forgotten my name; oh no. She had *completely* forgotten it. I stuck out my hand towards the man. 'Matt Moore,' I said.

'Jean-Philippe Durand,' he replied.

'You're French,' I said cleverly.

Jean-Philippe Durand looked at me. 'Yes,' he said. 'I am.'

'That's nice,' I said.

'Yes,' he agreed. 'It is.'

'Jean-Philippe is here for a year on a scholarship,' explained Anna brightly.

'Golly,' I said hollowly. 'Congratulations.' My soul had begun to shred itself into tiny, forlorn pieces.

Jean-Philippe Durand inclined his head slightly. 'Thank you. *Matt.*' Was that a small sneer?

Anna looked at her watch. 'We should be going.'

'Off anywhere nice?' I asked, not wanting to let her out of my sight.

'The cinema,' she answered. 'Jean-Philippe insists that only the French make decent films. We decided to put his theory to the test. Yesterday we saw a Truffaut, and today it's my turn. We're going to watch *The Third Man*, which was directed by Carol Reed. *Then* we'll see if he still stands by his theory.' She grinned archly at Jean-Philippe, who had not taken his beautiful eyes off me.

I nodded, hopelessly out of my depth. 'Ah, the great Carol Reed. One of my personal favourites, funnily enough. I think she's wonderful.'

Disconcertingly, Anna frowned at me for a moment, then decided I was joking and laughed politely. 'We really should be going,' she said again.

'Well, it was nice to meet you both,' I said. 'Have a great time.'

'We will,' said Jean-Philippe Durand with such unflappable certainty that I wanted to punch him on his beautifully sculpted nose.

'Bye,' said Anna, flashing me a heartbreaking smile before grabbing Jean-Philippe's hand and turning to go out of the bar.

And that was that.

That wasn't that, of course.

The reason why Jean-Philippe Durand will not remember me, why his brow will furrow as he sees my blade swoop down towards him in that darkened side street, is because we never spoke to each other again.

After my humiliation at the bar, I began to brood hopelessly. Anna rapidly developed into a fully-fledged obsession. All other thought or action was suddenly pretty much impossible, and pretty much meaningless. I was hopelessly in love. I spent hours staring longingly out of my window, which gave me a terrific view of the bins at the back of the college kitchens, wistfully contemplating what might have been. Rather than doing the sensible thing and forgetting about Anna by chasing after any of the hundreds of other nubile young female undergraduates, I decided to remain chaste, loyal to the girl of my dreams. I was, rather speculatively, saving myself for her.

In the meantime, I watched Anna and Jean-Philippe parade around the college, holding hands and whispering in each other's ears. The innocent tenderness that the two of them displayed towards each other in public didn't fool me for a moment. I knew they were at it all the time. Dirty bastards, the pair of them. They were shagging as if it were the end of the world, with wanton, lustful, pornographic abandon. I just knew it.

It was around this time that I started to write seriously, and I suppose in a way I have Jean-Philippe to thank for it. I sat down one afternoon, intending to compose a tragic love poem to Anna. The idea was that when she read it she would realise just how sensitive I was; she would then dump Jean-Philippe, pledge her heart to me for eternity, and we would live happily ever after. After thirty minutes of doodling I gave up on that idea and instead wrote a terrible and rather bleak short story which culminated in the grisly death of every single character, all of whom happened to be French.

I showed the story to Ian. He sat on my bed and read it in silence.

'What do you think?' I asked.

'I think it's quite good,' replied Ian.

'Thanks,' I said.

'I also think,' he continued, 'that you need help.'

I nodded. 'It's just a first draft.'

'No.' Ian shook his head. 'Not with the writing. With you.' He waved my story at me and tapped his finger against the side of his head. 'You are one sick puppy.'

Encouraged, I began to write in earnest. The one leitmotif in all my work at that time was the gruesome demise of a good-looking Frenchman at the end of each story. In this way I killed Jean-Philippe Durand off several times, exacting revenge for the misery he had unwittingly heaped upon me. He was crushed, poisoned, shot, asphyxiated, garrotted, drowned, buried alive, exsanguinated, dismembered, hanged, electrocuted, cannibalised, starved to death, beheaded, pushed in front of an oncoming train, disembowelled, and crucified. As I reached the gory climax of each story, my handwriting would degenerate into an illegible scrawl as I rushed gleefully towards the *coup de grâce*, cackling maniacally as I did so.

Like Ian said, one sick puppy.

It wasn't a good year.

I spent unhealthy amounts of time hanging around the college quads, waiting for a sighting of the happy couple. I would gaze at them wordlessly, my heart beating blackly as my envy of Jean-Philippe flourished and developed into fully-fledged hatred. Looking back on it now, I can see that he wasn't really doing anything *wrong*. But that was irrelevant. He was having sex with the woman I loved. That was quite enough.

I couldn't bring myself to approach either of them. Occasionally I would pass Anna as I scuttled through college, but she showed no signs of recognising me after my artless overtures in the college bar. The obvious thing to do was to stay away, but I couldn't help myself. I kept going back for more, quietly crucifying myself.

Finally, the summer holidays arrived. I escaped back home, and spent three months lying on my bed, staring at the ceiling, waiting for the summer to end. I was unable to think of anything but my return to Oxford, and the chance to see Anna again. I couldn't wait to inflict more pain on myself.

*　　*　　*

When we reconvened for the new academic year, Jean-Philippe Durand had returned to Paris, leaving the way open for me to try my luck with Anna again. It took several false starts before I summoned up enough courage to speak to her. Thankfully she didn't remember our earlier encounter. I did, though. Remembering Truffaut and Carol Reed, I started chatting to her about movies, hoping to catch her interest. It worked. After our trip to see *Citizen Kane* and a successful dinner date a few days later, we began to see each other regularly. Every time we arranged to meet, I blinked in amazement when Anna actually appeared, clutching her thick, brightly coloured legal textbooks. This was really happening; Anna was walking down the narrow Oxford streets on her way back from the law faculty, thinking about *me*. Her smiles as we shyly greeted each other stunned me into delirious, weak-kneed awe. I spun with happiness, fizzing with the ceaseless, internal momentum of my raging ardour. My arm was blue from disbelieving pinches.

Unfortunately, though, the damage had already been done.

Long after Jean-Philippe Durand had waltzed out of my life, I found myself unable to stop thinking about him, even once Anna and I had begun our own romantic adventure. A year of all-consuming jealousy proved difficult to shake off. His presence lingered on, casting a pall over my happiness. Those perfect teeth haunted me. That alluring French accent kept whispering in my ear: *She could have been mine.* His mesmerising eyes twinkled on in my memory, tormenting me. I couldn't shake the ghastly suspicion that I was merely Anna's compromise candidate. Jean-Philippe had gone, and I was the runner's-up prize, second best.

In this way the Frenchman left an indelible stain on the crisp white sheet of our romance, an ineradicable reminder of our lives before Anna and I came together. Our fairy tale had been tarnished before it had even begun. That is why, one day, I will wreak my terrible revenge on him.

Of course, Anna knows nothing of all this, even now. I couldn't bring myself to admit my disquiet to her at the time, terrified that if I even mentioned Jean-Philippe's name, she would suddenly realise that I *was* second best, and go straight back to him. Instead I suffered in silence, and the more my suspicions festered, the more impossible it became to broach the subject. Finally I understood that if I was ever to escape Jean-Philippe Durand's insidious clutches, I would have to do it on my own.

And, who knows? Perhaps, one day, I will.

So, it has been decided. Anna is off to France. She leaves tomorrow morning.

After supper, she spends the rest of the evening packing, unpacking, and repacking. I sit on the end of the bed, watching. As she folds her clothes carefully into the suit-case, she tells me that she will be staying at the Hotel Léon, near the Louvre. She is travelling to Paris with three of her colleagues, Andy, Graham and Richard. They are, she says, all lovely chaps. They enjoy a laugh, good food, that sort of thing, so I mustn't worry that she will be spending the evenings sitting alone and bored in her hotel room. Far from it. They will, she informs me with a grin, be painting the town a fabulous shade of *rouge*. I nod, blinking.

A taxi to Waterloo is ordered for the morning; we have a final glass of wine and go to bed. Anna wordlessly turns out her bedside light and pulls the duvet over her, leaving me propped up on an expectant elbow. So. There will be no drink before the war. She leans over and kisses me on the forehead as I slump into my pillow.

'Sorry. Early start tomorrow.'

'Not for me.'

'Well, count yourself lucky,' she replies, wriggling into a comfortable position, her back towards me.

'Will you wake me up before you go?' I ask.

'Why?'

'Because I'm not going to see you for the rest of the week. I'd like to say goodbye properly.'

With a sigh, Anna rolls back over to face me. She looks sleepy and adorable. 'But the cab's coming at a quarter to *six*,' she says. 'It's inhuman. There's no need to ruin your day.'

I shrug. 'I'd like to ruin my day, if it's all the same to you.'

Anna softens. 'You're mad,' she says. 'Sweet, but mad.' She smiles. Her hand strokes my cheek.

'So you'll wake me?' I persist.

She rolls away from me again. 'All right,' comes the muffled reply. I sense her body relaxing for sleep.

A pause. 'Goodnight, then.'

'Night, sweetheart,' yawns Anna.

She shifts again, and then remains still. Her gentle, sleep-heavy breath soon becomes rhythmic and smooth. I stare at the blackness around me.

I do not sleep well. When I finally wake, pummelled by a bruising sequence of unremembered dreams, I glance at my clock. It is eight o'clock. Anna is long gone.

In the kitchen is a note.

Sorry I didn't wake you, Matthew. Couldn't do it, in the end. You looked so peaceful, I couldn't bear to disturb you.

Hope you don't mind. I'll call you this evening from the hotel. Have fun. Wish me luck!

A

PS   It's Noon's birthday on Saturday. Can you please send her a card from both of us? Thanks. (She'll be 93.)

Noon is Anna's grandmother. Everybody in her family dotes on her, which I find bemusing, as she is the most vituperative, cantankerous old crone I have ever met. Still, sending the rebarbative old trout a birthday card won't kill me, I suppose.

I make myself a cup of tea, wishing that Anna had woken me before she left. This isn't the first time she has gone abroad on business, of course; she's flown all over the world in the past few years. But this trip feels different. Her absence needles me. It may be due to the lack of fond goodbyes, but I cannot help wondering whether there is something wider than just a stretch of water between us now.

I walk back into the bedroom and open the wardrobe. Anna's work suits are hung neatly in a row, a palette of demure pastels, muted greys and blacks, and one or two startling blasts of primary colour. I find yesterday's choice, an elegant charcoal trouser suit, and pull it out. My fingers dip fleetingly into the suit, as nimble as a pickpocket's. As I perform my search I hum tunelessly to myself, as if this were quite the most ordinary thing in the world. There is a book of matches in the left jacket pocket, glossily embossed with the name of a restaurant near the Barbican. I open the flap. Four matches have been pulled out from the right hand side. Four cigarettes after lunch? Perhaps more. Maybe less. I stare at the matches, willing them to reveal their meaning to me. What conclusions should I draw from this? What do four post-lunch fags actually mean? Shouldn't Anna have mentioned that she went out for lunch yesterday? Who did she go with?

I hang the charcoal suit back in its place. This amateur detective work is ridiculously self-destructive. It just sends me into vertiginous tailspins of bewildered despair. But I am powerless to resist the call of those untended pockets; every day, the possibility of new information draws me back, like the cruellest addiction.

I wish Anna were here now. There is so much I want to talk to her about. We used to have endless, earnest conversations which stretched on long into the night, as we forgot the time and the rest of the world – everything except each other. But those talks are a thing of the past; all Anna wants to do now in the evenings is collapse on the sofa with a glass of wine and watch television until it's time to go to sleep.

I open my saxophone case and begin to practise for this evening's rehearsal, but I cannot muster any interest for the pretty patterns of notes that I am producing. The saxophone keys feel heavy beneath my fingers. I am relieved when the telephone interrupts me. It is Sean.

'Hey, fella,' he chirps.

'Sean. How are you?'

'I'm fine. But the six million dollar question is how are *you*?'

'All right, I suppose. Anna's gone to Paris for the rest of the week, and the world hasn't exactly been set alight by the publication of *Licked*, but other than that I'm fine.'

'Shouldn't lose too much sleep about the book,' says

Sean carelessly. 'These things take time. Rome wasn't built in a day, you know. Has Anna gone to Paris on business?'

'No, Sean, she's gone with her fucking knitting circle,' I snap. 'Of course she's gone on business.'

'Anyway, listen,' says Sean blithely. 'I've got some news that's going to make your day.'

'OK,' I say, seriously doubting this.

'I've arranged a reading for you.'

I almost drop the phone. 'That's fantastic, Sean! Where?'

There is a pause. 'In a bookshop.'

'OK. Where's the bookshop?'

'Look,' says Sean, 'before we go any further, can we discuss dates?'

'Sure. I'm available pretty much any time.'

'Ah. Footloose and fancy free. Lucky old you.'

'When is this all fixed for?' I am delighted. One thing is for certain: Neville never would have dreamed of arranging anything as vulgarly populist as a reading. Good old Sean. For a moment, I find myself almost liking him. Thanks to him, I'm going to get to read my work to a real audience. Who, at the end, will *clap*.

'Probably in about a week or so,' answers Sean. 'There or thereabouts.'

'Great! Where's this bookshop?'

'And I think we can safely assume that you'll be guaranteed a good reception. I've been talking to the manager of the shop, and he's very keen on the book.'

'God,' I exclaim. 'Someone's actually read it. Miracles will never cease.'

'Oh, he hasn't actually *read* it,' replies Sean, 'but he loves the *idea* of it. The whole, you know, stamp thing.' Sean is on thin ice here, since he hasn't read it either.

'Well,' I say. 'Stamp enthusiasts are OK. I'm not fussy. If my audience calls, then I must go. Where did you say the bookshop was again?'

'And this, I would think, will be the tip of the iceberg. Once you get a few readings under your belt –'

'Sean,' I interrupt. 'Where's the fucking bookshop?'

There is a long pause before Sean finally says, 'Preston.'

I take a deep breath. 'Pardon?'

'It's in Preston. The bookshop.'

'OK,' I say evenly. 'Why Preston, precisely?'

'Well.' I hear Sean weighing up his excuses. 'Basically, they're the only place so far that's agreed to have you.'

Jesus. A fine time for him to start telling me the truth. 'I was hoping for something a bit more, I don't know, *local*. At least within the M25, say.'

'All in good time. Everything comes to he who waits. But at the moment it's Preston.'

'Christ.' I take a deep breath. 'All right. I'll do it.'

'Oh *good*. Stuart *will* be pleased.'

'Who's Stuart?'

'He's the shop manager. My cousin, actually. He owes me a favour.'

'Ah.' So Sean is press-ganging one of his family into hosting my first reading. What am I saying? My *only* reading. In *Preston*. It wasn't quite what I had in mind. 'Thanks, Sean,' I say, far too late for him to believe that I could possibly mean it.

'Right, then,' says Sean. 'I'll let you know as soon as I have a date.' He rings off.

I put down the telephone and survey the flat. Now that Anna will be away for a few days, there seems little point in carrying out the usual battery of daily domestic tasks. I can live like a pig, and nobody will know. The prospect fills me with a hollow thrill. I wonder what Anna is doing right now.

Suddenly I remember that in all the excitement caused by the announcement of Anna's trip to Paris last night, I never asked her about the cufflinks in her underwear drawer. I was so relieved when I realised that she wasn't leaving me for ever that my brain must have subconsciously decided to shelve that issue for a more apposite occasion. I swear softly to myself. Now I will have to wait until next weekend. I walk into the bedroom for another look at the cufflinks. Anna's underwear drawer is emptier than before; she has packed a lot for her trip, including, I notice, some of her more alluring items. I begin to riffle through what is left.

Minutes later I sit down on the bed, lost.

The Tiffany bag has gone.

Anna has gone to Paris with Andy, Graham and Richard, her colleagues, lovely chaps all. They are, she told me last night, all up for a laugh, *that sort of thing*.

My mind whirls.

What sort of thing?

I stare into space, my heart racing.

Anna has gone to Paris, and she has taken a pair of Tiffany cufflinks with her.

Each piece of the jigsaw slams into place with a resounding smash. The dreamy silences, all those late nights at the office – suddenly everything begins to make terrible sense.

Is one of her Paris-bound colleagues a gym enthusiast with a thing for Ravel?

It would explain why Anna was hiding the cufflinks in the first place, and it would explain why she didn't wake me up this morning. She wanted to avoid the embarrassment of a flamboyantly uxorious goodbye if she is off to Paris to shag like a jack rabbit with somebody else.

I spend the rest of the day struggling to find alternative explanations for everything I've seen, everything I know. The more I wrestle with the facts, the more they obstinately shape themselves towards the unthinkable.

Is Anna having an *affair*?

I haven't even got to the gut-busting punch line yet, the little detail that makes this all so especially sad:

We went to Paris on our honeymoon.

See? You couldn't make it up.

Our jazz quartet rehearses every Tuesday evening at Gavin's loft. At six o'clock I pack up my saxophone and catch the Tube to Old Street, numb from a dayful of worry.

Gavin is a graphic designer of some sort. He's obviously good at it, because he's loaded. He lives in a vast loft conversion on the fringes of Clerkenwell, all exposed brick, double-height ceilings, and stripped pine floors. There's a baby grand piano in one corner. He even has a *Raiders of the Lost Ark* pinball machine. It feels more like a film set than a place where a real person should actually live. It's every bachelor's fantasy wankpad.

Gavin's homogenised but expensive taste is derived in large part from the glossy magazines to which he is addicted. I have seen him rip open the latest edition of *GQ*, salivating as he gazes with barely suppressed ardour at the most recent techno-gizmo or the newest Paul Smith loafers. You can see his eyes glinting with deranged lust as he compulsively turns the pages. He just loves labels. He just loves *stuff*.

I press the doorbell, gazing anxiously in both directions as I wait to be buzzed inside. The entrance to Gavin's building is shrouded in dark shadows which give me the creeps. Shifty characters with tattoos on their arms hang around on street corners, talking into mobile phones and staring menacingly at passers-by. I am waiting for the inevitable day when I am robbed and brutally murdered, all within pressing distance of Gavin's doorbell. The atmosphere of palpable violence doesn't seem to bother Gavin. Perhaps the attendant dangers of living here are immaterial, given the hipness of the milieu. Perhaps the attendant dangers of living here are the *reason* for the hipness of the milieu.

Gavin's voice crackles out of the small metal box by the front door. 'All right,' he says cheerfully. He knows it's me; I am being scrutinised by the unblinking eye of a small security camera above the intercom. I make sure the front door closes firmly behind me before climbing the stairs to Gavin's loft.

He is standing by the door, waiting for me.

'Hi Gav,' I say.

'Matt. How's tricks?'

'Tricks are dandy. My novel's just been published, actually.'

'Really,' says Gavin.

'It's called *Licked*,' I tell him.

'Nice title.'

I perform a playful shuffle. 'You could buy a copy if you liked,' I say.

'Yeah,' agrees Gavin, laughing. 'Course I could. Come on, the others are already here.'

I follow Gavin in. The twins, Ronnie and Abdullah, are setting up their instruments at the other end of the room, next to the piano. 'All right Matt, you poncy fucker!' shouts Ron Fries from behind his half-erected drum kit.

'Do you want a beer?' asks Gavin. 'I've got this fantastic bottled stuff from Korea. It's made by albino monks in this isolated monastery on top of a mountain. They trample the hops with their feet.'

'Yeah, go on then,' I reply doubtfully.

Gavin goes to his beautiful open-plan kitchen and opens an enormous Smeg fridge, which is taller than I am. Apart from about twenty bottles of beer, the fridge is empty. He takes out a bottle, prises the cap off, and hands it to me. I take a tentative sip. As I swallow, I start to believe the story about the monks trampling the hops. The beer has a distinct odour of smelly feet. I carry my saxophone towards the twins at the far end of the room.

As twins go, Ron and Abdullah Fries could not be less identical. Ron is a huge, stocky bear of a man; Abdullah is tall and thin. Abdullah's wild shock of unruly red hair and mash of orange freckles make him look at least five years younger than his brother, but in fact he is the older of the two, by about forty-five minutes.

'All right, Matt,' says Abdullah as I approach. He raises his own bottle of Korean beer to me in friendly salute. I'm sure that Abdullah isn't supposed to drink: he became a Buddhist years ago.

The Fries twins were born in East London in the middle of the Sixties. For newly-born twin brothers it was an unfortunate confluence of time and place, as there were only ever two names that they were going to be given. Ron was all right, but the subsequent proliferation of McDonalds restaurants, and Abdullah's adoption of a *Muslim* name, has always led me to suspect that his conversion to Buddhism was due less to any spiritual conviction than a simple but heartfelt desire to change his name from Reg Fries.

Ron finishes setting up, and pulls out his drumsticks. He plays a few press rolls, and then puts on a pair of dark glasses. As soon as the shades go on, Ron is firmly installed in his own jazz dream world, where he is American, and black. While he acts out this peculiar fantasy, he insists on speaking some ghastly argot of his imagination, an excruciating cocktail of bastardised Harlem jive and flat estuary vowels.

'You sorry-assed bitches ready to get down and play some shit?' he drawls, sounding like Sammy Davis Jr marooned in Basildon. Gavin and I exchange glances.

'Getting there,' says Gavin, riffling through pages of sheet music by the piano.

Abdullah gives his double bass a heavy twang and looks at his brother. 'Ready and waiting,' he reports.

'Fuck it, motherfucker,' says Ron to nobody in particular, pushing his dark glasses a little further up his nose.

A few minutes later, we are ready to begin. We decide to play a Charlie Parker tune, 'Au Privave', to warm up.

Gavin breathes a count of four and we launch into the music.

Saturday evening, the jazz cellar beneath the Oxford Union, two weeks after *Citizen Kane* and a week and a half after that first dinner date. My quintet was performing in front of a chattering student audience drinking cheap, creamy cocktails. The lights were so low and the smoke so thick that the band couldn't see the tables at the far end of the long, narrow room. I had invited Anna to come and listen to us play. She sat at a table near the front, watching me through a veil of smoke as I tried to pretend that she wasn't there. I failed horribly, of course: I took long, indulgent solos, showing off, strutting about the cramped stage. Rather awfully, I dedicated a song to her. It was 'Embraceable You'. Anna, of course, bore it all with equanimity and grace, gazing down at her Pink Flamingo as I made a stupendous tit of myself, silly with infatuation. Nobody in the audience paid much attention; they were there for the cheap booze, not the floorshow.

Despite my excruciating behaviour, when the band finally finished in the early hours of Sunday morning, Anna was still there. We walked up the stairs and out into the night without saying a word. As the doors swung shut behind us, she turned to me.

'I'm impressed,' she said. 'That was beautiful.'

'Really?' I asked, wanting her to say it again.

A nod. 'Beautiful. Really. Thank you, Matthew.'

Up until then we had confined ourselves to chaste but lingering kisses on the cheek, as Anna patiently waited for me to make my move, but now she took half a step forward, her lips parted slightly as she tilted her face towards mine. We stayed motionless for an age, suspended out of time, both wanting to prolong the moment. It was only later that I understood what had happened: our emotional nexus had arrived moments before the physical. As we stood there in the dark, the greatest leap of our lives had already been made.

A sense of calm descended on me. I slowly lowered my

mouth on to hers, and the quiet fireworks began. Her lips felt unbearably soft on mine. There was no mashing of yawning mouths, slippery with lust. Every tiny movement was desperately erotic. The restrained tenderness made my head pound with blood. We looked gravely into each other's eyes as we kissed. We both knew that this was a moment we would want to remember.

Finally, Anna pulled away with a small laugh. A moan escaped me: immediately, it was unbearable not to be kissing her. I knew then that nothing was ever going to be the same again. I leant forwards, seeking more. My stomach contracted in anguish as she held up a hand.

'That's enough for now, I think.'

I looked down. 'Oh.'

Anna's hand went up to my cheek. 'That was a *fantastic* snog,' she murmured. 'Thank you.'

I felt ill with undiluted longing. 'Anna –'

She shook her head calmly. 'I need my beauty sleep.'

I nodded, distraught. 'Right. I understand.'

There was a pause as we looked at each other.

'Are you coming?' asked Anna.

'What?'

She grinned. 'Well, beauty sleep is much more fun with two.'

I blinked. 'Really?'

She took my hand and squeezed it. 'Really. Come on.'

I hauled my case on to my shoulder. My saxophone felt lighter than air.

As my fingers fly over the saxophone's keys, its tone fills Gavin's loft, and my worries about Anna are eclipsed.

Immersed in my solo, I shed everything but the music. Finally, we draw to a close. Ron's cymbal rings on after we have stopped. There is a contemplative silence. It is the sweetest moment of the week.

After this, we get down to business. We decide to run through Gavin's new composition, 'Urban Machinations – the Plight of the Zeitgeist'.

I watch Gavin as he plays, hunched over the keyboard. Breathtaking flurries of notes cascade from his fingers. The rest of us are competent musicians, but Gavin is the real thing. Musical ideas proliferate at a bewildering rate, as he tries out a phrase, a mood, pulling the tune this way and that. It is an extraordinary performance. When we get to the end of the tune, Ron leans back on his stool in satisfaction and says, 'Mother*fucker*.'

'That was pretty good,' says Gavin.

'Nice solo,' I tell him.

'Nice solo yourself,' he replies with a grin. He's lying, and we both know it, but I am grateful all the same.

'Abdullah, ma man,' says Ron from behind his drum kit, pointing a stick at his brother, 'don't be pussyin' around with your goddam bass, you dig? Play that motherfucker like you mean it, nigger.'

Abdullah looks at his twin and sighs.

'Er, right,' says Gavin. 'Shall we try it again?'

'One question,' says Abdullah.

Gavin raises his eyebrows.

'It's the title.' Abdullah looks embarrassed. He is doing his best to hide behind the wide wooden body of his instrument.

Gavin stiffens. 'What about it?'

'Well. What does it *mean*?'

There is a pause.

'Isn't it obvious?' asks Gavin in an aggrieved tone.

'Not really,' answers Abdullah, blushing furiously.

Gavin sighs. 'OK. First of all, right, Urban Machinations are the forces that make the city go round.'

'Which city?' I ask.

'It doesn't matter which city. *Any* city. We're talking about the hidden forces of society, yeah, the impetus behind major conurbations, the social adhesive which glues the lives of individuals together.'

We look at Gavin blankly. With a pained sigh, he continues.

'So, that's the Urban Machinations part, OK? The stuff none of us knows about. Then you have the Plight of the Zeitgeist. And that's basically saying that the trouble with the way we live today, yeah, is that, well, none of us *do* know what binds human beings together any more. I mean, shouldn't we all be striving towards a more profound understanding of who we are and how we live?'

We leave this rhetorical question well alone and wait for him to continue.

'And, like, nowadays we just carry on, without understanding anything, with no conception of the reality of the human condition. Which is, you know, sad.'

'Hang on,' I interject. 'Are you saying that it's sad that we no longer understand the human condition, or that the human condition itself is sad?'

Gavin looks at me suspiciously. 'Both,' he says.

'And that's because of the Urban Machinations?' I ask.

'Right.'

'And *that* is the Plight of the Zeitgeist?'

Gavin nods slowly, no longer quite sure himself. I know

this is all bollocks. Gavin called it 'Plight of the Zeitgeist' because he thinks it sounds good. Because it rhymes.

'Well,' I say, 'it's a pretty tune.'

'Yeah,' agrees Abdullah. 'Very nice.'

'It's not supposed to be *pretty*,' snaps Gavin. 'This is sad stuff we're talking about here. These are serious social issues.' He waves the music at us. 'This piece raises important queries about the way we live our lives.' He pauses. 'It's very *profound*.'

'Oh, OK,' I say.

'Sorry,' mumbles Abdullah.

'You are one *crazy* motherfucker,' Ron tells Gavin.

We run through the tune again. This time I try and impart some degree of Gavin's socio-existentialist worries into my solo. At least, that is how I justify all those wrong notes to myself.

Two hours later, we are tired and all played out. The rehearsal has gone reasonably well. The dynamics of the group rarely change. Gavin takes charge, I make occasional suggestions, Abdullah does what he is told, and Ron contributes his rich vein of patois invective, which the rest of us do our best to ignore.

I pack up my saxophone and wait for Ron to put away his drums. As soon as he takes off his dark glasses, he mercifully reverts back to his normal self and we are treated to his usual swaggering banter. 'So, when's the next gig?' he asks, as he does every week.

'Actually,' says Gavin, 'we may have one early next year.'

'Really?' All three of us turn to look at him.

Gavin nods. 'A mate of mine is opening a bar round the corner from here. He said we could play there if we liked. It's due to open in early January.'

'A bar in Clerkenwell?' I ask doubtfully. 'Won't it be full of wankers?'

'Fuck, Gav,' shouts Ron, ignoring me. He slams a fist into his palm. 'That's *great* news. Well done, man. Nice one.' Gavin shrugs, pleased.

On average, we play in front of an audience about twice a year. None of us, with the possible exception of Gavin, particularly minds the fact that the public-at-large has limited opportunities to hear our efforts. I just love to listen to the music we create. At some point during each tune the thought occurs to me, fucking hell, that's *us*. That's enough for me. Playing jazz is one area of my life where I don't need an audience to ratify and applaud my endeavours.

Finally Ron is ready to go. We say goodbye to Gavin and Abdullah, and I help Ron load his drums into his car. He has probably the worst car in the world for carrying drums around. It's a Ford Crouton, the penis translated into automotive form. Ron is extremely proud of his car. He never tires of pointing out its alluringly low-slung lines, its seductive interior trim, the throaty roar of the souped-up engine as he squeals away from traffic lights. After a struggle we manage to shove all of the drums and cymbals into the back of the Crouton, and I climb into the passenger seat. I fasten the seatbelt securely. (I know what Ron's driving is like.) Ron clambers in behind the wheel. He sniffs deeply, with satisfaction. 'Fucking great car, this,' he says.

I nod. A certain amount of fawning is expected from me in consideration of my lift home. 'It certainly is.'

'Not only that.' Ron leans towards me. 'It's a fucking *fanny magnet*. Girls can't get enough of a motor like this. They love it. I have to beat them off.'

'I'll bet,' I say dutifully.

This is precisely the same conversation that we always have when we climb into Ron's Crouton. We sit there for a few seconds in reverential silence, contemplating just how much of a fucking fanny magnet Ron's car really is. Then he slips the key into the ignition, turns on the stereo, and we're off.

The noise from the car's speakers buffets me physically. It reminds me of the noise that Anna's computer makes as it connects up to the internet, a raucous, high-pitched squeal, except that this is also punctuated by the rib-shattering thump of pre-programmed drums. In self-defence, I reach over and turn the stereo off.

'Oi,' says Ron mildly. 'I was listening to that.'

It baffles me how Ron can play the drums with such subtlety and grace and then climb into his car and listen to this lobotomy-inducing shit. 'Can't we listen to something else?' I ask.

Ron shrugs. 'I – fuck me, look at the tits on *that*.' Ron has lost all interest in the stereo, the road, and the surrounding cars. He is staring at a woman who is standing at a bus stop about thirty yards ahead of us, reading a book. He is now concentrating on changing lanes so that we will pass as close to the woman as possible. After much gesticulating and swearing, he edges into the left-hand lane just before we reach the bus stop.

'She's reading a fucking *book*,' whistles Ron. 'Nice. Bit of posh.'

Ron slows down to a complete halt immediately in front of the woman, and presses a button on the dashboard. My window slides smoothly down. As it does so, Ron pumps the throttle, making the Ford Crouton roar. The woman looks up.

Ron leans across me and smiles out of the window. 'Hello *darling*,' he says.

'Fuck off,' says the woman.

I stare straight ahead, trying to get a look at the woman out of the corner of my eye. She is averagely pretty, I suppose, but the way Ron is behaving you'd be forgiven for thinking that she was Claudia Schiffer. I look at the book she's reading. It's *Virgin on Mergin'* by Bernadette Brannigan. Of course it is.

Ron winks at me. 'Fancy a lift, sweetheart?' he asks the woman. 'I can take you to Heaven and back, if you like.'

I debate whether I should ask Ron if I can borrow his dark glasses.

'Fuck off,' says the woman again.

'Bet you like the motor, eh?' demands Ron jovially. 'She's a beauty, isn't she?'

'Fuck off,' says the woman for the third time, returning to her book.

Ron, for some reason, seems delighted with this response, but unfortunately shows no signs of fucking off just yet. 'What do you say?' he asks, revving the engine again. 'Fancy greasing my pistons some time?'

The woman now simply ignores Ron, keeping her eyes fixed firmly on her book. I resolve to take the Tube home in future.

'Look, love, I can't hang around here all day,' says Ron. Still there is no response. 'All right, babe. Maybe next time, yeah? Stay beautiful.' With a roar we disappear into the traffic.

I am momentarily struck dumb, mesmerised by Ron's Neanderthal mating technique. After a few moments I regain my powers of speech. 'Hard luck,' I mumble.

Ron, though, is grinning from ear to ear. 'Nah,' he says, changing gears with a flourish. 'She was up for it.'

I blink. 'She was?'

'Christ yeah. No question. Did you see the way she looked at me? She was mine for the taking, mate.' Ron rolls his eyes and lets out a small whoop of testosterone-flooded elation. I wonder how it can be that Ron and I appear to have witnessed totally different exchanges back there by the bus stop. Was one of us momentarily transported to some parallel universe? Or is Ron merely deranged?

'She didn't seem awfully keen to me,' I say tentatively.

'Well, no, of course not,' agrees Ron. 'They don't, do they? That's all part of the fun. It's a game, innit?'

'Ah,' I say, waiting for further elucidation.

'Look. You and I *know* that all women want it, right, pretty much all the time. But they like to play hard to get. They like to be chased. And so we chase 'em.' Ron grins happily.

'You think all women want it all of the time?' I ask doubtfully.

'Fuck, *yeah*,' replies Ron. 'Birds are always horny. It's their natural state. Christ alive, they're *gagging* for it, twenty-four fucking seven.'

I settle silently back into my seat. Ron's theory, however implausibly optimistic, has reminded me of Anna, and all at once I am lost. The jazz has set me free for a few hours, but now I am plunged again into a maelstrom of suspicion and worry. Where are the cufflinks? I glance at my watch. Eleven o'clock. Midnight in Paris. Anna's laughing face floats in front of me, promising to paint the town red with her colleagues. What is she doing now? And with whom? Perhaps Ron is right. Perhaps women can't help themselves; they need to play the field.

I begin to feel sick.

We make it back to Camden without further incident.

Waving Ron a hollow thanks, I unlock the front door of the flat. I walk through the rooms, switching on lights, trying to transform our home into a warm repository of familiar comfort. It isn't easy. My worries about Anna cast a cold pall over everything.

In the hall the answering machine is winking. I press the button.

'Hi, darling, it's me. Hope your rehearsal went well. Just to say that we've arrived safely. We got here mid-morning and have been in meetings ever since. Unbelievably tedious. These French. Anyway, we've just got back to our hotel. Room 523, if you need to get in touch. We haven't eaten yet, so we're going to go out for a bite to eat soon. Hope you're OK. Don't get too lonely. Speak to you soon. Lots of love.'

I listen to the message four times. Anna sounds as brisk and businesslike as usual, but it's as if she no longer exists as an individual entity. The first person singular has been eradicated from her speech. She has been subsumed by the collective; now she is a team player, one of the gang.

87

I look at my watch. Quarter past eleven. Quarter past midnight in France. I stand in front of the telephone, debating whether to call her. I'm used enough to her being away from home, but right now I badly need to hear her voice. I dial the hotel's phone number.

A voice answers in crisply enunciated French.

I take a deep breath. 'May I speak to Anna Given, please?'

(When we got married, Anna flatly refused to change her surname. People knew her as Anna Given, she said, and there was no reason why she should become Anna Moore just because we'd got married. Well, no, I said, hurt, except that that's what married people *do*. Anna mocked me gently for being so old-fashioned, and refused to change her mind. In professional circles, then, our marriage is not recognised. I put this thought out of my mind as I think of her in Paris with her colleagues – Andy, Graham and Richard, that unholy horny trinity.)

The receptionist responds smoothly in perfect English. 'Certainly, monsieur. One moment, please.'

I stare at the ceiling as I wait to be put through. There is a rattle in my ear. I brace myself.

'Monsieur? I'm sorry, I'm getting no reply from Miss Given's room.'

This information registers numbly. 'Right,' I say.

'Would you like to leave a message for her?'

'No, don't worry. I'll call again tomorrow.'

'Very good, monsieur. Good evening.' Unruffled Gallic professionalism. The phone goes dead.

I go into the kitchen. There's an open bottle of white wine in the fridge, and I pour myself a glassful. I sit down at the kitchen table, and hungrily light a cigarette. The smoke cuts the back of my throat.

It's past midnight in Paris, and Anna is not in her room.

Perhaps she's asleep and didn't hear the phone ring. Perhaps she's enjoying a last drink with the boys before retiring for the night. Perhaps their meal has dragged on.

Perhaps.

It's past midnight in Paris, and Anna is not in her room.

I feel as if I'm moving through a sea of cotton wool. Nothing seems quite real.

Until recently Anna and I were chugging happily along the same rails, but someone has thrown a switch, changed the points. Now we seem to be flying away from each other, steaming down separate, unjumpable tracks. We have been uncoupled.

Where is she?

I grind my cigarette into the ashtray in front of me. A heavy lethargy fixes my bones and freezes my spirits at their lowest ebb. I feel myself wink slowly into shutdown. Inertia threatens to flatten me. I smoke another cigarette, staring at my reflection in the darkness of the kitchen window. My face stares back at me, on the outside, peering in.

The next morning, I wake up with a sharp jolt. Cold dread flushes through me. Waking from a bad dream should be a welcome relief, as reality soothingly washes away the darker excesses of the subconscious. This time, though, reality and nightmare correspond.

I lie in bed and consider my position. I can't go on like this for the rest of the week, wondering what is going on across the Channel. I pull back the duvet and sit on the edge of the bed, my head in my hands. This is hopeless. I have to do *something*.

I go and look for my passport.

An hour and a half later, I find myself at Waterloo station, passing over my credit card to a young Eurostar desk clerk, immaculate in her yellow and blue uniform.

Inside the terminal, there is a frenetic buzz of activity. Groups of baggily-trousered teenagers stare sullenly at the other passengers. Harried businessmen talk urgently on mobile phones. There is a long, chattering queue at the ersatz Parisian *boulangerie*, which is doing a fine trade in soggy croissants and *pains au chocolat*. In the bar area sits a refined coterie of immaculate middle-aged French women, resplendent in their Chanel suits and granite perms. They survey the milling crowds with a frosty hauteur. Heavily minted baubles adorn their wrists and finely wattled necks.

I finger my passport absent-mindedly, and decide to buy something to read on the journey to Paris, something which will take my mind off Anna. In the newsagents there are several shelves of novels. I move cautiously along the pristine spines.

My book is not there, obviously.

Bernadette Brannigan's stupid book, on the other hand, is piled high on its own separate table near the till. I cannot bring myself to go near it. There must be at least a hundred copies stacked there. As I watch, a woman with a heavy rucksack picks one up. She takes it to the till and hands it to the cashier, who smiles approvingly. The two women exchange enthusiastic words about what a wonderful writer Bernadette Brannigan is. I experience a pang of anguish. How can so many people be so *very* wrong?

Grumpily I cross the shop and inspect the racks of magazines. The most prominently displayed title has a pouting blonde on the cover, her breasts bursting out of a skimpy bikini top. This is *Bloke*, Gavin's secular scripture. It calls itself a 'lifestyle' magazine, but this is somewhat disingenuous, as nobody – not even nose-to-the-coal-face-of-cutting-edge-trendiness Gavin – has a lifestyle which gets within sniffing distance of the sort of nonsense which it peddles. *Bloke* panders to men's masochistic urge to have their inferiority complexes rammed pitilessly down their throats. It only features men who are high-powered commodities brokers or architects and who write award-winning film scripts or are Olympic gymnasts in their spare time. They only date supermodels with PhDs. Oh yes, and they all own *at least* one restaurant. Or a bar.

The gulf between theoretical and actual readership demographics for *Bloke* is akin to *Just 17*, whose average reader is twelve and a half years old. It's aspirational publishing at its most cynical. But if men are happy to fork out more than three quid a month to drool over someone else's collection of Hermès ties, then let them. Idiots.

I buy a copy.

I settle down and begin to flick through the heavy pages. I am unable to find the contents page, or indeed any content. There are just endless glossy photographs of beautiful models, male and female, and lots of advertisements for aftershave, which all have an annoying sachet glued to the middle of the page. I begin to work my way methodically through the magazine, pulling out every insert and sachet I find. By the time I have finished, there is an inch-high pile of fragrant debris on the seat next to me.

One picture in particular catches my eye. It's a grainy, black and white photograph of a man dressed in a pale linen suit and white shirt. He looks vaguely familiar. He is sitting at a table of a pavement café, a tiny cup of coffee in his well-manicured hand. The man is pushing his other hand through his glossy dark hair, which is just beginning to go grey at the temples. He looks distracted, his eyes gazing off into the middle distance. There is an aura of crumpled distinction about him. Vulnerable greatness, perhaps. This is a man, you think, who has probably just completed a distinguished philosophical novel. He is sensitive, yet unquestionably masculine. He is cerebral, but physically perfect. He's basically everything that the sad bastards who read this stupid magazine want to be. What perplexes me is that I don't have the faintest idea what this is an advert *for*. At the bottom of the page, in discreet type, is the word, 'Hødelfütt'. That's all. No address, no details, nothing.

I look at the photograph for several minutes, wondering what this picture is trying to make me buy. The linen suit? The shirt? Coffee? Am I being obtuse, or is this just too subtle?

About twenty pages in, I finally discover what might, in the loosest sense, be described as editorial content, and begin to read about What's Hot This Month. Before long, a fey Dalek with an outrageous French accent announces over the intercom that our train is ready for boarding. There is an immediate flurry of movement. I hoik my bag on to my shoulder, and join the throng.

My carriage is at the front of the train. The only seat available at such short notice was in a First Class compartment. The man immediately opposite me has already opened his laptop, which is humming quietly. He squints at the screen, occasionally tapping at the keyboard. The man next to him is hidden behind the *Financial Times*. The final man in our travelling quartet, my immediate neighbour, has a copy of the *Express* folded on the table in front of him. He has a moustache which languishes forlornly in the fleshy gulf between two expanses of chubby jowl. The frayed end of his tie lies on the vast plateau of his bulging gut. As I sit down, a whiff of stale sweat assails my nostrils. The man smiles at me. I ignore him, and pointedly put my magazine down on the table, giving my travelling companions a good look at what I'm reading. Yes! I *am* that script-writing architect!

After a few minutes, we pull out of Waterloo. I try not to think about where we are going, and why. I have settled into heavy, absolute denial about the purpose of my trip. We make our way towards the coast, gliding through the Kent countryside. Out of the window I gaze at the alien fields and extraterrestrial sheep. Our passports are checked by gruff Frenchmen, their ties already loosened despite the early hour. They are followed by wondrously svelte and beautiful French women who ask us prettily what we would like for breakfast. I wonder what on earth these delectable creatures are doing here. Our waitress should be sashaying up a catwalk in an exotic Jean-Paul Gaultier creation, not serving us coffee. Her skin is as smooth as the china cups which we humbly proffer up towards her. She has exquisite cheekbones that suddenly make me feel wearily insignificant, mundanely second-rate. Best of all is her gloriously sensuous mouth with its vast expanses of dark red, hugely kissable lips. She looks as if she's just stepped out of a Robert Palmer video. Even *sans maquillage*, this goddess of the coffee pot would have any man hornily salivating. I peer at her badge as she leans across to serve the man behind the *Financial Times*. Her name is Virginie. Virginie!

Virginie's brilliant black hair is tied up in a tight bun. I imagine her shaking it loose before she jumps on me, hot with rapacious desire. The yellow and blue uniform now seems impossibly alluring, promising untold treasures beneath the crackling polyester. God, I think, *uniforms*. I had always thought myself above such hackneyed sexual fantasies, but in the end it seems I'm a slave to the same pedestrian passions as everyone else. My brain haemorrhages with intoxicating images of Virginie's stocking tops.

The man next to me is staring too. When Virginie finally moves on to the next lucky group of diners, he lets out a low moan of real longing. To my horror, he nudges me gently.

'What do you think of that, then?' he whispers, his syllables thickened with lust.

I look away, addressing my pre-sliced grapefruit.

'Isn't she gorgeous?' continues the man. His moustache wobbles with desire.

I pick up my small spoon and primly begin to eat.

'No, really,' he persists, nudging me again. 'She's beautiful, isn't she?'

I put down my spoon and half turn towards him. 'She was quite pretty, yes,' I say through a mouthful of fruit.

'Quite *pretty*?' breathes the man. A low, guttural noise emerges from the back of his throat.

'Well,' I say self-righteously, 'I'm a married man.'

'Oh, of course,' he replies. 'Absolutely. Me too. Twenty-eight happy years.' He holds up a podgy hand to show off a fat band of tarnished gold. 'Still. Eh?' He winks.

Suspicious eyes regard us from behind the *Financial Times*. Idle chat is doubtless infra dig in First Class, particularly idle chat about French waitresses. I look at my neighbour with irritation. What really annoys me is that we were thinking the same salacious thoughts about the delectable Virginie, he and I. We are cut from the same hormonal cloth. I am reluctant to admit this to myself, let alone to him.

Then he sticks out a hand. 'Gordon Hayes,' he says.

There is a disapproving sigh from behind the *Financial Times*.

'Er, Matthew Moore,' I say, shaking his clammy paw.

Gordon Hayes reaches into his suit pocket and extracts a card, which he hands to me. 'Shower accessories,' he explains. I glance at the card. Gordon Hayes is, it tells me, a Senior Sales Executive (Europe). In his fifties and still on the road. I feel an unexpected pang of pity for him. At his age he should be tucked up comfortably behind a desk, the conquering of foreign shores left to younger blades. 'What's your field?' he asks.

'Actually, I'm a writer,' I reply.

'Really?' exclaims Gordon Hayes. 'What do you write?'

'Novels.' I allow myself the plural.

'Are you published?'

I nod as if this is the silliest question imaginable.

'I've never met a real writer before,' says Gordon Hayes, impressed.

I smile reassuringly. 'It's just a job. We're like everyone else, really.' There is a pause. 'My first novel is called *Licked*,' I add.

'Can't say I've heard of it,' says Gordon Hayes.

'No, well,' I reply, sanguine. 'It's only just come out. Published this week, in fact.'

'*Really*. How interesting.'

I smile modestly.

'So, go on, then,' says Gordon Hayes. 'Do your sales pitch. What's it about?'

I frown. 'I'm not sure —'

'Is it a thriller? Comedy? Detective story? Romance?'

I suddenly realise I don't have a clue what *sort* of book it is. 'It doesn't fit into any of the usual categories,' I say. 'It's, er, genre-defying.' Gordon Hayes waits for me to elucidate. 'You might say that *Licked* is a fable for modern times. It's an exploration of some of the baser elements of the human psyche. And it's deeply allegorical.' I grind to a sticky halt. Fuck. What is my bloody book about? Sex. That's it. 'It raises some disturbing questions about our subconscious libidinous impulses. But,' I say quickly, seeing Gordon Hayes's eyes begin to fog over, 'it's also funny. In a sort of bleak, sophisticated way.'

'What, like *Porridge*?'

There is a pause.

'Yes,' I mumble. 'Like *Porridge*.'

'Well,' says Gordon Hayes kindly. 'It sounds good. What's the plot?'

What's the *plot*? I close my eyes in frustration. Plots are for John Grisham and Jilly Cooper, for heaven's sake. *Literature* doesn't concern itself with plots. 'Well,' I sniff. 'It's a bit complicated.'

'Don't want to give too much away, is that it?' says Gordon Hayes, winking at me. 'Fair enough. I'll just have to buy a copy for myself, won't I?' He pulls out a cheap notebook from his inside pocket and carefully writes down my name and the title of the book. I watch closely as he does so.

'Well,' I say, 'I hope you enjoy it.' I rather doubt that he will, if he's interested in *plots*. How on earth have I managed to get myself trapped in conversation with this awful man? I start to eat my breakfast. To my relief, he does the same.

Silence descends for, oh, twenty seconds.

'So what brings you to Paris?' asks Gordon Hayes, his mouth full of croissant.

I put down my spoon again. 'I'm going to see my wife,' I say.

'Ah. Nice. I'm on this train all the time, myself,' he confides. 'Back and forth, back and forth.'

'Really.' I ostentatiously open my magazine and pretend to read. I look at the Hødelfütt advert again. Shoes? Hair products? Shower accessories? I gaze at the handsome model, trying to work out why he looks familiar. And then I get it.

I blink in horrified disbelief.

It's Jean-Philippe Durand.

No wonder I noticed those eyes. They have mocked me in my dreams for long enough. He's grown his hair, which fooled me before, but now I recognise his arrogant moue. Shit. Awful timing. Staring at this photograph of my romantic nemesis brings back all sorts of unwanted thoughts about Anna and exactly why I am on this train. I examine the picture again. Jean-Philippe has actually got better looking as he has got older, something I had not previously thought possible. Perhaps Anna has arranged to meet up with her old flame while she's in Paris. My sphincter tightens in terror. After all – oh shit! – Ravel was French, wasn't he? For a few seconds a diabolical web of intercontinental deception and betrayal spins itself across my brain.

Finally, reason asserts itself. Ridiculous, of course. Anna hasn't seen Jean-Philippe Durand for over a decade. At least, I don't think she has.

I can sense Gordon Hayes looking at me, but I really don't want to talk to him right now. I keep my eyes firmly on the page in front of me. Out of the corner of my eye I can see Gordon Hayes consider our two neighbours, who retreat further behind the *Financial Times* and the laptop. Finally, he reluctantly shakes open his *Express* and begins to read.

The other three of us relax a little.

I find an article in my magazine entitled 'High Infidelity – What to Do When She Cheats on You.' Not *if*, you'll notice, but *when*. This is fatuous, quickly knocked-off rubbish masquerading as meaningful journalism so that men can convince themselves (and their girlfriends) that they don't just buy the magazine for the pictures of models in their underwear. I begin to read.

Ten minutes later, I am thoroughly depressed.

The article examines the testimony of three men who have been cheated on by their wives or girlfriends. Each has the same story to tell: his partner's emotional disengagement, the gnawing doubts, the quest for evidence, the terrible uncertainty. And then, the climactic confrontation

– and in all three cases, to my dismay, the messy disintegration of the relationship.

Of course, admitted all three men with cheerful, after-the-event glibness, they realise now that they're much better off without the cheating bitch; in fact they never really liked her very much in the first place. Anyway, now they're all going out with supermodels with PhDs.

I had hoped that in at least one instance the woman would have begged the man to forgive her. After much soul-searching, he would have taken her back, and their relationship would have subsequently blossomed. As a graceful coda to the piece, there would be a baby or two to cement their newly-rediscovered happiness.

But no.

Instead we learn that all women are selfish, cold-hearted harridans, and that no man with any integrity or self-respect would be able to live with a woman who had cheated on him.

Fantastic.

I flick through the magazine for something to take my mind off this gloomy conclusion. I find the book review page, and my spirits sink lower still. *Licked* has passed beneath the magazine's literary radar and is nowhere to be seen, but, worse, there is a glowing, five-star review of *Virgin on Mergin'*, brimming with unwarranted superlatives. The piece is nauseatingly sycophantic, describing Bernadette Brannigan as 'the leading lit chick of her generation, sexy, sassy, foxy, sultry, *superb*.' Inside I am silently puking. Some hapless subeditor will doubtless get his balls roasted for allowing that 'foxy' to slip through the alliterative dragnet. Disgusted, I move on and read an article about why gingham shirts will be *the* thing to wear next spring.

Our imminent arrival in Paris is heralded by our passage through acres of desolate industrial wasteland to the north of the city. We sweep past the grey platforms of deserted commuter stations, rush hour long since past. Sagging black cables crisscross the low skies. Hyper-inflated letters of graffiti festoon every wall.

Finally the train pulls into the Gare du Nord. Without a backward glance at my three travelling companions, I pick up my bag and clamber off the train as quickly as I can. At the barrier I pass the ranks of people who are peering hopefully past me, waiting to welcome friends, colleagues and loved ones. There is nobody waiting to welcome me.

Clusters of beefy armed gendarmes patrol the concourse, radiating unfocused menace. These boys in *bleu*, putteed up and bovver boots a-glistening, proudly wear their sleek black automatic weapons on their hips as they stride muscularly through the crowds, who pay them little attention.

I put my bag down, and breathe deeply. Through the front doors of the station I can see a man unloading suitcases from the back of a dirty taxi.

'There you are,' wheezes Gordon Hayes, rolling up behind me, out of breath. 'Thought I'd lost you for a moment.'

I spin round. 'What? Oh, yes, so did I,' I stammer.

Gordon Hayes looks at his watch. 'Look, fancy a coffee? I've got a while before my first meeting.'

I glance at the large clock behind his shoulder. It is early afternoon. Anna will be in meetings now. There is nothing I can usefully do before she returns to her hotel this evening. I have the rest of the day to kill.

'Sure,' I say. 'Why not?'

I follow Gordon Hayes to a crowded café outside the station. The English believe that all French cafés have wooden tables, yellow *Ricard* ashtrays and antique posters of the Michelin Man on the walls, but the only places that look like that are in England. The genuine article is more functional, and far more prosaic. This one has metal tables and chairs and a dirty linoleum flooring, scarred by years of use. Regulars lean against the *zinc*, drinking tiny cups of steaming espresso and tall glasses of pastis in between pulls on their filterless Gitanes. Waiters with complicated, multi-pocketed black waistcoats stride purposefully between tables, shouting out orders to their colleagues behind the bar. They are unflappable, efficient, and dead behind the eyes.

While we drink our coffee, Gordon Hayes acts as an effective cerebral anaesthetic, cauterising my brain with his relentlessly banal chatter. As he talks, I do a mental run-through of my acquaintances and conclude that he is without doubt the most boring man I have ever met. There is no let up in the unremitting tedium of his conversation. As he regales me with stories about his adventures in the shower accessory trade, my weary brain gratefully slips into stand-by mode.

Finally he glances at his watch, and with an unfathomably wistful look on his face, he shakes my hand and wishes me a pleasant stay in Paris. He picks up his briefcase and plods out of my life. I watch him go with relief, and order another coffee. I'm in no hurry, after all.

Eventually I leave the café and enter the rabbit warren of the Parisian Métro beneath the Gare du Nord. The sweet aroma of roasting chestnuts hangs in the tunnels. On the platform, a posse of arrogant-looking youths lounge close by, staring at me from beneath their reptilian eyelids. They all sport identical Adidas tracksuits, the stripes on their arms worn with military pride.

A train finally rolls into the station, its tiny carriages and rubber wheels quaint after the vast, sleek efficiency of the Eurostar. The group of youths get into the carriage behind me. I sit down and look out of the window, ignoring their stares. A horn echoes through the train, and we pull off into the darkness.

Our progress towards the middle of the city is rapid. At Etienne Marcel, the tracksuits saunter off the train in moody silence, and I relax a little. Some of the stations are covered in gleaming white tiles, which lend them a certain lavatorial ambience. I finally emerge into the overcast Parisian afternoon near the rue de Rivoli, the fast-moving thoroughfare which is the northern boundary of the sprawling palace of the Louvre.

It is easy enough to find Anna's hotel. It haughtily eclipses everything nearby with its ornate finery – no mean feat in this part of Paris. By the entrance, a liveried doorman stands guard, watching the passers-by. It all looks untouchably grand. My own wife suddenly seems way out of my league.

Five minutes' walk away, I find a smaller hotel, and book a single room for the night. I lie on my bed, staring blindly at the ceiling, wondering what on earth I am doing here.

I still have the rest of the afternoon to fill, and I decide to revisit some of the places that Anna and I went to on our honeymoon, hoping that memories of happier times will calm my anxiety. In the Latin Quarter I find the stall where we bought egg and cheese *crêpes* five years ago. I order another one now. Standing self-consciously on the cold street, I eat it too quickly and burn the roof of my mouth.

On the banks of the Seine I inspect the wares of the *bouquinistes*, where Anna and I bought an antique edition of *Playboy*, from the seventies. Soon after that we went back to our hotel and screwed, furiously turned on by the soft-focus photographs and the rude excitement of each other. Today the magazines are still there, but now they're wrapped in cellophane to ward off browsers. As I walk through the grey afternoon, immersed in wistful memories, a bitter wind sweeps through the streets. I pass couples, huddled together for warmth, their heads turned towards each other as they walk.

In Montparnasse I tour the cafés where Hemingway and his acolytes drank themselves into oblivion and literary legend, hoping that these felicitous surroundings will inspire me and release me from the heavy shackles of my writer's block. At the window of Le Select, sipping my espresso and peering across the Boulevard Montparnasse, I watch the traffic hurtle past. My brain remains obdurately blank, utterly void of ideas. I do my best to look like a roguish *flâneur*, staring moodily at the passers-by. Every woman over fifty is accompanied by a small rat-like creature on a lead, members of the huge canine army of *crottes ambulantes* that make Parisian pavements such hazardous minefields, booby-trapped with endless piles of dog shit. Still no ideas come. Instead I succumb to the inevitable, and think about Anna.

I waited well over a year into our relationship before I dared show Anna any of my stories. I talked a good game, though. I told her, at interminable length, of my literary ambitions and hopes, but I was reluctant to jeopardise the favourable impression that I had worked so hard to create by actually showing her anything I had written.

Anna was gratifyingly curious to read my work (as I had learned to call it) and constantly pestered me to show her something. When I knew that I could prevaricate no longer, I spent an unhappy afternoon agonising over which stories to give her to read. I had fondly imagined that they were all quite good (actually I thought that a few of them bordered on genius), but now I was dismayed to find every one of them clodhoppingly pedestrian; for the first time, I was assailed by the alien arrows of self-doubt. I eventually chose five stories which seemed marginally less awful than the rest. That evening, Anna's eyes shone as she snatched them off me. She insisted on reading them straight away, and promised to deliver her verdict the following morning.

I didn't sleep much that night. I had begun to regret my hysterical sales pitch. I knew Anna would be disappointed; there was no way anything could possibly live up to all the hyperbole. But I was also worried about what would happen then. Would she accuse me of being a stuck-up, pretentious fraud, and declare angrily that she never wanted to see me again? Or would she let me down gently, and treat me with well-meaning pity? Neither alternative seemed awfully alluring. As I lay in my bed, trying not to think about it, there was an urgent knock on my door. I switched on my bedside light and glanced at the clock. It was well after midnight. When I opened the door, Anna was standing in front of me, clutching the sheaf of paper I had given her earlier.

'Hi,' I said, immediately worried.

Anna stepped into the room, closed the door behind her, and without saying a word, kissed me. As she did so, she dropped my stories on to the floor and began to pull her clothes off. Within a minute we were both more or less naked. Anna pushed me on to the bed.

'Is everything all right?' I asked.

She put a finger to my lips, and then landed gracefully on top of me, straddling my groin. We stayed like that for a moment, motionless. Then she started to cry.

'Anna? What's wrong?'

She blinked, and smiled at me through her tears. 'Nothing's wrong. Everything's perfect.' She pointed at herself. 'Tears of happiness,' she explained.

'Oh, OK,' I said.

'Let's see, what else?' she continued. 'Tears of pride, of admiration, of jealousy. But mostly pride.' She waved at the paper that was now strewn over the floor. 'That you could write stories like that.'

I stared at her. 'You liked them?'

She sat back and laughed. 'Matthew, you goon, I *loved*

them. They're the most beautiful things I've ever read in my life. They're wonderful.' She wiped away a tear. 'I've read each of them three times, and I couldn't wait until the morning to tell you what I thought. I wanted to come over here and look you in the eye and tell you that you're a genius.'

I beamed at her. 'Really?'

'Really. Of course, I'm just an illiterate law student, so I'm probably not best qualified to give you an opinion.'

'Oh, rubbish,' I replied. 'Minor technical detail. Quite irrelevant.'

Anna grinned. 'Well, now that I've seen what all the fuss is about, I definitely think you should write full time when you leave here.'

I struggled up on to my elbows. 'You do? Honestly?'

She nodded seriously. 'You have too much talent to waste it on anything else, Matthew. You owe it to yourself – and to everyone who is going to read you in the future.'

My heart felt as if it would burst from happiness and relief. 'Wow,' I said.

Anna reached over my head and switched the light off.

I still don't quite know what I am going to do when Anna returns to her hotel this evening. Indulge in some sort of tawdry espionage, I suppose. I don't know what, if anything, I am expecting to discover. I vacillate between a savage, self-destructive desire to catch her in flagrante delicto, and the desperate wish to learn that all my suspicions are utterly groundless.

After several cups of industrial-strength coffee, caffeine is screaming through my veins, and my head starts to buzz like a microlite aircraft. I feel ready to ping-pong down the pavement between the lamp posts. As I walk back towards Vavin station, my heart begins to batter against my ribcage, and I suddenly become quite dizzy. I collapse on to the nearest bench and sit quietly with my head in my hands for a few minutes.

I need to escape the hurried cacophony of the Parisian streets, and so I walk down Boulevard Raspail and enter Montparnasse Cemetery. Soon I lose myself in the silent maze of tombstones and crypts.

I love cemeteries. The French do death so *well*. English graveyards are timidly populated by anonymous, mossy tombstones, but over here they prefer a more dramatic approach. Gargantuan slabs of pristine black marble, a silent symphony of abandoned grand pianos, commemorate the recently departed. Ornate vaults, Gothic masterpieces of self-aggrandising fantasy, house the families of the *haute bourgeoisie*. A silent army of carved angels watches over the cemetery's visitors, the tourists bearing cameras and the widows bearing new flowers and old memories.

The monolithic black shock of the Montparnasse Tower looms over the graves, an inescapable reminder of the brash, scuttling present beyond the cemetery's stone walls. I meander aimlessly, revelling in the silence, becalmed by death. My heart stops its jackhammering. Eventually I make my way back to the exit. In front of the tombstone of Jean-Paul Sartre and Simone de Beauvoir, someone has carefully placed a pair of cheap black biros. Say what you like about the French, but at least they revere their artists. In France, writers are national treasures. They name streets, theatres and libraries after them. I remember photographs of the scenes at Sartre's funeral. It was as if a rock star had died. Simone de Beauvoir, herself old and frail by then, was mobbed by well-wishers, delirious with grief.

I ponder my own funeral. Delirium seems unlikely, somehow.

I walk northwards through the formal, wintry splendour of the Luxembourg Gardens, and make my way back towards the Seine. Along the banks of the river, barren trees bend in the November wind.

Some time later I arrive in front of Anna's hotel, ready for the evening's reconnaissance. I sit in a smart café on the other side of the street and eat an early supper. I am ravenously hungry, but can hardly taste the food. When I have finished eating, I order a carafe of red wine, and begin to chain-smoke with mystery and flair.

An hour and a half later, two things have happened. Firstly, I have become quite light-headed, the cumulative effect of all of the day's coffee and wine. Secondly, I've begun to wonder whether I've already missed Anna and her cheery crew of legal breadheads. As time stretches on, my aura of untouchable cool vanishes. I am no longer a feral creature driven by unspoken passion; I'm now just a sad and jealous husband, desperate and lonely in a foreign land. I stub out my half-smoked cigarette and stare at the overflowing ashtray in front of me. My lungs feel awful, bloated repositories of carcinogenic gunk, and for what? I look around. Nobody is casting furtive but admiring glances in my direction. Of course not. Who have I been trying to impress? I've been playing to a gallery with nobody in it. This whole episode, the instinctive rush to Paris, the solitary waiting, has been nothing more than an exercise in fond self-gratification. Reality crashes around me. My sorry story is no different to countless others, no matter how many Gauloises I dangle from my lips.

As I am contemplating ignominious retreat, a car draws up in front of the hotel, and Anna climbs out of it, followed by three men in dark suits. I sit at my table, paralysed by surprise. It's just before nine o'clock: they *have* been working hard. The four of them walk past the doorman, heads down, not speaking. They look exhausted. My spirits balloon. Perhaps all of Anna's talk of wild nights has been wishful thinking. She looks too tired to do much more than settle down in her room with a mug of *chocolat chaud*. I light another cigarette, and decide to see what happens next.

Twenty minutes later, the younger two men of Anna's quartet leave the hotel, chatting to each other. Anna has obviously passed up the chance to go with them. I revel meanly in her exhaustion. So much for painting the town *rouge*, I think triumphantly. I begin to relax a little.

Then Anna appears with her remaining colleague. Her earlier tiredness seems to have vanished; she has changed clothes and looks happy and refreshed. Stunned, I watch her smile at something the man has said. They turn southwards towards the Seine. I hurriedly pay my bill and rush out of the café, not waiting for my change.

There are still a surprising number of people thronging the winter streets at this time of night, and it is easy to follow the couple without risk of detection. They cross the river and turn east, walking towards Saint Germain. They stop in front of a small restaurant on the *quai*, and, after a brief inspection of the menu, go inside.

Numb with apprehension, I hide behind a tree on the pavement opposite. Anna and her companion sit near the window. A river of shrieking cars rushes between us. After a brief consultation with the waiter, the man nods, and turns to Anna. He says something that makes her laugh. Her eyes sparkle. She looks ravishing. My heart slips. The waiter returns to the table bearing a bottle of champagne. Anna and the man raise their glasses to each other and merrily drink.

It starts to rain.

Two hours later, I step backwards into a puddle.

I look down. The bottom of my right trouser leg is now richly mottled with Parisian mud. I swear. The puddle wasn't there last time I looked. The rain is falling so heavily now that it has created the small lagoon of treacherous sludge while I have been watching the other side of the road.

My step backwards was an instinctive, defensive reaction. Anna and her dining companion have finished their desserts, and I have just seen my wife cup her fingers around the hand of this other man and look directly at him as she leant forward to light her cigarette from the match he held for her. It was the look in her eye that triggered my involuntary retreat into the puddle: it was a look of brazen, undiluted lust.

The man is also gazing at Anna with unabashed carnality. Like her, he is wearing a wedding ring. Tonight, though, is obviously not the night for arid fidelity. Tonight they are playing a different game, seeking furtive thrills away from home. I know that I am just witnessing the overture to the main event. Before much longer the couple in the window of this chichi restaurant on the Quai des Grands Augustins will progress to gentle hand-holding, soft compliments over coffee, and then they will walk back to their hotel for the real performance, the long, hard fuck.

My jacket clings to my shoulders. Parisian rain is astonishingly wet. There is none of the flaccid drizzle of London winters; when it rains in Paris, it rains without pity or charm. The water lies heavily clogged in my clothes, dragging me down.

I continue to watch Anna and her colleague – Andy, Graham, or Richard; I don't know which. The knowledge that he is married as well, that I am not the only one being hurt by all this, gives me a sour satisfaction. I picture his wife at home with three kids and a Golden Retriever, a dutiful life of school runs and weary submission to the demands of her husband's job. I wonder how much she knows, or how much she cares.

The man has now lit his own cigarette, and is leaning back, talking with the air of one who is used to being listened to. He is, I estimate, at least fifteen years older than Anna. The boss. God, I think, how depressingly tawdry.

Anna smiles as she listens to him talk. She is obviously having a wonderful time, utterly unburdened by guilt. I wonder bitterly when she last thought about me.

As I watch, I try and identify what has gone wrong in our marriage, that it should have come to this. I analyse, dissect, and conjecture, but there is an unfathomable lacuna which escapes me, whipping me up into a frenzy of jangling dread. I am a mass of exposed, raw emotional synapses. I am, frankly, a fucking mess.

Anna's companion, on the other hand, here in Paris with a woman who is not his wife, looks happy and relaxed. His hair has begun to turn a distinguished grey, his eyes crease into rugged wrinkles when he smiles. He is attractive, and he knows it. He is calm, elegant, unruffled. He seems, as the French would say, *bien dans sa peau*. As he flirts with my wife, he gives the impression of unshakeable confidence. Confidence, or arrogance? Or does he just know a sure thing when he sees it?

The bill has been paid. They are lingering over coffee, although the man has begun to glance at his watch. He looks eager to get down to business. I retreat fifty yards down the street, alert and quite sober now.

A few minutes later, the couple step out on to the pavement. It suddenly stops raining. (I cast a dirty look heavenwards.) As they stroll along the river, back towards the hotel, I watch to see whether they will hold hands. They do not. It's all too cynical for words. There's no passion, not even fondness. Just the sordid excitement of the extracurricular thrill, a quick snatch of the strictly *verboten*.

I cautiously follow them across the Pont des Arts, trying to decide what to do next. I still have a choice, after all. I can still beat a retreat to my own hotel, and pretend that none of this ever happened.

Suddenly I stop walking, as a cold realisation strikes me in the chest: I can't ignore this now. After what I have witnessed this evening, things have changed for good. A chill of dreadful understanding shoots through me. There's no retreat from here, not even to the mistrustful ignorance of yesterday. I have to finish what I have begun. I start walking again.

Anna and the man skip friskily up the steps of Hotel Léon and into the foyer. I pass by once, then back again, trying to peer inside. There is nothing to see. The guests pay for their sanctuary, and are well shielded from inquisitive stares from out here on the street.

Finally, after about twenty minutes, I summon up the courage to go inside. They should be hard at it by now. I take a deep breath and stride up to the doorman, who regards me with suspicion. After hours of standing in torrential rain, I look dreadful. He moves smoothly in front of me.

'*Vous-êtes un client de l'hôtel, monsieur?*' he demands.

I smile apologetically. 'I'm *terribly* sorry,' I say, sounding as English as I can manage, all fruity vowels and languid delivery, 'I'm afraid I don't speak a word of French.' I shiver for him and point skywards. 'Dreadful weather. I went out without my umbrella. Silly me.' I roll my eyes good-naturedly.

The doorman promptly steps back to his appointed spot. Whatever I am, I'm not a Parisian tramp looking for some warmth. 'Excuse me, monsieur,' he says in an accent as thick as treacle as he holds the door open for me.

There is a bank of lifts on the far side of the foyer. I stride towards it as if I own the place, and hit the call button. A door opens immediately, and I step gratefully inside the empty lift. As the doors glide smoothly shut behind me, I do my best not to think: to consider my actions now would be to court disaster. At the fifth floor, I step out. On the wall opposite is a sign, directing me to the left for rooms 511 to 544. I must be more cautious now. I am listening for every footfall, every warning of an opening door.

I glance at my watch. It's a quarter to one. The corridor is deserted.

Finally I reach Room 523. It occurs to me that the four lawyers will probably have adjacent rooms. I think of the other two members of the team. Do they know about Anna and their colleague? Is it common knowledge at work, openly discussed and joked about over the coffee machine? Am I pitied, or roundly mocked?

On the door of Room 523, a plastic sign has been placed over the door handle, '*Prière de ne pas déranger*'. Oh-ho. I'm going to disturb them, all right.

Standing there, as I prepare myself to catch my wife committing adultery, I experience a curious epiphany. I am about to bring everything I cherish crashing down around me; I am about to confront the truth I have been struggling so hard to avoid. And rather than terror, I feel strangely elated. This is an end; but it is also a new beginning. A new beginning without lies, distrust, and betrayal. I feel a sudden resolve flash through me.

I step up to the door.

PART TWO

'Hello?'

'No. This was after the pub. And a bottle of Lambrusco back at his. So, yeah, we were pretty well gone. But still. Cheeky *bastard*.'

'I ran into Piers last night. Super chap.'

'Where are you?'

'Anyway, so I told him, look Terry, there's *no way* I'm putting that thing anywhere near me.'

'Stockbroker, I think. But terrifically nice.'

'Can you hear me? Hello?'

'And that was when he produced the snorkel.'

'No, but he used to go out with the sister of a chum of mine.'

'Hello?'

'No, unfortunately. It only went halfway in. But I refused to go to the hospital with him.'

'That's what I heard, too. But give the man credit. I mean, what else are you going to do in Chamonix with nothing except a chalet girl from Dorset, two bottles of Pimms and a tub of sun-screen lotion?'

'Are you there?'

'Nothing permanent, more's the pity, but he won't be able to sit down for a week or two.'

'Mmm. I've been to that clinic, too. Bloody awful business. Tells you something about girls from Dorset, though.'

'Hello?'

I am on the bus.

I am back in London.

My hotel door epiphany did not last long.

I stood in front of Anna's door and took a deep breath. As I raised my hand to knock, there was an almighty clatter from the end of the corridor. I spun around. An old man was weaving precariously towards me, ricocheting back and forth between the walls.

Horrified, I watched his unsteady progress, unsure what to do. As he approached, his eyes focused on me, and he began to say something unintelligible. I frantically motioned at him to be quiet, but he ignored me. Before I could stop him, he collided with me, wrapping an arm around my shoulders to steady himself. He smelled as if he had been submerged in a vat of Pernod. His sepia-tinged eyes were riddled with orange deltas of broken veins. He leant in towards me. 'Eh,' he slurred in my ear. '*Eh.*' As he spoke, a fat blast of sour garlic rolled off his tongue. At this I took a step backwards, which nearly caused us both to crash into Anna's door. I tugged him away at the last minute, but the momentum sent him spinning across the corridor. He slammed awkwardly into the opposite wall, where he remained for a moment, his head resting peacefully against the wallpaper.

'Sorry,' I whispered.

'Eh-*heh*!' cackled the old man, as he began to totter back towards me once again. I tried to shoo him away, without success. He began to talk to me in slurred French. I looked desperately up and down the corridor, terrified that he would wake someone up. I certainly didn't want my confrontation with Anna and her lover to be conducted in front of an audience. The old man began to implore me to join him for a quick tango in the middle of the corridor.

In the end, I fled. I left my assailant slumped against the wall, gesturing uselessly at my disappearing back, entreating me not to go.

As I walked back to my hotel, I wondered whether the drunken old man's sudden appearance at the crucial moment wasn't some sort of sign from above, a gentle celestial suggestion that I was going about things the wrong way. I had been all set to jump, bravely but wrongly, and Fate had clawed me back to safety, patted me down, and handed me a second chance.

I considered my position. Anna still had no idea that I was in Paris. The best thing I could do now was to escape back to London while I had the chance, with my dignity still intact. This was not the time for intemperate, ill-considered behaviour. I needed to be calm, in control. I also needed time to digest what I had seen. As I undressed and crawled shivering under the covers of my bed, I tried to decide what I should do next. The fact that Anna didn't know that I suspected anything was a definite tactical advantage. I could choose exactly when and how to confront her. For the moment, though, I needed to continue to play my cards close to my chest.

The next morning, I quickly packed my bag and left the

hotel before breakfast. Overnight I had developed a dreadful cold from my rain-drenched vigil on the Quai des Grands Augustins. I hailed a taxi to the Gare du Nord and took the next available train back to London.

Back in the flat, there was a cheerful message from Anna on the answering machine. She had called the previous evening, just before she had left the hotel to go out for her romantic dinner.

I hit the erase button.

Sitting on the bus amidst the cacophony of mobile phones later the same afternoon, I am on my way to see Sean in his office in Soho.

It is immediately apparent upon my arrival that Sean isn't really concentrating today. He has a dreadful hangover. It was the launch party for Bernadette Brannigan's new book last night, a star-studded bash at the Ivy. Sean's conversation, never exactly scintillating, is all the more disjointed because the telephone keeps interrupting him. These phone calls are all the same:

'Hello? Yes, speaking.' A conspiratorial roll of the eyes towards me. 'No. I'm afraid Miss Brannigan doesn't give interviews. No, not at all. No. No, not even to *The Times*. Look, pal, I'm not going to beat about the bush. She's just turned down an invitation to appear on *Parkinson*. Yeah. So, no disrespect or anything, but she's hardly likely to want to talk to *you*, is she? She's got bigger fish to fry. She's an intensely private lady. Her view is that people should concentrate on the books, not the person. OK? Yeah, I know.' A wink at me. 'Listen, I'm her agent. I wish she would too, believe me. But she *will* hide her light under a bushel.

And, at the end of the day, when all's said and done, she's the boss. He who pays the piper, and all that. All right. Not at all. Bye.'

I sit in my chair, trying to stem the unremitting tide of snot that is cascading lavishly out of my nose. As I listen to this conversation again and again, indignation and outrage well in my chest. The arrogance! Who the fuck does Bernadette Brannigan think she is? The next J.D. Salinger? Thomas Bloody Pynchon? She writes barely literate pap for intellectual pygmies, for God's sake. Anyone would think she was the most significant writer of her generation with all this tripe about *concentrating on the books*.

Of course, this internal stream of vitriol is fuelled, to no small degree, by the fact that not a single journalist has expressed the slightest interest in interviewing *me*. As I sit listening to Sean fend off every broadsheet newspaper in England, not to mention several from the States and a few highbrow literary quarterlies from Europe, I am consumed by envy. I dab my nose with a handkerchief and listen miserably.

In between telephone calls, Sean tells me about the party at the Ivy.

'It was a really lavish do,' he says. 'Fit for a king. They did Bernadette proud. No expense spared. Champagne, caviar, the lot.'

I think of Neville's desultory effort at the White Horse. 'That's nice,' I remark sourly.

'Yeah. Talk about the lap of luxury.' Sean rubs his temples. 'Which explains why I feel a bit like something the cat brought in.'

'Poor you,' I reply, not awfully sympathetically, and sneeze.

'Yeah, well,' says Sean cheerfully. 'Nobody to blame but myself. You pays your money and you takes your choice. Shame Bernadette missed it.'

'She *missed* it?'

Sean nods. 'She never goes to her launch parties.'

'Why on earth not?'

'She doesn't like all the attention.'

For fuck's sake. This is a bit bloody much.

Sean takes a swig of water, fizzing with Alka Seltzer. 'I had an interesting conversation with Salman,' he says.

My stomach spasms in incredulous misery. '*Rushdie?*' I whisper.

'Yeah. Nice bloke.' Sean yawns. 'Anyway, *he* said that the canapés were the best he'd had at a launch party. And Christ knows, he's been to a few.'

I, though, am no longer interested.

Salman Rushdie went to Bernadette Brannigan's launch party?

I plunge into a vortex of bleak despair.

It is only when Sean bangs his fists on the desk that I snap out of it. 'Anyway,' he says. 'Listen to me prattling on as if there's no tomorrow. We're here to talk about *you*.'

'Uh, right.'

'I've put my thinking cap on,' continues Sean. 'And now that the book has been published, I think we need to raise your profile. You know, strike while the iron is hot.'

'Sean,' I point out, 'the iron hasn't even been switched *on*.'

He raises his hands. 'Granted, the coverage for *Licked* has been a bit thin on the ground so far.'

'A bit thin on the ground? It's nonexistent.'

'All right. That's true. You've hit the nail on the head. Although you should bear in mind that the grass is always greener on –'

'What do you have in mind, Sean?'

'Well,' he says, 'I've had an idea how we can get you noticed.'

'Go on,' I say cautiously, sniffing.

He rubs his hands together. 'What you need is a movement.'

'A movement? What sort of movement?'

'A *literary* movement.'

I frown. 'What, like the Bloomsbury Set?'

'Something like that.'

'What do you have in mind, exactly?'

Sean shrugs. 'I don't know. It's up to you. But something *radical*. Declare war on adverbs, that sort of thing. You need to spearhead a move into uncharted territory.'

I blink. 'Are you being serious?'

'Look,' says Sean, 'I'm not going to do your thinking for you. I'm just telling you what your career needs right now. The best way for you to get noticed is to rock the boat, ring the changes, break the mould.'

'What about concentrating on the book?' I ask.

'Don't be ridiculous. You need a *movement*. And in order to be a proper movement, you need a manifesto.'

'A manifesto? Are you sure?' I ask doubtfully.

Sean nods confidently. 'Trust me.'

'All right,' I say. 'I'll think about it.'

'Now go home and go to bed. You sound awful. What have you been doing? Standing around in the rain?'

*　　　*　　　*

Later that afternoon, back in the flat, I am pacing about the sitting room in a state of high excitement. I should be thinking about my new literary movement, concocting a radical manifesto which will catapult me into the literary limelight, but my mind is elsewhere. At the end of our meeting, Sean told me a priceless secret, which I am presently rolling around my brain, as I consider its implications.

It's a three-times-distilled, top-grade secret, the sort of thing that ordinary people just aren't supposed to know. It's the biggest secret in literary London. It's dynamite.

Here it is: Bernadette Brannigan is a *bloke*.

The quintessential female novelist of recent years is in fact a middle-aged man who lives in Swindon. He spotted a gap in the fiction market for undemanding drivel for women, but astutely realised that in order to be successful, the books would have to be written *by* a woman. So that is what he pretended to be. All that stuff about panty-liners and period pains was rubbish. He was making the whole bloody thing up. The much-lauded 'confessional tone' of Bernadette Brannigan's novels was, as it were, all bollocks.

Chick-lit was nothing of the sort. It was prick-lit.

This, of course, is why Bernadette Brannigan has always refused to speak to journalists and never attends launch parties. It's got nothing to do with disdain for the publicity process or a desire for privacy. It's because the guy doesn't want to be found out. He's been duping his adoring readers for years. I almost feel sorry for them. If this ever became public knowledge, there would be outrage, universal condemnation. Bernadette Brannigan would metamorphose

from a much-loved writer to monstrously cynical, misogyn-
istic ogre.

In the wrong hands, this knowledge could cause mass
hysteria, tabloid carnage. In the wrong hands, this knowledge could wreck Bernadette Brannigan's career.

I am wondering whether my hands might be the wrong
hands.

Finally, I sit down in front of my typewriter. Before I make
any decision about Bernadette Brannigan, I must concentrate on my own career. It's time to give birth to my new
literary movement. I stare blankly at the table. In the
absence of any better ideas, I decide to try Sean's suggestion of declaring war on adverbs. In the spirit of the new
radicalism that my movement will encapsulate, I resolve
to declare war on adjectives, too. I retype my opening paragraph:

```
The peasant rested his weight on the stick
that he carried with him everywhere he went
- Illic had never seen him without it some-
where on his body - and gazed up towards the
clouds that were amassing in the sky above
the terrain upon which they stood and emitted
a breath before intoning in that voice that
the boy loved and admired almost as much as
the man himself, 'All I am saying, Illic, my
boy, is that we should give peace a chance.'
```

I read through the paragraph with a growing sense of
dismay. This is vastly inferior to the original version. What

was Sean thinking? 'Swarthily crooked ash walking stick' is self-evidently better than boring old 'stick'. I look at my emasculated paragraph in despair. I have ripped out its guts; I have stolen its soul. No: I will not, *cannot*, declare war on adverbs and adjectives. They are the pivotal tools of my trade, the adhesive that binds my prose together. I would be rendered artistically bankrupt.

Perhaps, I reflect, the answer is to go the other way. I could become a *champion* of adverbs, an advocate of adjectives. I grab another piece of paper and begin to type.

```
        CAMDEN ADJECTIVE REVIVAL PROJECT

          C.A.R.P. - THE MANIFESTO

 1. We believe that adverbs and adjectives
    are the lifeblood of literature; they
    expand and elucidate; they magnify and
    illuminate. They should be celebrated and
    relished for their richness and variety
    and their descriptive force. Therefore to
    every noun should be appended at least
    one adjective; every verb should be
    enriched by an adverb. Where possible,
    adjectives should be enhanced by a sup-
    plemental adverb.

 2. Characters should, where possible, hail from
    Eastern Europe.
```

I sit back, satisfied. This is definitely a step in the right direction. It is far more sensible to construct a manifesto around what I have already written. Altering my work to comply with an arbitrary set of rules would be artistically corrupt. This way, I get to preserve my integrity. Still, a few further embellishments to my original paragraph are now called for. Another piece of paper goes into the typewriter.

```
The flamboyantly moustachioed peasant, Goran
Dmitrossovic, gratefully rested his not
inconsiderable weight on the swarthily
crooked ash walking stick that he proudly
carried with him everywhere he slowly went
- Illic had never seen him without it some-
where on his astonishingly corpulent body -
and gazed longingly up towards the towering
nimbus clouds that were amassing ominously
overhead in the low sky above the gnarled
terrain upon which they quietly stood
together, side by side, and slowly emitted
a raspy breath before carefully intoning in
that quietly authoritative voice that the
young boy so dearly loved and ardently admired
almost as much as the wise old man himself,
'All I am saying, Illic, my young, impetuous
boy, is that we should give longed-for peace
a fighting chance.'
```

I am excited. The prose is denser, richer, more deeply coloured. Its aftertaste lingers longer on the cerebral palate. Why had I not thought of this before? Perversely, I feel liberated by the thought of adherence to a strict set of rules. I am crackling with creative energy, eager to develop both my story and the manifesto. This is precisely the sort of impetus I need to get over my writer's block. I sit staring at the keys of the typewriter, wondering what to do next.

After about twenty minutes, I haven't written another word. I walk into the kitchen and switch on the kettle. As I make a mug of Lemsip, I notice that it is time for *Fifteen To One* on Channel 4.

Back in the sitting room, I settle down on the sofa and turn on the television.

I spend the rest of the day watching television, thinking about my new literary manifesto, and considering the implications of what I have learned about Bernadette Brannigan's true identity. In this way, I succeed in almost forgetting about Anna. Consequently I remain in relatively high spirits until halfway through the evening, when the telephone rings.

'Hi, sweetheart,' says Anna.

'Hi,' I reply, immediately awash with a nauseating cocktail of guilt and fear. 'How is everything?'

'Everything's fine. I'm fine. It's hard to believe it's Thursday already.'

'Well, time flies when you're having fun,' I say brightly, thinking about all the fun she had last night.

'Listen, Matthew,' says Anna. 'I have some bad news.'

My fingers curl tightly around the receiver. 'OK.'

'The thing is, we've run into a few problems. The deal is almost done, but there are one or two outstanding points that we still need to iron out.'

'Oh.'

'Anyway, it looks as if we're going to finish a day later

than we had planned. We're hoping to tie up all the loose ends during the course of tomorrow, and then try and have everything signed on Saturday.'

'Oh dear,' I say, frothing with suspicion.

'It can't be helped, I suppose. And it could be worse. There was a point yesterday when it looked as if we would be here for most of next week as well.'

'God,' I say, thinking of all the extra cosy dinners she could have squeezed in.

'Quite,' agrees Anna. 'Anyway, assuming that everything goes smoothly, we'll probably go out for a small celebration on Saturday evening. I'm provisionally booked on the first train back on Sunday.'

'Great.' I pause. 'I can't wait to see you. I've missed you.'

'I've missed you, too,' replies Anna, almost too quickly. 'By the way, where were you last night? I had to leave a message on the answering machine.'

'I was out with Sean,' I say, shifting this afternoon's meeting back a day. 'We were planning my next step to world domination.'

'Oh, right,' says Anna. 'Where did you go?'

'Just out for a bite to eat near his office. What, are you keeping tabs on me now?' I ask jovially.

Anna laughs. 'You bet. Beware the jealous wife. God knows what you've been getting up to without me there to keep an eye on you. When I get home I shall expect a full account of your movements while I've been away, together with corroborative evidence and independent third party testimony.'

I laugh to hide my horror. 'What about you?' I ask. 'Been painting the town red, as promised?'

There is the smallest of pauses.

'Not really. Generally by the end of the day I've been too tired. We've been getting back to the hotel pretty late. Last night I just went for a quick meal and hopped into bed.'

I feel a pulse roaring in my head, as I think of her little supper *à deux* yesterday evening. 'Oh well,' I say. 'Never mind.'

'Still, Saturday night should be better,' she continues. 'I dare say we'll make up for lost time.'

'Will your colleagues be joining you?' I ask.

'God, yes. They all love a party.'

Oh, splendid. 'Well, have fun.' I sneeze violently.

'Good grief,' says Anna. 'That sounds dreadful. Are you all right?'

'It's just a cold.'

'Have you not been wrapping up warmly when you go out?' demands Anna, mock stern. 'Is this what happens the moment I leave you on your own?'

'Well,' I say awkwardly, 'I got caught in the rain.'

Anna sighs sympathetically. 'It's been raining here, too.'

'Really,' I say hollowly.

'Well, listen, I should get going,' says Anna briskly. 'I'll see you on Sunday.'

'OK. See you then.'

'Can't wait.'

I swallow. 'Hope you manage to sort everything out.' I pause. 'Make sure you don't do anything I wouldn't do on Saturday night.'

Anna snorts. 'I'll take that as carte blanche, then,' she laughs, before ringing off.

I put the phone down and stare into space.

My brain has been hijacked by hyperbolic paranoia.

I think of Anna spending a raucous evening of celebration with her male colleagues, including, *naturellement*, her dapper dining companion of last night.

Carte blanche?

I sit on the sofa and put my head in my hands.

On Sunday morning I am waiting for Anna when she arrives at Waterloo.

'Hello, you,' she says, wrapping her arms around my neck and kissing me.

'Hello, *you*,' I reply, feeling her lips on mine and trying to reassure myself that everything, somehow, is going to be all right. 'Long time, no etc.'

'Long time,' agrees Anna, grinning.

As we queue for a taxi, Anna keeps up a constant stream of animated chatter. She tells me about last night's celebrations. After a meal at a very expensive restaurant they went to a casino, and then to a club. She finally fell into bed at about four o'clock in the morning. I smile indulgently at all this, wondering whose bed she fell into. A few cautious questions establish that, yes, Andy, Graham and Richard all stayed right to the end.

I didn't get much sleep, either. I spent last night lying awake in bed, perspiring poisonous thoughts, imagining Anna's grotesquely pornographic infidelities, and longing desperately for the sanctuary of sleep. When I finally drifted into jagged unconsciousness, my dreams were worse. My subconscious, unfettered by any instinct for self-preservation, whipped up a dreadful cornucopia of baroquely obscene horrors to torment me. Anna reached unspeakable depths of depravity with an army of faceless men, their torsos freely tattooed and their members stupendously swollen. She was rampant, insatiable, a whore. To my dismay, I awoke with an unflagging erection.

When we arrive back in Camden I carry Anna's suitcase into the flat while she pays the taxi driver. She steps through the front door and takes a deep breath. 'Home sweet home,' she says. 'It's good to be back.' We walk into the kitchen, and I switch on the kettle.

'Tea?' I offer.

'Please.' Anna sits down at the table and idly inspects yesterday's newspaper. I busy myself with milk and tea bags. A few minutes later I hand her a steaming mug. She takes a sip. 'Ah, good old British tea. I've missed this.'

'You're pleased to be back, then.'

'You bet.'

There is a pause.

'I've missed you,' I prompt.

She smiles at me. 'I've missed you, too.'

Seeing Anna finally here in front of me, back where she belongs, I am suddenly hamstrung by both fear and fury. The mephitic pyre that has been smouldering inside me since my trip to Paris threatens to erupt, inflamed by this cool charade of innocence. I stare out of the window, scarcely believing the words I am speaking: 'In that case, perhaps we should repair to the bedroom for a reunion celebration.'

Anna's face falls. 'Oh, sweetheart. Do you mind if we wait until later?'

I turn to face her. Suspicion fogs my vision. 'What's wrong with now?'

'Well, apart from anything else, I'm exhausted. I've been up half the night.'

In the circumstances, this is not the best answer she could have given.

'Yes, I know,' I begin, 'but surely —'

'Can't we wait until this evening?'

'But I've already been waiting for a week,' I say quietly.

Anna looks sympathetic. 'I know. You've been terribly patient and good.'

'And this is all the thanks I get.'

'Matthew, listen,' says Anna, standing up. She puts her arms around me. 'I'm sorry I've been away. I know it can't be easy for you, being stuck in the flat on your own.'

I look away. 'It's not that.'

'I don't know what you think I get up to on these trips,' Anna continues, squeezing me. 'But it's not much fun for me, either. I'd rather come home to you every night – but it's part of the job, you know that. I have to go where I'm sent.'

'I understand that,' I reply.

Anna continues. 'All I'm asking is that you give me a little time to recover from last week, OK? I'm shattered. Please don't be put out if I don't want to be jumped on the moment I get through the door. I understand your frustration, honestly I do, but I'm asking *you* to be understanding, too. Give me until this evening, and I promise I'll make it worth your while.' She tries a lewd wink, which doesn't really work.

'I see,' I say after a moment.

'Is that all right?'

I look at her. 'Of course. You must be exhausted.'

'Thanks, pet.' Anna releases me from her hug and sits back down at the table.

I watch her drink her tea, trying to fathom what all this means. Maybe she's had enough sex over the past few days. Maybe she's still sore from last night. I feel sick. I adopt a mock-inquisitorial tone. 'So do you not fancy me any more, then?'

'Don't be daft.' She doesn't look up.

'I can remember a time when you wouldn't have been able to keep your hands off me if we'd been away from each other for a week.'

At this, Anna looks at me, a pained expression on her face. 'Of *course* I still fancy you.' She pauses, weighing her words. 'Like I said, I'm knackered. And – well, look at us.'

Uh-oh.

'What about us?' I ask anxiously.

'Well, we're both fully dressed.'

'And?'

Anna shrugs. 'It seems a bit of a fag to take all our clothes off, since we'll just have to put them on again afterwards.'

I blink. 'A bit of a fag?'

'Don't you think?'

'I didn't realise sex with me was such a *chore* for you,' I say huffily.

'Oh, come on,' sighs Anna. 'You know that's not what I'm saying.'

'It sounds like it to me.'

'God, Matthew, don't sulk. It doesn't suit you.'

'I'm not asking for much,' I reply, stung. 'But suddenly it's a bit of a *fag*.'

'You're overreacting.'

'No I'm not.'

'Yes,' says Anna calmly, 'you *are*.'

Suddenly I am unable to let this go. 'Anna,' I plead. 'I've missed you. All I want —'

'I know what you *want*, Matthew, and I've already explained that I'd rather wait. Aren't you listening? What is *wrong* with you?'

There is a pause.

'There's nothing wrong,' I say quietly.

'Then what's the big deal? Why is having sex so important all of a sudden?'

'You *don't* think sex is important?' I ask.

'Jesus.' Anna lights a cigarette. 'Don't be ridiculous. You're putting words into my mouth. Of course it's important.' She pauses. 'I just don't see why we have to do it this instant.'

'Well, it seems pretty natural to me, seeing as how we're married and everything, and given that we haven't seen each other for ages.' I pause. 'I mean, we're not quite at the stage when we only do it on high days and holidays, are we?'

'Oh, that reminds me,' says Anna suddenly. 'It was Noon's birthday yesterday. You did send her a card, didn't you?'

I stare at her in horror.

'Oh, *God*, Matthew.'

'I'm sorry. I completely forgot.'

Anna looks at me angrily. 'I asked you to do *one thing* while I was away.'

'It was just —'

'No.' She holds up a hand. 'I don't want to hear your

excuses. Christ, how difficult is it to send a birthday card? And to *Noon*, of all people.'

'Anna —'

'How many more birthdays do you think she's going to *have*?'

I am left speechless. Anna goes into the hall and retrieves the telephone. Without looking at me she punches the keys with venom. 'Mum? It's me. Yes, fine. Got back this morning. Well, the place is still standing. Is Noon there? Could I have a word? Oh, is she? Yes, well, I can't say I blame her. Thanks for the warning.' I am beyond redemption on this one. I completely forgot about Noon's birthday when I discovered that the cufflinks had vanished, but I can hardly tell Anna that. 'Noon. How are you?' Anna listens. 'I was just calling to wish you a happy birthday for yesterday, and to say sorry for not sending you a card. I've been away working in Paris this week.' There is a pause. Anna doesn't look at me. 'Oh, Noon, don't ever say such a thing. Of course you will. Yes. No, I understand. I'm very sorry. All right. We'll see you in a few weeks, anyway, for Christmas. I promise I'll make it up to you then. OK. Bye.'

Anna puts the phone down.

'I'm sorry,' I murmur.

'Forget it,' she says shortly.

'She wasn't happy, I take it.'

Anna sighs. 'You know Noon. There's nothing she enjoys better than a spot of emotional blackmail.' She takes a deep breath, and then looks at me for the first time in minutes. 'I think I'll go and change out of these clothes.'

There is no point trying to resume our discussion. She is angry enough with me already. 'OK,' I say.

Anna stops at the door, and turns to face me. 'Oh, that reminds me. We're going out for dinner this evening.'

'Tonight? Who with?'

'One of the guys I went to Paris with. Graham. He's my boss. One of the senior partners. And his wife. We thought it might be a nice thing to do, to celebrate our return.'

I stare at Anna. She walks out of the kitchen and shuts the bedroom door behind her.

Graham?

We've fought before, of course, but neither of us really has the appetite for the epic wars of attrition and operatic battles that some couples indulge in on a regular basis. We always found that it was more fun to kiss and make up.

The summer after our wedding, we booked a small cottage in Cornwall for a fortnight's holiday. The weather in London before we set off was unremittingly terrible, an endless succession of grey, cloud-covered days, but our arrival in Padstow was heralded by glorious sunshine. On our first afternoon, we drove to Tintagel to wander around the remains of King Arthur's castle. Dismayed by the crowds of gum-chewing tourists who were being ushered through the ruins like herds of placid sheep, we escaped to the nearby cliff tops and walked for miles along the coastline. It was windy, but blissfully warm. We watched the waves smash against the rocks below us. I stared out at the ocean and reflected that for all of the hugeness of Nature, and the irrelevance of two tiny humans compared to the might of the Atlantic Ocean, Anna and I had a bond, a strength, a love, which could stop the earth spinning on its axis.

Then we began to squabble.

It was fairly soon after my brief flirtation with full-time employment as an advertising copywriter. I was back at my typewriter, in the foothills of the first draft of my fourth novel, *Who Knows Where the Angels Live?*, and suffering from chronic self-doubt at the mammoth task ahead of me. I sighed as I watched the white spume froth and fly below us. 'I don't know, Anna,' I said. 'Perhaps this writing thing is a waste of time. Maybe I should get a proper job and be done with it.'

Anna turned and looked at me. 'Didn't you just do that?'

'A *proper* job,' I said tightly. 'One with sober, sensible colleagues and a pension plan.'

Anna frowned. 'But Matthew, I've already got one of those.'

'Exactly.' I picked up a small stone and threw it. '*You've* got one. I want one, too.'

She looked at me, bewildered. '*Why?*'

'I just do. Perhaps it's time that *I* started providing for us.'

'Hang on. Wasn't the whole idea that you wouldn't have to do that? You can't fulfil your creative potential while you're worrying about putting bread on the table.' Anna paused. 'Anyway, we do all right. I earn enough for us to get by until that million pound advance comes through.'

'But that's the point, Anna,' I replied, turning towards her. 'There hasn't *been* a million pound advance.'

She grinned as the wind whipped her hair across her face. 'Not yet.'

'The point is, at the moment there's no money there. And it's just not right. It's not natural.'

Anna's lips tightened. 'What isn't?'

'Look, try and understand this from my perspective. I'm a man, OK? And sometimes I just think that we've got this all the wrong way round.'

'What do you mean? Are you saying that I'm the one who should be sitting at home all day while you go out and work?'

'Not really. What I –'

Anna threw a clump of grass at me. 'You ungrateful, sexist shit. I work my tits off so you can write your books in peace and now you calmly turn around and tell me that my place is actually at home, cooking you supper. What do you think gives you the right to start spouting such antiquated, Victorian *bollocks*?'

'All I'm trying to say is that it's not unusual for a man to want to provide for his loved ones. It's natural instinct. That's all. There's no need to jump down my bloody throat.'

'Natural instinct?' she replied, eyes flashing, furious. 'Are you suggesting that you have a Darwinian right to sound like a bigoted pig? Is that it?'

'No, of course not,' I sighed.

'You should have thought about all this years ago when we first set off down this road. You can't tell me now that you feel emasculated and that Nature should be allowed to prevail. It's a bit bloody late for that. Christ. You sound positively *primitive*, Matthew. I mean, what next? You'll be telling me that you've just clubbed the neighbours to death.'

'Anna, please. Calm down.' I stared out at the sea for a moment. 'Please try and understand. Your income is really helpful, obviously, and it's great that you have a career and you know how proud of you I am. But I'm the man. I'm *supposed* to be the prime provider. I know we're meant to be terribly modern and beyond all those old-fashioned rules, but maybe there's a good reason why those rules were there in the first place. Maybe it's because they're actually – where are you going?'

Anna had stood up, and was looking at me, too angry to speak. Finally, she managed to say, 'My income is *really helpful*?'

I nodded. 'Of course it is. It's a real bonus.'

'A *bonus*?' She took a step backwards. 'That's really what you think?'

Somewhere in the back of my brain it registered that this was probably not a serious enquiry but in fact an indication of impending marital meltdown. Too late, the alarm bells began to ring. 'Ah, no, no, not really. Much more than just –'

'Fuck off, just fuck off!' shouted Anna. 'How *dare* you be so patronising? You *prick*.' She stormed off back towards the car without another word, forgetting that the car keys were in my pocket. I gave her a ten-minute start, and then set off behind her. When I arrived in the car park, she was sitting cross-legged on the bonnet of the car, smoking a cigarette. Her eyes were shut, her face turned towards the sun.

'Sorry,' I said.

Anna opened one eye and looked at me. 'You should be.'

'You're wonderful. You're amazing. I'm worthless.'

'Keep going.'

I sagged. 'Must I?'

She giggled. 'No more Neanderthal Man?'

'Scout's honour, ma'am.' I saluted.

'I forgive you, then.' She waved her cigarette at me in

some vague benediction. I curtsied meekly. 'Come on,' she said suddenly, banging the bonnet with her free hand.

'Where are we going?' I asked.

She looked at me beadily. 'Take me back to the cottage, *now.*'

'Why? Are you feeling all right?' I asked as I unlocked the car. 'What's wrong?'

Anna settled into the passenger seat and gazed straight ahead. 'Matthew, we've just had a fight,' she said pointedly.

'Yes, I realise that,' I said, climbing in behind the wheel, 'but I thought we'd –'

'In such circumstances,' she interrupted, 'the standard procedure to conclude the dispute resolution process is for us to go back to the cottage and spend the rest of the afternoon in bed.'

'Oh, right,' I said, turning the ignition. 'Now you come to mention it, I do remember that bit of the manual.'

Today, though, is different. When we fought in the past, we did so safe in the knowledge that a simple apology was all that was ever needed to restore the status quo. The only question was who would relent first. We could give rein to our tempers knowing that there was always an easy way back. Now, though, I am not so sure. The look of frosty disdain in Anna's eyes, that new, scornful edge to her voice, make me wonder whether the rules of engagement have changed. This time I dare not capitulate, terrified that she will not accept my apology. If she rejects my overtures for peace, what then?

Nor do I feel quite brave enough to confront Anna about Wednesday night. Not yet. I am trapped, locked in silence with my suspicions. There is nothing I can say, nothing I can do.

The rest of the day passes in a close fug of simmering resentment. Anna stays in the bedroom, the door resolutely shut. I prowl around the flat, too distracted to concentrate on anything. I listen to a handful of Ellington records, killing time, furious and frightened at the prospect of this evening's dinner. Nobody thought to ask me whether *I* thought it was a good idea. Was it really too much for me to hope for a quiet night alone with my wife, after a week apart?

Worries rain down on me remorselessly, a never-ending barrage of suspicion and fearful conjecture.

Is Graham her suave dinner companion of Wednesday night?

What is going on?

We are late. Of course we are; and it is my fault.

'Come *on*,' hisses Anna. She stands by the door, anxious to be off. I am looking at myself critically in the mirror, adjusting my tie.

'Shan't be a minute,' I mumble, as I raise my chin to examine the knot. The atmosphere in the flat got even frostier when Anna announced that I would have to wear a shirt and tie this evening. It is, apparently, *that* sort of restaurant.

'You look fine,' says Anna, her voice flat. 'Can we *please* go?'

I'm not satisfied with my tie, but it will have to do. I follow Anna out of the flat. The taxi ride to the restaurant is coldly silent. Anna spends most of the journey looking pointedly at her watch, and checking her lipstick. My shirt collar chafes my neck. I feel uncomfortable, and bloody-minded. On the pavement in front of the restaurant, Anna takes my hand, and squeezes it a shade too tightly. 'Right,' she says, staring straight ahead of her. 'Let's try and enjoy this, shall we?'

I squeeze back. 'OK,' I reply. 'Let's try.'

She turns to me and flashes a small smile. I am suddenly overwhelmed with the urge to confess my spying and tell Anna that I know what went on in Paris. With an effort I hold my tongue. We step inside.

Lighting in the restaurant is tasteful and subdued. The tables are laden with candles, heavy-looking cutlery and cleverly origamied serviettes. The low murmur of culti-vated conversation floats through the air.

'There they are,' says Anna brightly, and waves.

I look towards where she is waving, and see Anna's mys-tery dining companion from Paris. Immediately my head starts to seethe in unfocused aggression. Opposite him sits a nervous-looking woman. The man spots us from across the room, and his face breaks into a movie star smile. I am transfixed by his dazzling grin, like a rodent before a swaying cobra.

The man stands as we approach the table. His shirt is perfectly ironed, his tie spotless, his jacket obviously bespoke. He takes Anna's hand, and they exchange kisses on each cheek. I watch, my stomach performing a com-plicated set of back-flips.

Anna takes a step backwards. 'Graham, this is my hus-band Matthew. Matthew, this is Graham.'

We stare at each other for a moment or two, and then Graham extends a hand. 'Matthew,' he exclaims. 'I've heard so much about you.' He grasps my hand warmly. A faint whiff of understated but elegant cologne caresses my nos-trils. For God's sake. He even *smells* good.

'Hello,' I say, captivated by his teeth.

'You must be pleased to have your wife back,' says Graham.

'Oh yes.'

'I'm sorry to have taken her away from you for so long.' His smile, impossibly, gets wider.

'Quite all right,' I reply.

'May I introduce my wife, Caroline?' says Graham. His wife remains seated and limply takes my proffered hand, unable to look me in the eye.

'Matthew, why don't you slide in there, next to Caroline?' suggests Anna. I do so. Graham and Anna sit down opposite us. Side by side, they look as if butter wouldn't melt in their mouths.

There is an awkward pause as everyone looks at everyone else. Caroline is probably in her early forties, and was obviously a real stunner a few years ago, although a few cracks are beginning to show now. She has on an elegant black dress. Apart from a wedding ring with an ostentatiously mammoth solitaire diamond, she is not wearing any jewellery.

'So, Matthew,' says Graham finally, clapping his hands together. 'Here you are. At long last I get to meet the great author himself.'

I smile blandly at him. 'Here I am.'

'I've heard a lot about your book,' continues Graham.

'Have you read it?' I ask.

Graham shifts in his seat. 'No. That is, not yet. But it sounds interesting.'

'Yes, I think it is, quite,' I say. I catch a warning look from Anna.

'I love books,' continues Graham blithely. 'As a matter of fact, I'm a voracious reader.'

'Really,' I say flatly. Anybody who describes himself as a voracious reader is, always and without exception, an imbecilic twat who takes himself and his opinions more seriously than he should. Next, Graham will tell me that he quite often reads whole novels *at one sitting*. Either that or —

'As a matter of fact,' he says, 'I've often thought about writing a book myself.'

My face remains impassive. 'Oh?' I say politely.

He nods. 'Can't be that difficult, can it? I could knock off a couple of pages a day. I'd be done in a few months.' He pauses to take a sip of his drink. 'Of course, my difficulty is that I never get the time.'

'Well,' I say carefully, 'I'm sure literature's loss is the legal profession's gain.'

'If you ask me, writing novels sounds more interesting than being a lawyer,' says Caroline. 'And *much* more interesting than housework and childcare, which are my specialities.' I look down modestly. 'Do you have any children?' asks Caroline after a moment.

There is an electric silence, until Anna shakes her head.

'We're *waiting*,' I explain. 'Anna's job comes first.'

'Oh,' says Caroline.

I see the colour rise in Anna's cheeks. We have been fighting about this for years. Despite my persistent pleas, Anna has always refused to consider starting a family, claiming that pregnancy would do irreparable harm to her career. She hasn't ruled out the possibility entirely, but any procreation will take place exclusively on her terms, when she is ready. I have done my best to be patient, but sometimes it's hard not to resent her skewed priorities.

'If I were you, old chap,' says Graham, 'I would enjoy your freedom while you still can. Once you've got kids, that's it. You're tied down for life. They're lovely, of course, but they come with a lot of responsibility. Your time is never your own.' He smiles benignly at me.

I grin back, nodding. Although he can't be more than fifteen years older than me, the patronising bastard is behaving as if he's my father. An unexpected calmness settles on me, as I suddenly realise that there is not the remotest chance that Anna could be tempted to have an affair with this man. He may be rich, attractive, and successful, but he is also an insufferable, top-of-the-drawer arsehole. Anna is no fool. She wouldn't fall for his vacuous, oily charms. I look across the table at her. I know that she is angry at all this talk of children, but she is still smiling brightly, the outward veneer of professional charm firmly in place. Anna knows what a cretin this man is. I relax.

'Does anyone mind if I smoke?' I ask. I pull out my packet of cigarettes, and offer the box to Caroline, who shakes her head. Anna takes one, of course, although with a slight frown. I offer the open box to Graham.

'No thanks,' he says. 'I don't.'

I start in surprise. Yes you *do*, I want to say. I've *seen* you smoke, after an intimate dinner with my wife. I glance towards Anna, whose countenance remains impassive in the face of Graham's lie. My spirits darken again at this calm conspiracy. I reach over the table with my lighter. Anna keeps her eyes fixed firmly on the flame. This is an anodyne, desiccated version of the sultry performance for Graham in Paris. There is no coquettish touch now.

I pull deeply on my own cigarette, lost in thought. Anna and Graham begin to trade office gossip. They are relaxed with each other, joking and leg-pulling easily. As I watch them, I feel myself falter doubtfully once again.

Finally a waiter appears bearing leather-bound menus. After a moment or two, Anna murmurs, 'Oh, *delicious*,' and this is met with a sigh of agreement from Caroline. I remain steadfastly silent, principally because, to my horror, the menus are entirely in French. I scan the pages for items that I recognise. Eventually I spot what I think is veal, and settle for that. Graham makes a big show of asking the sommelier to come to our table and engages in a long discussion of the merits of the wines at the expensive end of the list. I look on, hating him.

We will, of course, be expected to ooh and ahh over the wine that Graham chooses. There will be much serious nodding of heads, many elaborate metaphors employed. It's just *wine*, for God's sake – although perhaps to Graham it's more than that. Perhaps it's also testament to his sophistication, his urbane taste, his status as all-round good egg. Suddenly I feel very tired. When the bottle is presented, the label is scrutinised and then a thimbleful of wine is reverentially poured into Graham's glass by the sommelier. All conversation stops as we watch Graham taste it. This is a drawn-out performance, as he sniffs, swirls and sips. Finally, with his eyes tightly shut, Graham nods slowly. We all (the sommelier included) breathe a sigh of relief. The sommelier fills our glasses. Cautiously I taste the wine. To my dismay, it is wonderful.

Graham sees my reaction. 'Good, isn't it?' he asks.

I nod. 'It's exquisite,' I agree sadly. Caroline drinks thirstily. Anna leaves her glass almost untouched.

Our first courses arrive, and we descend into grateful silence as we address our food. I have ordered an endive salad peppered with croutons, which seemed to offer the smallest possibility of linguistic or gastronomic traps.

Conversation is restricted to compliments about the wine, and polite enquiries as to each other's food. When our main courses are served, the waiter slides a plate in front of me. I stare at it curiously. The meat doesn't look much like veal to me. I lean forwards for a closer look, and realise with horror that I appear to have ordered a vast, ungarnished slab of *liver*.

I have always hated liver. When I was at school, every Friday lunch time we were fed great leathery lumps of it, garlanded with small mounds of fried onions. While the school kitchen assiduously eradicated the last molecule of taste from every other dish, by some ghastly gastronomic joke our Friday liver always made it to the table *quivering* with its dreadful, moribund flavour. I would cut up the meat into tiny pieces and then catapult them down my throat with my knife in an attempt to bypass my taste buds.

Now I am staring in disbelief at the largest piece of liver I have ever seen. There aren't even any onions.

Graham has seen my face. 'Everything all right?' he asks.

'Fine,' I mutter.

'I didn't think you *liked* liver,' says Anna, tucking into a delicious-looking piece of monkfish.

'Well, you know,' I say brightly, determined not to be beaten by the menu's treachery. 'I fancied a change. Haven't had it in *ages*.' I carefully cut a thin strip off the grey slab on my plate. The meat is very tender. Perhaps, I think, I have misjudged liver. Perhaps I will actually enjoy this. I take a tentative bite.

The familiar, awful taste floods over my tongue. The meat clogs up my jaws with its cloying richness. Reluctantly, I begin to chew. When I finally manage to swallow, the unmistakable taste of *deadness* lingers in my mouth. I take a large swig of wine to wash it away.

I struggle as best I can through the rest of my meal. Finally, I put my knife and fork down with relief.

'How was it?' asks Graham, who is just finishing his duck *confit*.

'Oh, lovely,' I grimace.

'Well, Matthew, you have quite a lady here,' he says, pointing towards Anna with his knife. 'She's really something. Quite a catch.'

'Isn't she?' I agree, watching her.

'She's been an absolute star this past week.'

Anna looks down. I see a flush of pleasure on her neck.

'Really,' I say.

Graham nods. 'You're a very lucky man,' he remarks genially. And then he *winks* at me. Oh, this is too much.

'Excuse me,' I blurt. I stand up. I need a few minutes' rest from this insufferable man. The nearest waiter discreetly points towards some stairs as I stumble past.

In the toilet, I splash some water in my face, and stare at myself in the mirror. Come on, I admonish myself. Don't let him get to you. He's just a monumentally pompous, patronising prick. I take a few more deep breaths, and feel a bit better. With a last glance at myself in the mirror, I open the door, ready to face them all again.

Caroline is waiting for me.

Unprepared, I am helpless. She performs a three-pronged assault: her left arm wraps around my shoulder, her mouth fastens sloppily on to mine, and her right hand goes between my legs and grasps my balls with an assured grip.

154

I struggle for a few moments, and then she puts her tongue into my mouth. At the same time she begins to knead my cock through my trousers. All of which would be mildly diverting, if it weren't for the look of utter misery and desperation in her eyes.

Finally I manage to push her off.

'Jesus, Caroline,' I gasp. 'What was that about?' Immediately she bursts into tears. I look on, helpless. Tentatively I put a hand on her shoulder. 'Caroline? What is it? What's wrong?'

'You know they're doing it, don't you?' she asks through her sobs.

'What? Who?' I ask stupidly.

'Those two.' Caroline jerks her head towards the stairs. 'My lovely husband and your lovely wife. They're at it like rabbits.'

'Oh, rubbish,' I say.

'Can't you see it?' she demands angrily. 'They're all over each other. And they've been in Paris all week. *Paris*. What else do you expect?'

'I'm sure you're wrong,' I say, more firmly than perhaps I feel.

For this I receive a look of pity. 'You'll see,' says Caroline. 'They'll get lazy. They always do. Then they start getting careless.' She sniffs. 'He always sleeps with his pretty assistants.'

I hold up my hands. 'No, Caroline. I'm sorry.' I pause. 'Not Anna,' I say, more for my benefit than hers.

'You don't think she'd cheat on you?' asks Caroline dully.

'No, I don't. We're very happy together.' I think of our argument this morning and my weeks of interminable worry. I think of Anna's closed hotel door and what might have been going on behind it. My stomach knots. '*Very* happy,' I repeat.

'Fine,' sighs Caroline. 'But don't say I didn't warn you.' Even with her smudged make-up, she still looks attractive. 'That's why I kissed you,' she explains. 'All I have left is revenge. I need to get my own back. And so do you.'

There is an awkward pause.

'Well,' I say falteringly, 'it was very nice, obviously, but I'm not sure if it's the right —'

Caroline takes a step towards me and kisses me again, more deeply this time, looking straight into my eyes as she does so. There is something so unspeakably erotic about such a brazen act that I cannot stop myself kissing her back. My brain momentarily abnegates responsibility; it allows my body its carnal, unthinking response. Her eyes flash in satisfaction, and her hand reaches for my groin again. At once I have a furious erection and Caroline's fingers begin to rub my trousers with an assured touch. We are standing outside the toilets of a smart London restaurant, the clink of crystal drifting down from the dining room above. Our respective spouses are waiting for us at our table, and we are necking like randy teenagers. Either Anna or Graham could come down the stairs at any moment.

I can't remember the last time I felt this alive.

After a moment Caroline relinquishes her grip and begins to grind her hips into me. I am deliriously horny. I want to fuck this woman right now, although whether out of lust, sympathy, or revenge I do not know. I am about to pull her into the men's toilets when I hear the sound of footsteps coming towards us.

Caroline and I disengage as if we've been electrocuted, just as a man arrives at the bottom of the stairs. We both stare at the ground, not wanting to look our interrupter in the eye. My face burns with shame and ferocious longing. The man pauses uncertainly for a moment to look at us, and then walks past me into the men's toilet. As the door shuts behind him, Caroline and I look at each other. The moment has been lost. Caroline points to the door of the ladies. 'I'd better, er —' she murmurs, indicating her smudged make-up. I nod. Without another word she turns and leaves me standing alone in the corridor. Numbly I climb the stairs back up to the restaurant, where Graham and Anna are chatting animatedly, their heads too close together. I slide wordlessly back into my seat, my heart racing.

Anna turns to me and smiles. 'Better?'

'Much better. No Caroline?'

'She's gone to "powder her nose",' says Graham, sardonically carving two sets of inverted commas out of the air with his fingers. Poor bloody Caroline, I think.

'Oh.' I nod. 'Right.'

A few minutes later, Caroline returns to the table, her cheeks flushed. She sits down without looking at me, and empties her wine glass in one swallow.

'Goodness, steady on darling,' remarks Graham, his jovial tone betrayed by an edge of irritation.

Caroline delivers a smile of terrifying, icy perfection. As she does so, she begins to rub her leg against mine. Immediately I feel a stirring in my trousers. I smile affably at Graham, who is looking strangely at his wife. 'May I have some more wine?' asks Caroline, holding out her empty glass. She has kicked off one of her shoes and is running her stocking-clad foot up my shin. My grin becomes more fixed. Graham grumpily pours some more wine into his wife's glass. Caroline suddenly seems to have destabilised. She is edgy, slightly out of control. I begin to worry that she is about to make rash accusations about what went on in Paris. Or worse, triumphant confessions about what just happened downstairs.

Graham glances at Anna, who nods at him, almost imperceptibly. 'Well,' he says, 'now that you're both back, I have a confession to make. There was a specific reason for the four of us getting together this evening.' He pauses. 'Anna and I have something to tell you both.'

Caroline's foot stops dead in its tracks, halfway towards my knee. 'Oh?' I say, watching Anna. She is staring at her empty plate.

'The fact is,' says Graham, 'we've been keeping something from you.'

I glance sideways at Caroline. She is quite still.

'We, that is Anna and I, have come to an important decision,' continues Graham. 'There's about to be a big change in our relationship.'

Caroline kicks my shin with surprising force. I almost don't notice the pain.

'I'm delighted to tell you,' says Graham, 'that we have asked Anna to become a partner in the firm. And that she's accepted.' He beams at me.

I am momentarily speechless. Anna is looking at me, her smile heartbreakingly wide.

'Really?' I manage.

She nods. 'Really.'

'That's it?'

She frowns. 'What do you mean?'

I look at Graham. 'That's your news? Nothing else?'

Graham looks confused. 'That's it.'

'Ah.' I sit back in my seat. 'Wow.' I lapse into thoughtful silence.

'Jesus, Matthew.' Anna looks distraught. 'Isn't it enough?'

'God. Sorry, of course it is. It's *wonderful* news.' And it is. I am filled with wonder and admiration for my wife. All those long nights, all those sacrificed weekends and inhuman workloads, have finally been worth it. At last Anna has got what she always wanted. Of *course* I am delighted for her. But I am also thinking: *This explains everything.*

This is why Anna has been distracted, why she has been working even harder than usual. And of course: this is why Graham ordered the champagne in the restaurant in Paris. They were celebrating!

I have been wrong, wrong, wrong.

I have been a seething repository of misplaced distrust. I glance triumphantly at Caroline, who is sitting completely still. Seeing her makes my heart lurch in icy guilt at our impromptu bout of dry humping downstairs. I put the thought behind me. I walk around the table to deliver a kiss on Anna's glowing cheek. As I bend down, she reaches for my hand, and holds it firmly.

Everything is going to be fine. Anna never needs to know what has been going on in my head. We're back on track.

'Now, how about some champagne to celebrate?' says Graham. He looks over his shoulder and imperiously clicks his fingers. Before long the four of us are fingering thin flutes of Dom Perignon. 'So,' declares Graham, 'a toast, then, to my new partner.' He raises his glass to Anna, then to Caroline and me. Before we can drink, however, Caroline puts her glass down, buries her head in her arms, and bursts into tears. We all look at her, dumbstruck.

'Is everything OK?' I ask after a moment.

Caroline raises her head off her arms and fixes me with an awful look. I swallow. 'You tell me,' she whispers.

'Right, then,' says Graham, suddenly grim. 'I think we should probably toddle off home.'

Anna looks shocked. 'Don't go,' she says. 'Please.'

'No, really, we must,' insists Graham, walking around the table towards his wife, a rigid smile on his face. 'It's been a long day.'

'Well,' says Anna uncertainly, 'if you're sure.'

Graham waves a hand. 'Of course. You two relax and celebrate on your own. You don't want us oldies about anyway, cramping your style.' He smiles without much humour, ignoring Caroline, who is staring at the table, a large tear rolling down each cheek. 'Polish off the champagne between you. You deserve it.' He delivers a perfunctory kiss on Anna's cheek. 'Enjoy the rest of the evening, Anna, and I'll see you in the office tomorrow morning. Matthew, it's been a pleasure.' I grin anxiously at him, keen for him to whisk Caroline out of our orbit. Graham extends his hand towards me.

And that is when I see, peeping out of the end of his beautifully tailored jacket, one of the Tiffany cufflinks.

Graham grasps my hand, looking me in the eye. I stare back at him, my stomach in instant free fall. My mouth opens and then shuts again. He looks enquiringly at me, and then with a quick smile steers his still sobbing wife out of the restaurant. I sit down again, stunned.

We sit quietly for a few moments.

'That was weird about Caroline, wasn't it?' says Anna.

I do not reply.

'She does that a lot, apparently. Always breaking into hysterics at awkward moments. Graham's terribly understanding. It must be hard sometimes.' Anna takes a swig of champagne. 'But that's just typical of her. I mean, of all the times to make a scene, she has to go and ruin my big moment. Silly bitch.'

I stare at Anna, my pulse racing. What have I just seen?

'She's probably tripped out on Prozac. Or Valium. Or any of the dozens of pills she's addicted to. What a sad little wife. Pick her up and she rattles.' Anna lights a cigarette as she speaks.

I take another swig of champagne, staring into space.

'Matthew?'

Graham was wearing the cufflinks that were hidden in Anna's underwear drawer.

'Sweetheart? Is everything all right?'

And so everything changes, again.

Some time later, we go outside and hail a taxi to take us home.

Anna snuggles up to me in the back seat. 'I hope you don't mind me not telling you about the partnership before tonight,' she murmurs.

'That's OK,' I reply neutrally.

She squeezes my arm. 'Graham likes to deliver the good news himself. That's why we arranged the dinner.'

'Ah.'

There is a long pause.

'He seems like a nice guy,' I say.

'Graham? He's all right. A bit pompous. He can be a bit of an old duffer sometimes.'

I grin, unfooled. The old duffer with the Tiffany cuff-links. Good old Graham.

'But yes,' continues Anna, 'otherwise he's fine. Certainly not the worst boss in the world. Although I suppose technically he's not my boss any more. So,' she breathes into my ear, 'are you ready for this?'

I stare straight ahead. 'Ready for what?'

'Well, isn't this going to be the first time you've made love to a partner in a big City law firm?'

I nod slowly. 'Oh, I see. Yes, first time I've done that, as far as I can remember.' The city night streaks past the taxi window. I cannot bring myself to look at Anna. Instead I watch the bright lights shimmer as we sweep by. Perhaps there is an innocent reason for all the flirting that took place over dinner in Paris. Perhaps there is an innocent reason why a pair of cufflinks should vanish from Anna's underwear drawer and materialise on the shirt sleeves of her suave, attractive boss. Perhaps it's simply a monumental coincidence that Caroline's suspicions should mirror my own fears so precisely.

Perhaps, perhaps.

If there are innocent reasons, I cannot see them.

Anna is having an affair.

As soon as we step inside the front door of the flat, Anna starts kissing me, pressing me up against the wall. Her lips taste bitter. She pushes herself against me. I cannot banish the thought of Graham's hands roaming freely over her body, and, worse, her excited responses to his caresses. Images of Anna's depravity dance before me, as she opens herself up, wetly primed for hard rutting.

I am dizzy with jealousy, bursting with bilious hate.

Happily unaware, Anna breaks off our embrace and goes into the kitchen. She opens the fridge and pulls out a bottle of wine.

I gulp. 'More?'

'Of course. We're celebrating.' She pours two glasses. 'Cheers.'

I feel utterly hollow. 'Cheers.'

Anna's eyes flash. 'I've got an idea.' She walks out of the room, and comes back a few moments later with a ready-rolled joint. 'Here's one I made earlier,' she giggles.

I stare at the joint, wondering where she was hiding it. 'Does Graham know you smoke this stuff?' I ask.

Anna fires up her lighter and touches the flame to the end of the spliff. 'Of course not. He'd go ballistic.' She pulls in a lungful of smoke and holds it, gazing levelly at me.

'So you don't tell him *absolutely* everything, then,' I say.

Anna frowns as she exhales. 'Why are we discussing Graham? Come and have some of this.' She walks towards me, holding the joint in front of her, offering it to me. Then she gives me that seductive smile, last delivered across the restaurant table in Paris. The sight of this tired old trick pushes my rage beyond my control. I hold up my hand.

'Anna, wait.'

She stops. 'What's wrong?'

A thought flashes through my head: I can still back down. I can still continue as if everything is fine. The idea dissipates as quickly as it arrives. There's no avoiding this now. My temples begin to throb. I look my wife in the eye.

'Anna, listen. I know about you and Graham.'

There.

Anna's face goes almost white. I close my eyes. That's all the evidence I need. The last fluttering vestiges of hope are swept cleanly out of my heart. I feel utterly sick with grief.

'What are you talking about?' she says.

'It's too late,' I say softly. 'There's no point pretending any more. I *know*.'

'Know?' She shakes her head. 'Know what?'

I swallow. 'You're having an affair.'

Anna turns away from me and sits down at the kitchen table, silent. She takes a long drag of the joint. I look at her, my pulse screaming. Up until now my paranoia has been cosily internal, but no more. Now there is no going back.

Finally, a small smile appears on Anna's face. 'With *Graham*? This is a joke, right?'

I say nothing.

'Tell me this is a joke, Matthew. A poor, unfunny joke, delivered with terrible timing, but still a joke.' Anna's eyes are suddenly filled with doubt.

I shake my head. 'No joke.'

Anna looks down at the table in front of her, her face expressionless. 'Would you care to explain to me,' she asks carefully, 'where you got this idea from?'

'I *saw* you,' I say. 'I went to Paris and I *saw* you. I followed the two of you to an intimate little restaurant on the Left Bank. It looked very cosy from where I was standing. Very *romantic*.'

Silence fills the room, blocking us in. Neither of us moves.

'Well?' I demand. 'Aren't you going to try and deny it?'

Anna raises her beautiful head. Her eyes fix me with a look of such icy detachment that I hardly recognise her. 'You went to Paris?' she says. 'You *followed* me?'

I wave a hand. 'I thought something was going on. But I needed to see for myself.'

Anna calmly rolls the ash off the end of the joint. 'So, come on. Tell me everything, then.' Her voice is cold. 'What happened, exactly? What did you *see*? You watched me go for dinner with Graham? Then what?'

'I watched you go back to the hotel together.'

Anna looks at me. 'And?'

I falter slightly. 'And nothing.'

'Nothing? What do you mean, *nothing*?'

'Well, there was nothing to see. I went back to my hotel.'

There is a long pause. 'You watched us walk back to the hotel, and then you left?' Anna looks bewildered.

I remain silent.

Her fist slams down on to the table. 'You just *left*?'

I remember my hesitation in front of Anna's hotel door, and the old man barrelling down the corridor towards me. 'I couldn't face you there and then,' I say.

'Matthew,' says Anna, her eyes dead. 'What sort of a man *are* you?'

I blink. 'What?'

'You think I'm having an affair, you watch me go back to my hotel with another man, and you do *nothing*?' She shakes her head. 'You do nothing at *all*?'

Why isn't she denying it?

'This isn't about *me*,' I protest. 'It's about you. And Graham.'

But Anna is not listening to me. 'You just left us to *get on* with it. Don't you give a fuck, is that it?'

'Jesus bloody Christ. Of course I give a fuck.'

'Then why didn't you *do* something?'

'Like what? What could I have done that would have made any difference?'

'You could have confronted us. Tried to stop us. *Something*.'

'So you admit it.'

Anna hasn't heard me. She is shouting. 'But no, you couldn't do that, could you? Didn't you have the nerve? Were you too scared?' She stands up. 'Maybe you got some sort of perverted thrill out of it all. Is that it? Did you actually *enjoy* imagining me with someone else? Did you?'

'You admit it?' I ask dully.

The distance between us, across this tiny kitchen, yawns impossibly wide. Anna carefully extinguishes the unfinished joint in the ashtray.

'Do you admit it, Anna?'

She sneers at me. 'You're pathetic.'

'Yes or no?' I persist.

'Listen to yourself.' There is cold scorn in her voice. 'What am I supposed to think, when you act like this?'

'What am *I* supposed to think, when you won't answer my question?'

Anna looks up at me. The withering gaze in her dry eyes burns me up inside. 'You want me to tell you whether I'm having an affair with Graham?'

I list slightly to my left. 'Yes.'

She stares at me in silence. The only sound is of the wall clock ticking.

'I'm sorry,' she says eventually. 'I won't do it.' She stands up calmly and walks out of the kitchen.

'Why *not*?' I shout, following her down the corridor.

Anna turns to me in the doorway of the bedroom. 'You can wallow in your sordid little fantasies on your own. I'm having nothing to do with them. If you think I'm going to stand here and deny your accusations, then you can think again.'

'You won't?'

'No, I won't.' She pauses. 'Matthew, listen to me. I want you to think very hard about what you've said. OK? You're going to have to sort this out on your own. It's not worthy of you, and it's *certainly* not worthy of me.'

'But if it's not *true*, why won't you just deny it?' I plead.

Anna points at me angrily. 'Is that all you can think about?'

'What do you mean? What else is there to think about, for God's sake?'

'You're just thinking about *yourself*. It obviously hasn't occurred to you that *I* might have a view about all of this as well.'

I cannot answer.

'Have you given even the first thought as to how *I* might feel, being accused of sleeping around like some common whore? Did you think for one second what this says about the way *you* feel about *me*?' Anna's eyes, finally, are shining with tears.

'But Anna,' I say, shocked, 'I *love* you.'

She snorts in disgust. 'Wait there,' she snaps, and walks into the bedroom. A minute later she reappears, her arms full. 'One duvet,' she says, walking past me into the sitting room. 'And a pillow.' She throws the bundle on to the floor and points at the sofa. 'You're sleeping there.'

I stare at the heap of bed linen. My brain clouds up with the injustice of it all. Which of us, I want to scream, is at fault here? Why am *I* the one being banished to the chilly gulag of the sitting room? Anna is staring at me, haughty and imperious. 'I'm not playing games, Matthew. I am *not* going to entertain your paranoid theories and accusations.' She takes a step backwards. 'I'm going to bed now. I've got a big day ahead of me tomorrow. It'll be my first as a partner.'

'Right,' I mumble bitterly.

Anna watches me pick up the duvet. 'You just walked away,' she whispers. She shuts the door behind her.

I sit on the sofa, numb.

So much for the grand confrontation. I had been

expecting reassuring words of comfort, angry denials, or a grim confession, but not this. Not scorn.

Why won't Anna deny the affair?

I prowl around the sitting room. Sleep is hours away now. Finally I go into the kitchen to retrieve the ashtray with the half-smoked joint in it. I run my finger along the spines of my record collection. I put on my headphones and switch the record player on. Soon I am immersed in the relentless, upbeat swing of Duke Ellington. The tunes come in quick succession, three minute pools of familiar wonder and enchantment. I lie on the floor, hungrily smoking the rest of the joint, and turn up the volume in my headphones. The massed ranks of mellow horns caress me; the trumpets, sweeter than Gabriel's, give me strength — but not even the music can erase the stain of Anna's scorn. After an hour I switch the record player off. My head spins thickly from the marijuana.

I sit on the sofa and stare miserably at the bowl full of Anna's cherished champagne corks. I carefully arrange each cork on the table in chronological order. By the time the bowl is empty, there are thirty-seven brown mushrooms in front of me. Suddenly these reminders of happier days are weighed down with significance and wistful nostalgia. The most recent cork still has a faint smell of alcohol about it; it is from the bottle that Sean brought with him on the evening of the launch party. The earliest, by contrast, looks worn and shrunken, its bursting contours eroded by the years. Anna's handwriting has almost faded into illegibility, but this cork I remember well.

We were still at Oxford; it was a few months before our finals were due to begin. We had decided to treat ourselves to one last night of romantic excess before knuckling down to interminable schedules of hellish revision. We went back to the small French restaurant where I had taken Anna for our first dinner together, more than eighteen months previously. Over the single flickering candle, reckless from the champagne, I confessed the secret that I had been anxiously harbouring for years: for the first time, I told Anna that I loved her. She cast her eyes down towards the tablecloth, smiling. Then she looked up, gently brushed my cheek with the back of her hand, and told me softly that she loved me, too.

I don't need a wizened piece of cork to remember this. It was, I see now, the moment in my life when I was happiest, untouchable and filled with grace. As my brain floods with memories of that evening, unreachable now, I squeeze the desiccated cork tightly in my fist, and begin to cry.

The following day, Anna and I agree to go for a walk in Regent's Park to discuss last night's fight. It is a bright but chilly winter's morning. The biting wind whistles past us as we walk. It has kept most people indoors: the only people we see are a few dog walkers, some brave mothers pushing prams, and a small convoy of slow-motion joggers in the distance. Just as I begin to explain to Anna about the Tiffany cufflinks, she suddenly turns to me and, without saying a word, slaps my face, astonishingly hard. I stare at her for a moment or two, rubbing my jaw. Then I slap her back, with all my strength. The blow knocks her to the ground. After a moment, she pulls herself unsteadily to her feet, and then hits me again, this time with her closed fist. Now it is my turn to fall over. We both remain silent throughout this exchange of blows. As I am recovering from Anna's punch, a car pulls up about fifty yards away. The door opens, and a man with a pencil-thin moustache climbs out. He approaches us, carrying a detonator box with a T-shaped handle sticking out of the top. The man places the box on the ground in front of him, and presses down the handle. There is a loud explosion. With a forceful crack my head is detached from the rest of my body, and is flung through the air, landing about ten yards away. It rolls for a further yard or two before coming to a gentle stop. I blink. I still have a good view of the rest of my body, which remains standing next to Anna. To my horror, she delivers a well-aimed kick to my groin. My body doubles over in agony. Anna kicks me again, toppling me to the ground. I look over at the man with the detonator. He has pulled off his moustache. It is Graham. He waves at me, or rather at my head, and smiles his perfect smile. He walks up to Anna, and begins to undress. An obscene, satisfied leer spreads across her face as she watches. She licks her lips in lascivious anticipation. Once naked, Graham's monstrous penis dangles nonchalantly down to his knee. Anna throws her head back and emits a throaty laugh of irrepressible lust. I begin to notice just how much having my head blown off has begun to hurt. Somewhere, a telephone starts to ring.

I lunge for the phone.

'Wur-hur?' I ask, my brain still mired in the depths of my nightmare.

'Rise and shine! Another day, another dollar!'

I blink sleep out of my eyes. My neck feels as if someone has tied a knot in it. 'Sean. Thank Christ.'

'What's up, buddy?' asks Sean. 'You sound the worse for wear.'

'No, I'm fine.' I sit up and rub my neck. Pain shoots upwards into my head and down my spine. The sofa is far too small for me to sleep on with any degree of comfort. 'You woke me up, that's all.'

'Ah well,' says Sean, 'the early bird gets the worm.'

I yawn. 'What time is it?'

'About nine forty-five.'

'*Shit.*' Anna has long since left for work. I wasn't awake to wish her luck for her first day as a partner. I sigh. Yet another black mark against my name. 'Well, Sean, what can I do for you?' I stand up unsteadily and make my way into the kitchen. I scan the room for a note. There is none. This is a first, I gloomily realise. Not a good sign. The awfulness of last night's argument comes back to me. Why wouldn't Anna deny the affair?

'How's your literary revolution going?' asks Sean.

'Not bad. I've got two rules so far, and an acronym.'

'Excellent. What's the acronym?'

'CARP.'

'Nice,' says Sean. 'What does it stand for?'

'The Camden Adjective Revival Project.'

'Adjective Revival?' says Sean, sounding worried.

'Yeah. We, that is, I, celebrate the use of adjectives. Every noun should have one. Adverbs too.'

'Ah,' says Sean doubtfully.

'I thought you'd approve,' I say, disappointed. 'Don't you think it's sufficiently radical?'

'Oh, it's not that.' Sean pauses. 'It's just that at the moment, people are going more the other way.'

I frown. 'The other way?'

'More ascetic. More pared down. Less lush.' He pauses. 'We're talking back to basics. We're talking dry, arid, puritan prose. It's terribly *chic* at the mo. It's the new black.'

'Sounds dreadful.'

'Oh yes,' agrees Sean cheerfully. 'It is. Boring as hell to read. Dull as dishwater. But it's cutting edge, and that's the important thing.'

'Look, Sean,' I say huffily. 'I'm not going to alter my manifesto just to fit in with this year's stylistic fad.'

'You're not?' Sean sounds disappointed.

'Of course not. I have my integrity to consider.'

'Your *integrity*?' chokes Sean.

'And besides, real visionaries, by definition, must swim against the tide of popular opinion, mustn't they?' I ask.

There is a pause on the other end of the line. 'Well,' says Sean eventually, 'it's your funeral.'

'I'm going to carry on with CARP,' I declare. 'It just feels *right*. You know?'

'OK. Whatever. But don't say I didn't warn you.'

'Was there anything else?'

'Actually,' says Sean, 'yes, there was.'

'Go on.' I rub my throbbing neck.

'Do you remember that reading in Preston?'

'What about it?'

'Well, there's been a development.'

'Oh dear. A development.'

'No, don't worry. They're still very keen to have you.'

A pause.

'Come on Sean. Spit it out.'

'Can you do it tonight?'

'*What*?'

'Can you go to Preston this afternoon? They'd love you to do your reading this evening.' Sean pauses. 'Go on. Please say yes. For me.'

'Why the short notice?'

'They had a cancellation. Another author fell ill.'

'And they want me?'

'They want *you*, buster. How can you say no?'

I think of Anna's face as she closed the bedroom door

on me last night. 'Well, Sean, the thing is, right, I'm not sure if Anna will –'

'And, just between you and me,' interrupts Sean, 'Stuart, the manager, did mention that if you couldn't go today then they might not be able to squeeze you in at a later date.'

Another evening of fighting with Anna is hardly an enticing prospect. 'Sean,' I say.

'Yeah, believe it or not, apparently Preston is a hot place for novelists to visit at the moment. People are queuing up like hot cakes.'

Anyway, I want to do a reading more than just about anything. 'Sean.'

'And you should never look a gift horse in the mouth. It may be an opportunity that you'll live to –'

'Sean. Shut up, for God's sake. I'll do it.'

'You will?'

'Sure. I'll go.'

'*Great*,' he says.

'Are you coming?'

'Oh, well, you know I'd *love* to, but I can't. I have an appointment. But I'll be thinking of you.' Sean gives me the address of the bookshop, tells me to be there for seven thirty, and rings off. I make myself a cup of tea and sit at the kitchen table.

Even the prospect of the reading in Preston cannot eradicate my awful mood as I contemplate last night's confrontation with Anna. Just about anything would have been better than her cold disdain, the insinuation that this is all simply *beneath* her. Why won't she deny my accusations? I didn't fall asleep until after half past two in the morning. My neck is in agony. At least the trip to Preston means that I won't spend tonight on the sofa. A soft hotel bed will be blissful, even alone. Especially alone.

I unpack my saxophone and angrily begin to play, honking and braying, allowing the tone to bend and distort. The sound is harsh and ugly, and just now it feels perfect. I funnel my anger into the bell of my saxophone. It emerges in a spiralling, boiling eddy of furious notes. After twenty minutes, however, I feel no better. I need another outlet for my frustration. I am hurting, and I want to lash out, share the pain, dilute my own grief. It's the wounded who are the most dangerous.

An idea occurs to me. I go into the hallway and flick through the telephone directory. I dial the main switchboard of the *Sun* newspaper and ask to be put through to the news desk. After a moment there is the sound of a receiver being picked up.

'Yes?' demands a bored voice.

'Hello,' I say hesitantly. 'I have a story that might interest you. It's about Bernadette Brannigan, the author.'

The train journey to Preston is relatively uneventful. I didn't ring Anna to tell her that I was going. Instead I just left a note on the kitchen table. Let her come home to an empty house tonight; that might make her think a bit. I flick through my copy of *Licked*, trying to find extracts which are appropriate for reading out loud. It's a harder decision than I anticipated. In the end I decide to read the opening of the novel, a breathless, intoxicating riff on the excitement of discovering a new stamp, tracing its provenance, and placing it in the right position, millimetre-perfect, on a fresh page of the stamp album. Ivo, the sadomasochist rubber fetishist who delivers this rhapsodic overture, pays maniacal attention to the smallest details of the philatelic process; this obsession is a metaphor for his hyper-critical self-analysis, which renders him socially dysfunctional. (It also explains why he has a thing for whips and tight-fitting shiny rubber suits.) I find a few other extracts to read, in case the crowd demands an encore.

I go to the train's buffet car to buy myself something to eat. The only thing available is a curried chicken sandwich in a crumpled triangular plastic container. The packet, ominously, has pale drops of condensation gathering on the inside, as if the luminous yellow sludge festering between the slices of bread is actually alive. I'm so hungry that I buy it anyway, along with four cans of Tennants Extra, and return to my seat to brood about the problems I have left behind me in London. By the time the train pulls into Preston station, I have drunk all four cans, and am feeling more resolute, if also less focused.

I climb into a cab and give the driver the address of the bookshop. As we go through the dark, rain-lashed streets, my excitement increases, and I try to forget about Anna for a while. I have descended from my ivory tower; I'm going to walk among my readers. I am terrified and exhilarated at the same time.

Finally we pull up in a deserted street next to a small bookshop. Inside, the lights are shining warmly. There is an enormous poster in the shop window advertising *Virgin on Mergin'*. My spirits dip a little. Inside the shop there is a hastily constructed sign.

Michael Moore will be reading from his new novel,

Locked

FREE WINE

There doesn't appear to be anybody in the shop except for me. I glance at my watch. It's seven forty-five. I look around. As I turn I almost knock over an old woman who has crept up silently behind me.

'I'm sorry,' I say. 'I didn't see you there.'

The old woman looks at me suspiciously. 'Can I help you?' she asks gruffly.

'Do you work here?' The old woman nods. 'Is Stuart about?'

There is a long pause, followed by another single but emphatic nod. The woman is looking me up and down with a critical eye as if I were a heifer at market. 'Stuart's my son,' she croaks.

'Really?' I pause. 'You must know his cousin Sean, then.'

'Sean?' The old woman's face darkens. 'He's a cheesy southern poof,' she whispers. She pronounces 'poof' to rhyme with 'roof'.

I am unsure how to respond to this. 'He's my agent,' I say apologetically.

'You look like a cheesy southern poof an' all,' she replies.

'Well, I'm Matthew Moore.' I point towards the sign at the front of the shop. 'I'm giving the reading this evening.'

'I'll go and fetch Stuart,' mutters the old woman. She turns and clomps heavily towards the back of the shop. I follow her.

Near the back of the bookshop, a space has been cleared. Four rows of plastic chairs have been set out. At the front stands a table, on which sit four bottles of wine and twenty or so neatly arranged wine glasses.

And five copies of my book.

It is a delicious moment when a novelist first sees his work in the context for which it was intended – in the cosy, warm atmosphere of a bookshop. It has been worth waiting for. Five copies of my work, my *baby*, stacked neatly one on top of the other, pristine, waiting for curious hands to prise them open and release the treasures within.

I take a step backwards to get a better look. There is a strangled yelp. I turn to face a man who is standing so close behind me that I have trodden heavily on his toe.

'Sorry,' I say. Behind the man lurks the old woman, who is staring at me suspiciously, doubtless mindful of the dangers posed to Preston society by cheesy southern poofs. 'You must be Stuart,' I say to the man.

The man nods. 'That's right.'

I put out my hand. 'Matthew Moore.'

He shakes it limply. 'Thanks for coming at such short notice,' he says. 'The guy who was meant to be giving the reading tonight isn't well, apparently.'

'Oh dear,' I say. Stuart looks about my age, but there is a palpable aura of drably resigned defeat about him that makes him seem ten years older. He is overweight, and wears his excess baggage awkwardly, bulging in helpless ostentation. Extra sausages of flab hang off his face like rolls of long-forgotten Plasticine. His tiny eyes squint unhappily at me. He is the most immediately depressing man I have ever met.

Stuart gestures towards the empty chairs. 'All ready for you.'

'Super,' I say, feeling the contents of the four cans of lager swilling about in my stomach.

'You won't read for too long, will you?' says Stuart. 'Only we don't like to stay open longer than we need to.'

'Oh. OK. How long do you think?'

Stuart stares at his grey shoes thoughtfully. 'Fifteen minutes?'

'Really? Is that all?'

'Well, you can try for longer if you like,' replies Stuart unenthusiastically. 'But people get a bit fidgety after a while.'

'I'll just play it by ear,' I suggest.

'Suit yourself. Do you want some wine?' Stuart walks over to the table and picks up a bottle.

'Thanks.'

He pours me a glass of red wine, and hands it to me. 'Cheers,' he intones, utterly cheerlessly.

'Cheers.' I glance at my watch. It is almost eight o'clock. Apart from the two of us and Stuart's mum, the shop is empty.

'Don't worry,' says Stuart. 'They'll be here in a minute. They're all in the pub over the road.'

'OK,' I say uncertainly. *They*? I take a gulp of wine, and point to the small stack of books on the table. 'Shall I sign those, before we start?'

Stuart hesitates. 'Actually, if you don't mind, I'd rather you didn't. If you sign them, I can't send them back if they're not sold.'

'Ah,' I say.

'If someone actually wants to buy a copy, then you can

sign it, obviously, no problem.' Stuart sounds as if the odds of someone wanting to buy my book are impossibly remote, little more than a statistically technical possibility.

Before I can reply, the door opens and three people walk in. 'Ahoy there!' shouts a middle-aged man, with greasy, shoulder-length hair, who is wearing just a T-shirt, despite the bitterly cold weather outside. 'Stuart, you fat fucker! Where's the booze?'

'All right, Rod,' says Stuart. He points to the table. 'Wine's over there. Hi, Ash. Cherie.' Stuart addresses the two women who have followed Rod into the shop. They nod at Stuart silently, and without looking at me join Rod in front of the table and help themselves to two glasses of wine each, before sitting down in the front row of seats.

Rod leans back on the two rear legs of his chair and emits a long, loud belch of singular unpleasantness, looking terribly pleased with himself. 'So, Stu, who have you got lined up for us tonight?'

Stuart looks at me enquiringly. I glance at Rod, Ash and Cherie. 'D'you think this will be it?' I whisper.

Stuart looks at me dolefully, and nods.

'Might as well get started then, I suppose,' I say, dejected. I shouldn't have bothered coming. This has been a complete waste of time.

'OK,' says Stuart. He perches on the edge of the table, which creaks in protest. I finish my glass of wine and administer a quick refill. 'Hello, everyone, and thank you all very much for coming,' says Stuart. As he is speaking, his mother slides into one of the empty chairs. 'We're very pleased to extend a warm welcome this evening to Michael Moore, who is not only a first-time novelist, but is also at the, er, vanguard of literary fashion with his new and radical literary theory, mackerel.'

I lean forward. 'CARP,' I say.

'Hmm?' Stuart turns towards me.

'It's CARP. The literary movement. The Camden Adjective Revival Project. And it's *Matthew* Moore.'

'Right. Of course.' Stuart turns blithely back to his audience. 'So, yes, as I was saying, it's a double honour to welcome, er, such a distinguished literary figure to Preston this evening. Michael Moore.' At this, Stuart turns to me. The trio in the front row are squabbling over the wine bottle that they are passing between them, and it is left to Stuart's mother to clap, which she does with a certain grim relish.

'Thank you very much, Stuart,' I say. 'It's very nice to be here tonight. I hope that you enjoy these readings from my first novel, *Licked*, which has just been published.' I point at the small stack of books on the table behind me. 'I thought I might begin with a brief —'

'Excuse me, pal.' Rod is speaking to me. 'Sorry to interrupt, yeah, but is this going to take long? Only I'm dying for a slash. And the pub shuts in three hours.'

This prompts sniggering from Ash and Cherie. 'Not long, no,' I mumble.

'Where are you from?' asks Cherie.

'London.'

'Hah!' Rod snorts triumphantly. 'I knew it. Cheesy southern poof.'

I look towards Stuart, who just shrugs at me. Stuart's mother, I notice, has got out her knitting, and is nodding in vigorous agreement. The quiet rhythmic click of her knitting needles floats through the bookshop. I take a large mouthful of wine and press on. 'I thought I might start with a passage from the beginning of the novel.'

I launch into Ivo's opening monologue. The reading is punctuated by loud yawns from Rod and the frequent clinking of bottle on glass as the front row pours more wine. After about five minutes, the shop door opens, and all five members of the audience turn to see who has come in. I continue resolutely on. From the corner of my eye a gaunt figure weaves its way towards us. Rather than slipping into a chair and settling down to listen, however, the new arrival approaches the table. From him emanates a potent odour of dustbins, sweat, and alcohol. He pours himself a glass of wine and starts to cough loudly.

I put my book down and stare at him. The man is a grey-haired, tousled tramp. He is wearing a heavy overcoat, soaked through from the rain and slaked with mud. His mismatched boots do not have laces, and his hands are covered by black fingerless gloves. Realising that I have stopped reading, he turns to me and smiles. What few teeth he has left emerge at improbable angles from around the periphery of his gums, like dilapidated yellow tombstones, collapsing into the ground in a sadly inelegant farewell.

'Don't mind me,' says the tramp.

'Do you mind if I continue?' I ask.

He gestures expansively. 'Please do.' I prepare to carry on reading. Just then, the door opens again.

This time there is an appreciative whistle from Rod. The newcomer is a pretty young woman, dressed in a black leather jacket, a short skirt and tight-fitting cerise top. As we all watch her approach, she smiles self-consciously, and slips quietly into the back row of chairs. 'Wouldn't you like a drink?' I say to her. 'Since we've stopped anyway.'

She looks down at her lap, blushing. 'No thanks,' she murmurs. 'I've just come for the reading.'

'Oh,' I say, beaming heartily. 'Right.' I begin reading again, and make it to the end of the passage without further interruption. The audience seems oddly unmoved by Ivo's adventures, and when I finish they do not react, so I close the book and smile modestly. There is still no response, so I say a pointed, 'Thank you very much'. The pretty girl at the back begins to applaud. She is slowly joined by the other members of the audience, except the tramp, who is now asleep, snoring gently, his head resting on his chest.

Stuart clears his throat and begins to clamber to his feet, but I am faster. 'And *now*, I'd like to read you another extract,' I say quickly. This is the only reading I've got, so I'm going to make the most of it. Stuart sits down again, exchanging looks with his mother. There is an outbreak of disbelieving sighs from Rod, Ash, and Cherie.

During this second reading, I start to stumble over my words, and occasionally lose the sense of the phrases I am reading. It dawns on me that after four cans of beer and several glasses of wine, I am now really quite drunk. A bleak emptiness settles on me. Anna isn't talking to me. My marriage, my whole bloody *life*, is acutely imperilled. So why the fuck am I wasting my time here? I should be at home with Anna, trying to resolve our problems, rather than prostituting myself in front of these unappreciative louts. Suddenly I am weighed down with a sense of terrible hopelessness, and abruptly end the reading in the middle of a paragraph. The narrative is halted in full flow, but nobody seems to notice.

This time Stuart wastes no time in coming to join me at the front. 'Well,' he says, 'that was, I'm sure you'll all agree, illuminating.'

The audience ignore him. Rod, Ash and Cherie are finishing off their wine and are making plans to go back to the pub; Stuart's mum is putting her knitting away; the tramp is fast asleep. The young woman who came in late is inspecting her fingernails. I feel ridiculous. As the alcohol begins to numb my brain, I start to feel extremely sorry for myself.

'OK,' says Stuart reluctantly. 'Any questions?'

The pretty girl at the back puts up her hand. 'I was wondering,' she says shyly, 'whether you used your own experiences when writing the book.'

I smile at her. It *is* the most hackneyed question imaginable, but at least she has asked it with due sincerity. 'It's an interesting point,' I say, trying not to slur my words. 'Certainly, I was a keen stamp collector when I was younger, and so yes, I did use that experience.'

There is a pause, and then the girl raises her hand again. 'Do you consider this book to be a big departure from *Before Your Very Eyes*?'

I stare at her, and shake my head. 'Sorry, what?'

'*Before Your Very Eyes*,' says the girl. 'Your last book.'

I look questioningly at Stuart.

'Ah, no, sorry,' says Stuart. 'Different author. That's Alex George. He was supposed to be here this evening, but couldn't make it.'

The girl's face drops. 'So you're not –'

'Alex George?' I snarl. 'No I'm bloody not.' Who the

fuck is Alex George, anyway? The look of disappointment on the girl's face is terrible to see. She thought I was someone else.

'Anyway,' interrupts Stuart, seeing his chance, 'that's been really interesting, and many thanks to Mike for coming all the way from London to see us this evening.'

There is a smattering of bored applause.

'Is that it?' asks Rod. Stuart nods. Rod, Ash, and Cherie stand up. 'Grand. Thanks a lot, Stu. See you over the road in a couple of minutes?'

'Yeah,' says Stuart glumly. 'I'll just close up here.' He walks over to the tramp and gently shakes him awake.

The tramp shuffles out of the shop, followed by Stuart's mother. The girl in the leather jacket has already left. We haven't sold a single copy of the book. I don't care any more. I just want to go to bed.

'So, Stuart,' I say. 'Where am I sleeping tonight?'

Stuart looks at me blankly. 'I have no idea.'

'You haven't arranged a hotel?'

He shakes his head. 'Sean didn't mention it, no.'

I blink. I am drunk, and marooned in Preston on a cold, rainy night in November. Stuart is turning the lights out. He looks at me, unblinking. 'Look, do you fancy a drink?'

A bitter wind whips past my ears as I struggle up the deserted platform. Finally I make it to the station concourse and stumble out into the night. It is one o'clock in the morning. I can hear a constant stream of traffic hurtling along the Euston Road.

I allow the rain to hit my face as I walk, hoping that it will sober me up a little for the cab ride home. I am murderously drunk. I stayed in the pub with Stuart, Rod, Ash and Cherie until the last possible moment before catching the last train back to London. On the journey home I bought four more cans of Tennants Extra, which I drank while I tried to work out what to do about Anna. And I have come to a decision.

I have been a fool.

Anna is the important thing. If she wants me to forget about this business with Graham, then I will do so. The important thing, I realised as loneliness swept over me, is that she and I are together. Everything else is irrelevant.

I will explain all this to her in the morning. I am prepared to forget that her affair with Graham ever happened, if she is. And then everything will be better.

Three empty cabs pass without stopping, the drivers shaking their heads at me as they go by. I start to walk home in the rain.

By the time I arrive back at the flat, I am very wet and very cold. I briefly debate whether I should wake Anna up now to discuss our problems. In the end, I decide against it. I am far too drunk. Instead I tiptoe quietly past the bedroom door and into the sitting room. I undress, and stretch out on the sofa as best I can. The blackness crowds in.

For once, I sleep peacefully.

When I awake, however, my head is throbbing, my mouth is parched, and my limbs are aching sourly. I look at my watch. It is almost nine o'clock. Anna left for work an hour ago. I have missed her again. Gingerly I sit upright, and wobble queasily for a moment. I need tea.

My note to Anna explaining my trip to Preston is still sitting on the kitchen table. I throw it into the bin. For the second morning in a row, there is no note from her. So, there has been no thawing on her part. Anna is still playing the ice queen. I switch on the kettle. We've just had the worst fight in our thirteen years together, but by the time Anna comes home tonight we won't have seen each other for forty-eight hours. This is no sort of marriage, I reflect miserably. We're living in the same home, but orbiting different planets. Well, tonight all that will change. I shall apologise and cravenly beg her forgiveness. I want my ice queen back.

In the sitting room, I sit on the sofa and try to remain as still as possible. My skin excretes a noxious sheen of alcohol. I think back to last night's reading in Preston. I had obviously stumbled upon some sort of debauched drinking club. None of the audience had been even remotely interested in my book. They were just there for the free wine – except for the girl in the leather jacket, and she had thought I was someone else.

I sip my tea, imagining how it should have been: the girl comes up to me afterwards, her pretty eyes shining with excitement, and shyly admits to being my greatest fan. I listen to her enthusiastic praise, and then magnanimously sign her well-thumbed copy of my novel. As we chat, her pupils dilate in lustful adoration.

There is a vague stirring in my boxer shorts. I've never considered the erotic charge of hero worship before. Imagine: click your fingers, and they're yours. I picture myself handing the signed book back to the girl; then I bend down and whisper in her ear. Her eyes widen, and then she nods.

Five minutes later, the girl and I are standing in a dark alley behind the shop. I press her up against a wall. She claws at my groin and I knead her breasts through her cerise top. After much fumbling she undoes my trousers and my cock springs into the cold evening air. She takes it in one hand, squeezing urgently. With her other hand she greedily hikes up her skirt and pulls down her knickers. The thin strip of black nylon hangs suspended between her knees. The girl rubs herself quickly. The white clouds of our mingled breath billow into the cold night air. Then she pulls me close, opens her legs, and guides me inside her, grunting in satisfaction as I enter her. Only now does she look me in the eye, as we begin to fuck, a satisfied look on her face as I fill her up. Cheesy southern poof, eh? Ha!

(Back on the sofa in London, I look down. I have a fair-to-middling erection, not too shoddy given the state of my hangover. It seems a shame to waste it. I wander into the bathroom and pull off half a yard of toilet paper, and then return to the sofa. I lower my boxer shorts.)

The girl and I fill the alley with the strangulated sounds of our passion. We are in separate worlds of carnal frenzy, each body its own axis of sensual, selfish pleasure. The girl's breathing gets heavier. Her thrusts become more urgent. Before long I feel the nerve endings bunching up at the base of my spine, amassing, preparing for the explosion of pleasure. I pump between the girl's legs, fucking her hard, fucking

'Jesus, Matthew, what are you *doing*?'

Anna is standing in the doorway in her pyjamas, staring at me.

Instinctively I roll over sideways, diving for the protective sanctuary of the duvet. 'Nothing,' I shout.

'It was a rhetorical question,' yawns Anna, turning away and going into the kitchen. 'I could *see* what you were doing. Charming.'

'It wasn't what it looked like,' I insist.

Anna's voice floats through from the kitchen. 'Matthew, you were wanking like a fourteen-year-old.'

'What are you doing here, anyway?' I demand, my face hot. 'You should have been at work ages ago.'

Anna walks back into the sitting room with a steaming cup of coffee. 'I know.' She sits down at the other end of the sofa. 'I feel like shit. I have the hangover from hell. And when the alarm went off this morning, I thought, "Well, sod it, I'm the boss now, aren't I?" So I awarded myself the day off to recover.' She gingerly sips her coffee.

'Hangover? What happened last night?'

'We went out to celebrate my promotion. Drinks, then more drinks, then posh Italian grub, then more drinks, then a club.' She pauses. 'I did call you to tell you, but you weren't in.'

'No.'

Anna puts her mug down and rubs her temples. 'Jesus, my head hurts,' she says quietly. 'Have we got any aspirin?'

'In the bathroom,' I reply. 'Do you want some?'

'Please.' Anna doesn't look up.

In the bathroom, I find the bottle of aspirin and tip out three pills. I am desperate to know more about what happened last night. Above all, I want to know if Graham went along for the fun. But any such enquiries will now be deemed too inquisitive, crossing that line from benign interest to paranoid interrogation. I will have to be patient and wait to see what scraps of information Anna chooses to pass my way. She takes the pills without a word, and gulps them down. After a moment she collapses back on to the sofa with a dramatic sigh.

'Everything OK?' I ask.

Anna groans, and rolls over. 'No,' comes the muffled reply. 'Awful.'

'Oh dear.' I wait for her to ask about my trip to Preston.

Anna turns back over and stares at the ceiling. 'Fucking hell,' she murmurs. 'Never again.'

She doesn't ask about my trip to Preston.

'Well,' I say, 'at least you'll be home today. That's good.'

She looks at me. 'Is it?'

'Of course.'

'Won't I be disturbing your writing?'

Oh, that's right: Anna still thinks I spend my days *writing*.

I shrug. 'One day off won't kill me,' I say. 'Anyway, don't you want to hear about Preston?'

Anna frowns. 'Preston?'

'The reading.'

She shakes her head. 'You've lost me.'

'What time did you get home last night?' I ask.

'Late. About three.'

'Ah. I see.' When I had crept so carefully past our bedroom last night, it had been empty. Anna was still out carousing. She hadn't even seen my note. I have gone all the way to Preston and back, and Anna has not even realised that I have been away. A feeling of utter irrelevance settles upon me. 'Well,' I say, 'I went to Preston yesterday. To a bookshop. For a reading.'

'Was it good?'

'Not especially.'

'Oh dear.' There is a pause. 'Is that why you've got stuff written on your forehead?' asks Anna.

'I beg your pardon?'

She looks at me. 'You didn't know?'

I stride into the bathroom and look at myself in the mirror. Sure enough, someone – probably Rod – has scrawled CHEESY SOUTHERN POOF across my forehead in black felt-tip pen, which would explain why the taxi drivers wouldn't pick me up last night.

'*Bastards*,' I mutter, walking back into the sitting room.

'Look,' says Anna, 'I really need to go back to sleep. Otherwise I'm going to be fantastically sick.'

'Before you go, there's something I want to say.'

Anna looks at me warily. 'What?'

'It's about our fight on Sunday evening. About, you know. What I said.'

Anna sighs. 'Matthew, I'm really not in the mood, or a fit state, for an argument just at the moment.'

I hold up my hand. 'I know. I know.' I take a deep breath. 'The thing is, while I was in Preston I had plenty of time to think.'

A cautious nod. 'Go on.'

'Anna, look, I know I've been a fool. I've been totally paranoid lately. It was wrong, and stupid, and I want to apologise. I made a terrible mistake. I was wrong. It won't happen again.'

'Really?' asks Anna quietly.

'Really.'

'So there'll be no more snooping about, and no more daft accusations?'

'None. I'm sorry I got myself into such a state. It was moronic. It's only because I care so much. Do you understand that?'

Anna ignores my question. 'No more doubts about what Graham and I were up to in Paris?'

I swallow. 'All gone.'

'Good.' Anna sips her coffee.

'Can we forget about all that stuff, then? Water under the bridge, and all that.'

There is a long pause.

'I don't know,' says Anna.

'What?'

'I don't know if I can just *forget* about it.' She looks at me. 'Don't look so shocked, Matthew. Think about it for a second. Think about what you've done.'

'I've just apologised, haven't I?'

Anna sighs. 'Yes, but it's not quite as simple as that. You accused me of sleeping with someone else. That's bad enough, but to make things worse you *spied* on me. And that pisses me off, actually, quite a hell of a lot.'

'I realise that, but —'

'Shut up. I'm trying to explain. Just listen to me. What I *hate*, what really bothers me, is the amount of lying that all this involved.'

'I *never* lied to you.'

'All right. I'll rephrase.' Her voice is coldly clinical. 'The amount of *dissembling* that all this involved. You must have been sitting here for *weeks* wrapped up in your poisonous suspicions, and you never said *anything*. Why couldn't you *ask* me, if it was so important?'

'You make it sound so easy. It's not as if it was just any old question.'

There is a long pause. She does not look at me.

'I was desperate, Anna,' I plead. 'I didn't know what to do.'

She shakes her head. 'You don't get it, do you?'

I cross my arms. 'Obviously not.'

'I still can't quite believe, after all these years, how little you actually trust me.'

'That's hardly —'

'Thirteen years.' Anna sighs. 'Thirteen years, and you're following me around as if I'm some sort of petty criminal. Do you have any idea how that makes me feel?'

I look at my feet. 'I suppose not.'

'You suppose not. You suppose correctly. You have no idea.' Anna's voice is starting to break. She remains motionless, staring straight ahead of her. 'You don't have the slightest clue how extraordinarily *shitty* you've made me feel, how very *hurtful* it is to discover that your husband doesn't trust you.'

'Anna,' I say, moving towards her, 'What can I –'

She waves me away as she begins to sob.

I am paralysed by the sight of Anna's tears. I watch her cry, unsure what to do. After a few minutes she raises her head and looks at me through bloodshot eyes. 'And what about *you*?' she asks.

'What about me?'

'How can you think so little of yourself?'

I frown. 'What do you –'

'If you really think that I'm having an affair with another man – especially a pompous twat like Graham – then what does that say about *you*, and how you feel about yourself? Where has your self-respect gone?'

'My self-respect? What has that got to do with anything?'

'*Everything*, Matthew, can't you *see*? If you had any self-respect, even an iota of belief in your own self-worth, then none of this would have happened.' She pauses. 'And as for your walking away from the hotel when you thought that Graham and I had gone upstairs to fuck each other's brains out, I don't really know *what* to say to you.'

I bristle. 'Are you suggesting that this is all my fault?'

Anna ignores me. 'How am *I* supposed to love someone who doesn't love himself? This sort of pathological self-loathing you've developed makes it hard for me, too.'

'What are you saying?'

'Nothing. I just thought you should know how I see it.'

I sigh. 'Well, like I say, there's no need to worry any more. All that stuff is in the past now.' The memory of Anna gazing seductively into Graham's eyes over coffee crashes into my head, immediately followed by the sight of the Tiffany cufflinks peeping out of Graham's jacket. 'In the past,' I repeat.

'I don't know if I can just *forget* it, Matthew,' whispers Anna. 'I need time to think.'

'Fine.' Inside I am choking.

Anna stands up. 'I don't want to talk about this any more. I'm going back to bed.' She stumbles out of the room.

I spend the rest of the morning quietly padding around the flat. I feel uneasy knowing that Anna is asleep in the bedroom. Is she really intending to punish me further? I've already apologised. What more does she want from me? I've done my bit; now it's her turn to reciprocate. I need something to take my mind off this mess.

I sit down in front of my typewriter and find the piece of paper with the first draft of the CARP manifesto. After much deliberation, I add:

```
3. We celebrate the English language in its
   glorious and varied complexity. We there-
   fore encourage elaborate, ambitious syntax,
   diversionary subordinate clauses, and other
   enriching linguistic techniques. Punctuation,
   like salt, is a necessary tool - it flavours
   and enhances the natural essence of our
   words. We do not shy away from this tool;
   we embrace it.
```

I read through my three rules. Already I can sense a general aesthetic emerging from these parameters, although I am not entirely convinced by the punctuation-as-salt metaphor. I return to the opening paragraph of my new novel and read it through once more, but then the usual petrified inactivity descends. I seem unable to move beyond this first sentence. It's as if I am hypnotised by its grace and power. Perhaps I am subconsciously afraid that nothing else I write will quite match it. I sit in front of my typewriter, dismayed. I still have no idea who Goran Dmitrossovic or young Illic actually *are*.

From behind the bedroom door, Anna's presence chides and scolds me. I decide to go for a walk. Outside, numbing gusts of icy wind take the edge off my headache. I meander aimlessly through Camden, past the open-fronted shops displaying their racks of tan leather coats and impractical footwear. Some places have enormous, papier maché models erected on their multicoloured exteriors to advertise their products: a giant boot, a rocking chair. Different strains of techno music blast into the street, each shop competing for sonic dominance of the pavement. Small crowds of people hang about on street corners. Unlike the frenetic scramble everywhere else in London, people loiter here, killing time. Compared to the rest of the city, Camden is like Jamaica, only colder. Most of the pavement habitués are heavily pierced and exotically garbed. Seeing them, I feel a small pang of nostalgia for my youth. Our neighbourhood is like a mildly anarchic student annexe. It's where people go when they don't want to grow up, a world of badly-dyed jumpers and multicoloured hair extensions. As I pass the market stalls of Camden Lock, the heavy smell of joss sticks floats by. I've always relished the uneasy edge to the area, the vague feeling of simmering chaos. Walk through Camden and you expose yourself to the rest of its slightly fucked-up population. You can never be sure what's going to happen next.

I step inside a shop whose grubby windows are filled

with LP covers. The shop usually has a pretty decent selection of second-hand jazz records. I regularly check the stock, more out of habit than hope, on the off-chance that a copy of Duke's mythical lament for Billy Strayhorn might appear as I riffle through the vinyl.

Today the shop is deserted except for the taciturn owner, who is sitting behind the wooden desk, smoking a cigarette, immersed in *NME*. He glances up as I walk in, and grunts a greeting. A piece of operatic prog-rock is blasting from the speakers. I move to the jazz section at the back of the shop and begin to flick through the closely-packed records, my fingers working to separate the cardboard sleeves. Most of what I see is familiar, the never-changing residue of unwanted vinyl which has been there for months. There is nothing new today, certainly no miracle acetate pressing to lift my spirits. After ten minutes, I step back on to the cold street. The prog-rock masterpiece is still in full flow.

I go into a newsagents for a packet of cigarettes. Beneath the racks of magazines lie today's newspapers. Suddenly I am electrified. The front page of the *Sun* screams:

BERNADETTE BRANNIGAN IS MAN SHOCK

Scarcely daring to breathe, I quickly scan the page. Glorious *Schadenfreude* beckons. It seems that the journalist I spoke to yesterday has already managed to identify the real Bernadette Brannigan and to track him down to a housing estate on the outskirts of Swindon. When the author opened his front door, he calmly confirmed that, yes, he was the author of the *Virgin* series, and that he had no further comment. I am slightly disappointed and reluctantly impressed by such a sanguine response to learning that his career was finished.

Still, I am exultant. This is sweeter than seeing my book in any bookshop. I quickly scoop up one copy of every paper and take them to the till, looking forward to reading about Bernadette Brannigan's ignominious fall from grace.

Back home, Anna has not yet surfaced. I sit in the kitchen and spread the newspapers on the table in front of me. With a delicious sense of anticipation, I choose one at random and begin to read.

Half an hour later, I am still sitting at the kitchen table. I can scarcely move. I am frozen in disbelieving, catatonic shock.

This cannot be happening.

Every newspaper has carried at least one item about Bernadette Brannigan. But rather than the career-crippling condemnations and attacks of outraged vitriol, there has been unanimous praise for this man from Swindon, whose real name is Alan Rossiter. Commentators have marvelled at the 'almost preternatural femininity' of the voice that the author has adopted, lauding his 'chameleonic and versatile narrative characterisation'. The principal character in the *Virgin* series, Poppy Flipflop, has been granted instant iconic status.

'There can be little doubt,' writes some moron from the *Daily Telegraph*, 'that Poppy Flipflop has now joined the ranks of truly legendary fictional greats. We must welcome this diminutive *faux-naïf* to the pantheon of modern fictional heroes along with Rabbit Angstrom, Raskolnikov and Leopold Bloom.'

Faux-naif? Poppy Flipflop isn't *faux-naif*. She's stupid. She's an imbecilic, one-dimensional tart, hackneyed beyond belief, fulfilling old-fashioned gender stereotypes in a regressive, damaging way. Unless, that is, you believe the *Guardian*: 'The genius of the *Virgin* series is the sly adoption and subversion of the language and iconography of the sexual cold war for its own ends. By adopting some of the traits which have for so long represented the female paradigm at the core of anti-feminist polemic, Poppy Flipflop has become a Trojan Horse for a new generation of women warriors, infiltrating enemy lines, only then to reveal her true colours, scattering the massed ranks of dismissive male supremacists with her honey-coated bullets of chaotic love.'

Unbelievable.

In every paper, a large photograph of Alan Rossiter smiles out at me, accepting the plaudits which are pouring in from all over the world. Martin Amis has hailed him as 'a fellow genius'. The *Financial Times* reports that *Virgin on Mergin'* has suddenly become the favourite for next year's Booker Prize.

I sit at the table, my head in my hands. This is a disaster. Bernadette Brannigan is no longer just an author. He or she is now a literary phenomenon. And I am responsible.

Some time later, the bedroom door opens and Anna stumbles out.

'Hello,' I say.

'All right?'

'Er, yeah, OK,' I say, sweeping up the newspapers off the table in one movement. 'How about you? Any better?'

'Not especially.' She sighs. 'Not at all, actually.'

I look at her, unsure how to proceed. 'Sorry to hear that,' I say cautiously.

'Look,' says Anna, 'do you want to go for a walk? If I'm playing hooky and you're giving yourself the day off writing, we should probably make the most of it. You know, *do* something.'

'Sure,' I say, 'that would be nice. The writing can wait.'

'I wish I could say the same for my clients,' grumbles Anna. 'Well, never mind. They're not getting a choice today. Let me have a quick shower and then we'll go.' She breathes deeply. 'It's kill or cure time. It's either me, or the hangover. One of us has got to go.'

Twenty minutes later we walk down Delancy Street and enter Regent's Park at its north-eastern corner. The day isn't one for casual walkers: we are almost alone on the vast expanse of green. I remember my disturbing dream of the night before last. We walk towards the middle of the park in silence.

Anna strides purposefully ahead. I want to continue this morning's conversation, but I can't push things. I have relinquished control of the dialogue; we will discuss things when Anna is ready, and not before.

We make our way towards the Victorian bandstand on the south side of the boating pond, forlornly deserted on this cold winter's day. We sit down on a bench and look out over the water. Congregations of wooden boats are moored in the middle of the lake, small islands of bright turquoise in the dark water. The weeping willows bend in the wind, kissing the surface of the lake. The scene is motionless except for the flurries of yellow and brown leaves which scamper along the water's edge.

Anna blows into her hands and looks out across the pond

towards the copper dome of the London Central Mosque. I sit quietly next to her. After a few minutes' silent contemplation Anna says, 'We need to talk about Christmas.'

'Christmas?' I repeat stupidly.

'Uh-huh.'

'OK.' I shiver. 'Shoot.'

'Obviously we'll go to Guildford.'

'Obviously.' One of the many disadvantages of my parents' pissing away my inheritance on their mammoth pan-global geriatric jolly is that we have no excuse not to spend every Christmas with Anna's family.

'I spoke to Mum yesterday,' says Anna.

'How's she feeling at the moment?' Anna's mother is a hypochondriac of such relentless inventiveness that she has worked her way through *Gray's Anatomy*, twice. In her quest for new ailments she recently bought a medical textbook which details obscure diseases of the indigenous tribes of the Kalahari. What I really object to is the way she uses her purported afflictions to exercise ruthless emotional blackmail over the rest of the family. She has a calculating, scheming way about her that makes Lady Macbeth look like Felicity Kendal.

'She's fine,' replies Anna. 'You know. For her. Anyway, she wanted to know when we would be coming down. The others are arriving on Christmas Eve. Is that all right with you?'

I shrug. 'I suppose so.'

'We should be able to escape the day after Boxing Day,' muses Anna.

'Right.' *Four days*. At the prospect of such extended exposure to Anna's family, my hangover begins to reassert itself. 'I take it everyone will be there?'

Anna nods. 'Oh yes.'

'Why don't your sister and her lot ever spend Christmas with Alistair's parents?' I ask plaintively. 'At the very least, shouldn't he be on duty somewhere? I would have thought that Christmas was the biggest event in his professional calendar, but he always seems to get the day off.' Alistair, our gormless brother-in-law, is a vicar. He and Anna's sister Theresa radiate smug perfection like a leak at Sellafield B.

'Funny you should ask,' says Anna. 'Apparently this year, he's going to conduct part of the service at St Mary's.'

St Mary's is the church in Surrey where my parents-in-law go. On Christmas Day we are all required to show up and carol lustily, putting on the annual display of familial harmony for the watching congregation. I turn to face Anna in horror. 'Oh no.'

'Oh yes.'

'Forget it, then,' I reply firmly. 'If he's got anything to do with the service then I'm not going. At all.'

Alistair's ministry is characterised by a conviction that the Church of England needs to be thoroughly modernised. The consequences of this trendier-than-thou approach are excruciating. As it says in Leviticus: beware the jean-clad vicar. Anna and I were corralled into letting him officiate at our wedding ceremony. It was one of the most embarrassing episodes of my life. Having watched me self-consciously peck Anna on the cheek after I had been enjoined to kiss the bride, Alistair delivered a small but thoughtful sermon about the importance of sex in marriage, remarking that he hoped that when we retired to our marital hotbed I would show a bit more enthusiasm than I had at the altar. We stood in front of the congregation of two hundred and fifty guests, squirming helplessly. With the exception of our own friends, the church was an addled symposium of double-barrelled corpulence, dressed up in bulging morning suits and ankle-length pastel. As Alistair's sermon rumbled on, I could sense the charge of electrified outrage rippling through the pews behind me. My own delirious embarrassment was almost worth it when we turned to process out of the church and I saw the radish-red faces of the men, blistered veins illuminating their cheeks in disbelieving apoplexy. Alistair followed us serenely down the aisle, hands clasped piously in front of him and a beatific smile on his face, oblivious to the stir he had created.

Anna turns to look at me. She has a pained smile on her face. 'I don't think Mum is too pleased about it, either. He offered, and she couldn't really refuse. You never know, though. It might be fun.'

I dread to think how Alistair will approach his Christmas sermon. Doubtless the issue of Mary's intact hymen will be analysed in detail. 'I suppose I might enjoy watching your parents while he does his stuff,' I concede.

'There you go. Every cloud.'

We sit in silence for a few moments. An elderly couple struggle by, tilting into the wind. Remembering our wedding reminds me how much we have to lose. 'So,' I say. 'About this morning. Are you going to forgive me for all that nonsense?'

Anna stands up. Gesturing that I should stay where I am, she crosses the grass to the empty bandstand and climbs the steps. She leans against the railings, gazing across the water. Framed by the bandstand's soaring pillars, she is a tiny figure, solitary among the fallen leaves.

The muted rumble of traffic percolates through the

trees. I shiver and stamp my feet as I watch her. The strip of grass between us seems a million miles wide.

Finally, Anna waves me over. I stand up and walk across to her. She watches me approach. Her cheeks are flushed red with the cold. As I arrive, she turns back to look at the water. I stand beside her, uncertain.

Then, without taking her eyes off the calm surface of the lake, she murmurs, 'Never again, Matthew. Never. Is that clear?'

Back at the flat, Anna picks up the duvet from the sofa and carries it back into the bedroom. Wordlessly I follow her. She turns and cracks a small smile. 'Welcome back.'

I look at her uncertainly. 'Thanks.'

Anna sits on her side of the bed and sighs, her head cast downwards. 'I still feel like shit,' she says.

'Sorry.'

'Not your fault.'

'Still.'

Anna smiles ruefully. 'Well, there's one hangover cure we haven't tried yet.' She pats the bed next to her.

'Really?'

'Yes, really. Come on, hurry up, before I change my mind.' Anna is bending down, untying the laces of her trainers as she speaks.

We undress quickly and slip beneath the duvet. Anna draws a finger down my arm. Tentatively I stroke her thigh. I feel deep in alien territory, terrified that one wrong move will bring all this crashing down. We do not kiss as we touch each other.

Finally, my hand creeps up to Anna's breast, and I feel her nipple harden beneath my fingers. I lower my mouth on to the small erect nub of brown skin. Anna stretches, arching her back, pushing herself further into my mouth. Moments later her hand is pushing on the top of my head, silently urging me downwards. Her face is turned away from me. With my tongue I trace a line from her breast to her groin. A low groan of supplication escapes her.

When Anna comes, she makes no sound other than a long hiss like escaping steam as her body stiffens. She smiles at me dreamily as I make my way back up the bed. 'That was *lovely*,' she whispers. 'Clever boy.' I grin. 'Now, your turn.' She pushes me on to my back, and crouches over me on all fours. Her hair falls in front of her face, obscuring my view. I exhale deeply. Everything is going to be all right. Everything is going to be all right.

Then I notice Anna's hand between her legs. She begins to gasp as her fingers fly back and forth. I look down the bed. This is new. I am forgotten; Anna's mouth has gone slack. A minute later, a second orgasm wracks her body.

When her spasms have subsided, Anna returns her attention to me, and the next thing I feel is a fingertip exploring my perineum. My pleasure is eclipsed by surprise. This is also new. Her finger creeps cautiously forwards.

And then, out of nowhere, I am blindsided:

Where have all these new tricks suddenly come from?

Devastation.

My imagination hurtles at full tilt into the abyss of self-destruction: my head is immediately filled with a picture of my wife, her lips wrapped around Graham's engorged tool and her forefinger delicately inserted into his anus. The effect is terrible, and immediate. The blood beats an ignominious retreat from my groin, and my penis starts to wilt like a wax candle in the full glare of the Death Valley sun. A strangled moan of frustration escapes my lips.

Anna is staring at my deflating cock. 'Matthew? What's wrong? Are you all right?' She peers up at my face in concern.

'I don't know,' I stammer. 'Something... doesn't seem quite right.'

Anna sits back on her heels, perplexed. 'Shit, Matthew.' She pauses. 'That's not very flattering.'

I stare at her miserably. 'I'm sorry.'

'I thought this was what you wanted,' she says, climbing off the bed and bending down to retrieve her underwear. 'I thought you wanted to sleep in our bed again. You know, resume normal service.'

'I am, I do, it's not –'

'Are you trying to tell me something?' She is getting angry now; her eyes darken as she speaks.

'Anna, please. I'm sorry about – this.' I gesture helplessly downwards. 'Perhaps it's just nerves. Performance anxiety.'

'You didn't seem to be having any trouble earlier on today,' she snaps.

'Yes, but –'

'I mean, what am I supposed to think? First I catch you furtively whacking off in the sitting room, and then *this* happens.' She is angrily pulling on her jeans.

I lie on the bed, naked. There is little point in arguing

with Anna in this mood. Without another word she steps out of the bedroom and closes the door firmly behind her. I roll over and bury my head in my pillow.

A new low, then.

Much as I would love to forget about Anna's affair with Graham, it is proving harder than I anticipated. No matter how much I try, how many diversionary tactics I adopt, I am unable to prevent my brain from generating a variety of graphic tableaux of the two of them together whenever the prospect of sex with my wife arises. The reaction is always the same, a catatonic limpness. My penis used to be a lively, unpredictable little fellow, always liable to pop up at inopportune moments, but now whenever I am near Anna a macabre, death-like aura surrounds its pendulous stillness. My wife is sullied to me now. To my dismay, I am revolted by her. In her presence my sexual drive dissipates instantly.

Impotence is a curious thing. As an ailment, it's well named. The feeling of abject helplessness stretches beyond the bedroom. The sense of failure, of duty shirked, taints everything with its shameful pall. As the days pass, the oppressive weight of disappointed expectation bears down more heavily upon me.

My plight is all the more frustrating because it is abundantly clear (although, thankfully, only to me) that the problem is psychological, rather than physiological: when I am alone, my trousers become a priapic temple. I begin to resort to an occasional bout of guilt-ridden onanism in an effort to make my erections go away. After a while I find myself addressing the problem three or four times a day. I am undiscriminating in my choice of partners for my masturbatory fantasies. The girl in the bookshop in Preston gets a few outings, and gradually I work my way through all of the female presenters on MTV, the cast of *Neighbours*, and finally the army of would-be celebrities who populate the bleak netherworld of daytime television. Then I start to plunder my memory banks, pillaging them for women, young and old, familiar and unknown. Like Bogart in *Casablanca*, when it comes to women, I'm a true democrat: even the gum-chewing girls at the checkout in Sainsbury's get a go. All that matters is that they aren't Anna.

In view of all of this extracurricular activity, my cock's unremitting flaccidity in my wife's presence is especially galling. It is living a double life, a genital Jekyll and Hyde, rampaging beast one moment, calm and docile the next. I have developed the world's first clinically schizophrenic penis.

At first, Anna does her best to be understanding. Each evening we hesitantly disrobe in front of each other, waiting to see what reaction is provoked in my undercarriage. After a few moments of staring at my inanimate tackle, Anna turns and puts on her pyjamas. The look of hurt on her face crucifies me, but if I explain the real cause of the problem and tell her that this is all still Graham's fault, I will be banished back to the sofa so quickly my head will spin. Instead I shrug apologetically and feign bafflement.

Slowly, Anna's hurt is replaced by scornful resentment. Our time together is filled with sullen, accusing silences. Now at bedtime, Anna undresses quickly without looking at me, and wordlessly climbs into bed.

I have woken up once in the middle of the night to realise with a shock that Anna was masturbating next to me. She was perfectly still except for the tiniest movement of her right hand. I pretended to be asleep. As she came, she gasped softly into her pillow. Afterwards, she rolled away from me and began to sob quietly. I lay next to her, unable to speak, wondering whom she was thinking about as she touched herself.

During this unhappy time I spend most of my days roaming through London, visiting bookshops. I have decided to conduct a survey of which shops have copies of *Licked* in stock. These outings do not improve my mood: after two weeks, I have not seen a single copy of my book.

I mention nothing of this to Anna. We scarcely talk now. The chasm between us yawns ever wider, filled by an awful, icy silence.

To my dismay, her affair with Graham actually starts to *make sense*.

As the weeks pass, I sink deeper into depressed introspection. Outside, bright lights and decorations hail the imminent arrival of Christmas. The streets of Camden are filled with unsteady packs of drinkers, shiny hats askew, marauding between restaurant and pub, mired in day-long Christmas parties. Their drunken good cheer torments me. I envy these people their holiday bonhomie. I have none of the ordinary human connections that frame a person within the society he inhabits, none of the usual reference points by which to orientate myself. I am contextless, unhappily spinning in the vacuum of my own indolence. For me, there *is* no holiday. I have nothing to holiday *from*.

I hate Christmas.

Anna begins to stay later and later at the office. She no longer eats at home; she has a busy schedule of Christmas wining and dining with clients. She arrives home, slightly drunk, long after I have gone to bed. My literary manifesto gathers dust, forgotten. The typewriter is ignored. Even my Ellington records remain unplayed. I am an empty bottle, discarded into the rancid effluent – rudderless, dragged relentlessly down as it is filled by the waste that surrounds it.

Of course, Anna isn't prepared to go on like this.

One evening I am lying on the sofa, idly watching a celebrity edition of *TV Scrabble* when I hear the front door open. Anna appears in the doorway.

'Hello,' I say. 'You're home early.'

Anna puts her briefcase down. 'We need to talk.' She takes off her coat and looks at me squarely.

I shift uncomfortably. 'OK.'

Anna sits down and takes a deep breath. 'I can't take any more of this, Matthew.'

'Any more of what?'

'Of living like this. Like we're, we're – *strangers*.' She pauses. 'I feel as if I don't know you any more. We hardly speak to each other. You've lost interest in *everything*. It's driving me crazy.'

'Oh,' I reply.

'Not to mention the fact that we haven't had sex for *weeks*,' she adds.

I am silent for a few moments. 'Yes, well. I don't know what to say about that.'

'Do you want to tell me what's *wrong*?'

I look at her, pained. Yes. No. 'Nothing's really wrong,' I say.

'Of *course* something's wrong. You know it as well as I do.' She pauses. 'Do you want to know what *I* think the problem is?'

I swallow. 'Go on.'

'It's the sex thing, isn't it? It's making you depressed.'

'Maybe,' I concede.

'Right. I thought so. Listen. I want you to go and see the doctor.'

'Oh, Anna —'

'It's nothing to be ashamed about. It happens all the time nowadays.'

'*It*?'

'Impotence. It's a symptom of modern life. Quite trendy, really.' She tries a grin.

I close my eyes and come to a decision. Anna deserves to know the truth. After all, things can hardly get worse. 'Listen, Anna. Going to the doctor won't solve anything.'

'Well, it can't hurt, can it? We have to do *something*.' She pauses. 'You're too young to be having those sorts of problems.'

I take a deep breath. 'I don't *have* those sorts of problems.' Anna's face clouds in confusion. 'That is, I do, but only with you.'

She stares. 'What do you mean, only with *me*? Are there *others*?'

'No. No, of course not.' I pause. 'I don't know quite how to explain it.'

Anna blinks. '*Try*.'

'Well, how can I put this? When you're not around, there isn't a problem. You know, getting an erection. But when I get near you, it just fizzles out. Gone. Vamoose.'

'Are you saying it's me? Is that it? You don't fancy me any more?'

'Quite the opposite,' I say. 'That's the problem. The difficulty is that I still fancy you rotten.'

Anna shakes her head. 'I don't understand.'

I look at her face. What I'm about to say will probably destroy everything – but what, really, is there left to destroy? We are rattling around in the husk of this relationship.

'OK. Well. You remember all that nonsense about you and Graham when you got back from Paris?'

Anna stiffens. 'Matthew –'

'The thing is, you see –'

'– I honestly think you should –'

'– that every time we get close to making love –'

'Please stop. I really don't want to hear –'

'– I can't help picturing you with him.'

There is a long silence.

Anna is looking at me, expressionless. 'I don't believe you,' she says finally.

'It's true. I'm sorry. It's true.'

She blinks in disbelief. 'You're still hung up about *Graham*?'

I look down.

'But you said that all that nonsense was finished.'

'I thought it was. But I can't get it out of my head.'

'Jesus,' sighs Anna. 'Why not?'

I take a deep breath. 'You never actually denied that you were having an affair.'

'But we *discussed* all this.'

'I know. And I know that I promised to forget about it. I did try, Anna. I did my best. But I couldn't. I mean, what was I supposed to think when you wouldn't deny it?'

'I told you. I didn't see why I *should*. You're supposed to *trust* me.'

I sigh. 'Yes, I know. I understand the theory. But you must admit it's a convenient argument if you don't want to answer a particular question.'

Anna looks shocked. 'Do you really imagine that's how I think?'

'But do you see my point?' I persist.

'Do you see *mine*? This idea of trust. It's not entirely alien to you, surely?'

'It didn't use to be.'

'What's *that* supposed to mean?'

'Well, it was your behaviour which started all this.'

Anna shakes her head. 'No. No. You're wrong. *You're* the one who followed me to Paris. *You're* the one who's fabricated this web of intrigue. You didn't even give me a chance to explain myself until you'd already quite made up your mind about what was going on.'

'Fine,' I snap. 'Go on, then. Tell me now. I'm all ears.'

'You want to know what went on in Paris?' says Anna quietly.

'Not just in Paris. I want you to tell me everything.'

She looks at me sadly. 'Everything? Are you sure?'

I am almost on my feet, escaping out of the door, away from the truth.

'Yes,' I say eventually. 'I'm sure.' I need an answer, after all. Nothing else is going to free me from this nightmare.

'So,' I say, keeping my voice flat. 'Did you sleep with Graham?'

Anna looks me in the eye. 'Yes.'

I am falling through space. Hurtling, plummeting. My stomach is in free fall, my head is pounding with the rush of blood.

I twist and spin, trying to escape this truth that I was so eager to learn. But wherever I turn, I am confronted by Anna's answer.

Yes.

Anna is sitting at the end of the sofa, looking at me. I stare back at her. Perhaps I have misunderstood? No. Her reply was clear, strong, and unequivocal. The word still rings in my ears, as clear as a well-struck bell.

Yes.

Anna shrugs. 'Sorry.'

My brain is unable to assimilate her response. Its circuits are threatening to overload. An illegal operation has been performed: I'm going into shutdown mode. Anna's single syllable of guilt echoes around my head, obliterating everything else, erasing files, wiping my hard disk.

I am at a place where I do not wish to be. I have pushed forward, and now my line of retreat has been cut off behind me. I am stranded, face to face with the truth that I did not want to know. There is no turning back now.

A flash of grim understanding: despite everything, I was expecting her to say no.

I have made a disastrous mistake.

Anna watches me with a sadly composed expression. 'Matthew,' she says levelly, 'just remember this. You insisted that I answer your question. You've nobody but yourself to blame. I was trying to protect you. But you gave me no choice. You handed me a loaded gun and asked me to pull the trigger.'

I sit back on the sofa, dead inside.

'What are you thinking?' asks Anna softly.

I look at my wife. 'Aren't you going to ask me if I forgive you?'

Anna nods solemnly. 'OK. Do you forgive me?'

'Yes,' I reply, hating myself. 'I forgive you.'

'Thank you.' There is a pause. 'Look,' she says, 'there's something else I want to discuss.' She is poised, in control. I, by contrast, am reeling, destabilised, desperately seeking some means of shoring myself up.

I blink. 'Something else?'

She nods. 'I want you to move back on to the sofa.'

'What? Why?'

'To teach you a lesson.'

'To teach *me* a lesson?' I shout. 'Why am *I* the one who needs to be taught a lesson?'

Anna ignores me. 'You're back out here. With immediate effect.'

This is all crazily distorted. She is the one who has been

unfaithful, but I am the one being punished. My eyes fill with tears.

Anna reaches out and puts a hand on my shoulder. 'Listen, Matthew. I'm not proud of what I did. I didn't want to hurt you. But it's done, and now we have to deal with it. I know I'm not perfect. But neither are you. We have to work out how we're going to get through this.'

'Aren't you just going to divorce me?' I ask bitterly. 'Aren't you going off to live happily ever after with the magnificent Graham?'

Anna sighs. 'Don't be stupid. It was just an affair. That's all. He has a family of his own.' She pauses. 'It's over, anyway. Graham and I are finished. Listen, Matthew. You and I are a family, too. You're *my* family. And I still want to make a go of this marriage if you do.'

I stare at her through my tears. 'You do?'

'Of course. Do you?' I nod. She stands up. 'Good. I'll get the duvet.' She turns and walks out of the room.

Once, playing Hide and Seek in my parents' house, instead of running off to hide from my playmate, I simply sat on my bed and shut my eyes. I assumed, with the implacable logic of a five-year-old, that if I couldn't see my pursuer, then he wouldn't be able to see me, either. I was excited; from now on I would be able to flit in and out of this world as I wished. It was only when I received a delighted pillow swipe in my face that I realised my experiment hadn't worked. Now all the hopes that blossomed as I waited in my childhood bed-room swarm back to me. If I close my eyes, will this all go away?

Anna drops the duvet on to the sofa next to me. 'I'm going to bed,' she says.

I gaze up at her. 'Right.'

'Good night, then,' murmurs Anna. 'And Matthew?' There is a pause as we both look at each other. 'I'm sorry.'

She closes the door.

I don't sleep, of course. I turn off the lights and lie down on the sofa, fully-clothed. I pull the duvet over my head, still wishing that I could shut all this out, perhaps effect a miraculous leap into another, kinder, parallel universe.

My brain remains resolutely awash with the ineluctable fact of Anna's confession. She had sex with Graham. She was wet, excited by him. The thought sluices through me, corroding me with black hate.

Finally I fall asleep. At least, I suppose I do; because the next thing I am aware of is a hand on my shoulder, shaking me awake. Anna is in her dressing gown, crouching down next to me, urgently saying my name. She has turned on the light; it is dark outside.

'What is it?' I mumble. 'What time is it?'

'It's about three o'clock,' says Anna.

'Jesus.' I groggily prop myself up on one elbow. 'What's the matter?'

'I need to talk to you.'

'Now?'

'Yes, now. Listen. I didn't sleep with Graham.'

I stare at her. 'You didn't?'

'Of course not.'

I struggle to wake up and concentrate. 'Why not?'

'Why didn't I sleep with Graham? Because I don't fancy him. Because he's actually rather a pillock. Oh yes, and because I'm married to you.' Anna pauses. 'And despite the fact that you've been behaving like a moron, I do actually love you. Quite a lot.'

I'm more awake now. I shake my head. 'I meant, if you didn't sleep with him, then why did you say that you did?'

'Because I wanted to punish you for being a prick.'

I sit up. 'For being —?'

'I wanted to hurt you,' says Anna slowly. 'I wanted to get back at you for not trusting me and for your little spying escapade.'

I allow this to register. 'So you *didn't* sleep with him?' I say.

Anna shakes her head. 'The thought never even occurred to me.'

'Oh. Right.'

'Also,' continues Anna, her voice hardening a little, 'I wanted to see if you'd believe me.' She pauses. 'And you did. You actually believed that I would sleep with someone else.'

'Yes, but come *on*,' I say defensively. 'It's not the sort of thing most people lie about. At least, not that way round.'

'That's not the point, Matthew.'

'Well, I'm sorry.'

'I'm sorry, too. I'm sorry I lied to you, but I was angry. I wanted to hurt you.'

'OK,' I say, rueful. 'You did.'

She stands up. 'Anyway, that's all. I just wanted you to know. I thought you'd probably suffered long enough.'

'Right.' I pause, utterly baffled. Did Anna really lie, just to punish me?

'I'll see you tomorrow, then,' she says, standing up. She closes the door behind her.

I walk over to the back door of the flat. I peer into the

darkness of our little walled garden for a few moments, until I notice that I'm staring at myself, superimposed on the outside world.

Why do I not feel relief?

I think back to my vigil on the rain-soaked boulevard in Paris as Graham and Anna ate together. I think of her flashing, siren eyes as Graham lit her cigarette. I think of Anna's late nights, of Ravel. I think of Caroline's hysterical accusations. Above all, I think of the Tiffany cufflinks.

I stare at my blackened reflection in the window.

I do not believe her.

So, now I know.

For all of her late night games and denials, I do not believe Anna's belated avowals of innocence. The weight of evidence against her is simply too strong. The time for worry and doubt is over. Now I have entered a new realm, that of awful certainty. I have my answer.

The next few days pass in a blood-tinged blur of fury. There is no longer room for sadness or self-pity. As the bald fact of Anna's betrayal spreads remorselessly across my consciousness like a virus, my anger is crystallised into jagged shards of bitterness. Her confession screams through my head, growing louder, more shrill, more callously mocking each time. Yes, yes, *yes*.

I am tormented by endless images of Anna, hotly inflamed, fucking with Graham in inventive and dirty ways. Crystal-clear close-ups of their writhing, fornicating bodies, the sweaty mash of their aroused groins, play on the big screen inside my head. There is no respite. This happened, *this happened*! I cannot think of Anna without seeing her being lustily penetrated by Graham's cock. She loves it. She *loves* it! She is being fatly filled by her lover, and she can't get enough. And Graham comes and comes, an unstoppable geyser of spunk, in every filthy hole that she offers him. Every deposit that he leaves lingers on, ineradicable, festering inside my wife, polluting her.

Try as I might, I cannot suppress these putrescent, suppurating thoughts. I can feel them gnawing away at me, relentlessly wearing me down. But that's not all. The looped pornographic film flickering inside my head hurts all the more because Anna has been deliberately toying with me: first there was the refusal to answer my accusation, then her belated admission, now her unconvincing denial. These sordid little games have robbed me of my dignity. Anna has sullied my faith; she has emasculated me, rendered me – literally – impotent. I am not sure which hurts more: the adultery, or the crucifying legacy of lies and disrespect that trails in its squalid wake.

Anna has begun to leave her morning notes again. In the evenings she seems tired, but cheerful enough. We are both pretending that everything has returned to normal, and quickly revert to a cordial domesticity. Anna says no more about her confession and subsequent denial: she assumes that I believe her. I press onwards, trying to ignore the pictures in my head.

I begin to understand the attitude of the men in *Bloke* magazine. I was wrong; their refusal to take their partners back wasn't due to misguided pride – it was the only response that would not destroy them completely. No matter how much I want our marriage to work, I cannot sustain this charade.

As the days pass, I wallow in despair, unsure where to turn for relief. My saxophone practice becomes obsessive.

I can hold Anna at bay, at least for a while, with the calming routine of scales and exercises, but as I pack away the horn I am immediately drawn back to the inescapable truth. *This happened!*

After a few days, Anna revokes my sentence of solitary confinement on the sofa, and I am invited back to bed. Suddenly a new danger presents itself, threatening this fragile chimera of new-found domestic harmony: when Anna sees that my impotence remains, still strangled by the grip of her infidelity, then this brief hiatus of calm will be exposed as a sham. I do not know what will happen then.

Faced with this new threat, this time bomb ticking in my trousers, I know that I must do *something*.

I cannot change the past. I can try to accept what has happened, but I will never be able to forgive Anna unless she confesses to what she has done. If she admits the affair, then perhaps there may still be a way back for us. Perhaps the pictures in my head will stop.

Anna, though, seems determinedly serene, untroubled by remorse. She behaves as if the episode is forgotten, our differences buried. I realise that the only way that I will make her confess now is to construct a watertight case against her, buttressed by irrefutable evidence. (If only I had knocked on her hotel door in Paris, I reflect ruefully, none of this would be necessary now.) I will amass forensic evidence of the affair, present my findings, and then sit back and see what happens.

And so my quest for hard evidence begins, yet again.

I resume my daily inspection of Anna's pockets. I also

begin to examine the previous day's underwear, sniffing her knickers for lustful secretions, scrutinising the tiny scraps of fabric against the light.

I begin a new vigil across the street from Anna's office, waiting for her to streak through the doors with Graham on her arm. She sometimes emerges from the building talking earnestly with people I do not recognise, laden down with bags and cases, and climbs into a waiting taxi. The only other times she leaves the office during my surveillance are to go to the gym. Once or twice a day I walk to a nearby phone box and dial Anna's direct line. Each time she answers with an efficient 'Anna Given', and I quickly replace the receiver.

In the evenings I loiter outside the restaurants where Anna entertains her clients in pre-Christmas festivities. At first she is always the composed professional, primly sipping her pre-prandial glass of Chardonnay. By the end of the evening she is smoking, knocking back the wine, laughing easily with men I have never seen before. The effortless intimacy chills me. Who are these people?

Not once do I see Anna with Graham. Perhaps she was telling the truth when she said that the affair was over. I become increasingly frustrated at my failure to unearth any evidence of their liaison. Time is running out: my penis is lurking furtively in the wings, poised to betray me with its moribund flaccidity.

I begin to cast around desperately for another way of provoking Anna into confessing her affair. Gradually, a plan coalesces in my mind.

I am going to step up to play at the top table, where the stakes can go no higher. I contemplate the prospect with a sad calmness. Because what choice do I really have? We cannot go on like this.

I must act.

The shop assistant's eyes widen as I push my purchase across the counter towards him.

He chews his lip for a moment before turning to the till. Coolly I open my wallet and extract my credit card, before thinking better of it. I decide to pay in cash instead.

The shop assistant takes my money. 'Haven't sold one of these for a while,' he remarks nervously.

'Oh?' I say.

He shakes his head. 'Not much call for ones that . . . size.'

'Reckon it'll work?' I ask.

'Oh yeah,' he replies hastily. 'These things are like Volvos. Completely reliable.'

I check the side of the box. 'Are batteries included?' The crenated plastic shimmers beneath the shop's lighting.

The man nods. 'Yeah. Batteries are included.' He puts the box into a brown paper bag and pushes it across the counter towards me. 'Merry Christmas.'

'*Here* they are! At last! Merry Christmas!'

'Merry Christmas!'

'Edmund, come and say hello to Uncle Matthew.'

'Hello Edmund. Merry – ow.'

'Oops! We'll make a prize fighter of you yet, won't we, Edmund?'

'Matthew? Are you all right?'

'Er, yes, I'm fine. That is – no, I think I'm OK.'

It is Christmas Eve. Anna and I have just arrived at the Given homestead in deepest Surrey, and I have been accorded the traditional welcome: Edmund, my two-year-old nephew, has landed an absolute peach of a punch in my eye. I stagger backwards, clutching my face. Edmund, hoisted high in his father's arms, watches my retreat with an inscrutable look on his face. We are standing in the kitchen. I haven't even taken my coat off yet.

'Well, now that you're *finally* here, we can start properly,' says Anna's mother. She puts her gin and tonic down on the kitchen table and steps forward, presenting herself to be kissed. She moves as if she is treading through a thicket of stinging nettles.

'Elizabeth,' I say, 'how super to see you.' As our cheeks brush together, a small cache of powder in one of her wrinkles is disturbed, creating a localised tornado of beige cloud.

'Yes, well,' replies Elizabeth unenthusiastically.

I step back. 'How are you?' I ask politely.

'Ah, well. Not too good. The joints are getting rusty. And I think I'm coming down with a rather unusual strain of bronchial pneumoconiosis.'

'Sounds serious,' I say.

'Oh yes,' agrees Elizabeth, brightening slightly, 'it is.'

I turn towards my father-in-law, who is standing next to his wife. I see him flexing his right hand in anticipation.

'David,' I say, bracing myself.

'Matthew,' grunts David Given, sticking out his enormous paw. Reluctantly I proffer my hand. He grasps it eagerly, and, as always, begins to crush my knuckles into a pulverised mush. There is an audible crack, which spurs him on. I, of course, am expected to stand there and smile, pretending that nothing is amiss.

'Sorry we're a bit late,' I gasp.

'What kept you?' he demands gruffly, a malicious glint in his eye as he grinds my fingers together in an excruciating rolling movement that he's been practising on me for years.

'The traffic was worse than we'd anticipated,' I explain as tears spring into my eyes.

It has taken us hours, literally, to crawl through the middle of London, round Wandsworth, and down the A3. In this season of goodwill, the level of ill-natured abuse between motorists as they sat in the traffic jams, simmering with impatience, was chilling. The principal reason for our tardy arrival is actually that Anna went out for drinks after work and arrived home slightly pissed and two hours late. Of course, I am not allowed to mention this. The responsibility for any delay must, applying the usual spousal/in-law guilt allocation rules, be lain firmly at my door.

'Never mind,' says Elizabeth, glacial. 'At least you're here now.'

My eye is throbbing from Edmund's well-aimed punch. Everyone is in the kitchen to greet us except for Hector. Noon is sitting in her usual chair by the Aga, watching me suspiciously through her thick spectacles. Her misty pupils constantly bobble and mutate behind the lenses like globules in a lava lamp. Distaste flickers over her wizened face as she catches my eye. I know that one is supposed to indulge the old and infirm, but I would be lying if I said that Noon was anything other than a cantankerous old bitch. She has never liked me.

I march up and bend down towards her. Her rheumy eyes blaze malignantly at me. 'Hello, Noon,' I say, and plant a sloppy kiss on each of her desiccated, leathery cheeks. She tries to wriggle away, but cannot escape. Kissing Noon is rather like licking the inside of an old boot, but it's worth it to see her squirm in displeasure.

I stand up. Immediately Edmund tries to head-butt my groin as he hurtles past. I watch him go with relief. My youngest nephew never really learned to walk. He proceeded directly from crawling to running, and now leaves a trail of destruction in his wake, like a tiny Visigoth.

There is a tug on my sleeve. It is Lavinia, Edmund's five-year-old sister. I bend down. 'Hello, Lavinia.'

Lavinia looks at me gravely. 'Hello, Matthew.'

'How are you?'

Lavinia considers this question. 'All right.'

'Can I have a kiss?'

Reluctantly she delivers a prim kiss on my cheek.

'Do you want one back?'

'No thank you.' Her response is polite, firm, and immediate.

'Where's Hector?'

'Reading somewhere.'

A maternally thick pair of legs appears next to us. Pulling a face at Lavinia, who gazes unblinkingly back, I straighten up to face Theresa, Anna's older sister. 'Hector's hidden himself away, as usual,' says Theresa, ploughing right into our conversation and appropriating it for herself. She leans forward for the double mwah. 'Reading again. Honestly, sometimes I wonder whether he's really our son at all. How are you, Matthew?'

'Oh, all right,' I say. 'Bit frazzled after the drive, but nothing that a stiff drink won't sort out.' Thanks to Edmund's punch, my eye feels as if it's been prised out of my head, jumped on, and then clumsily reinserted into its socket, but it seems unseasonably churlish to mention it. Nobody looks about to offer me a drink, though.

Theresa lets out a long sigh of contentment. 'I love Christmas. Don't you?'

I smile brightly. 'Adore it.'

'We're so lucky to have the whole family around us every year.'

I eye Noon cautiously. 'Yes, we're very lucky,' I mumble.

'Of course, it would be *so* lovely to have another addition to the family before much longer,' says Theresa, her eyes twinkling. 'When are you two going to get your act together and give our lot a little cousin to play with?'

This is absolutely vintage Theresa. Being the very model of domestic perfection herself, there is little left for her to do in life except point out where she thinks other people are going wrong – which, in our case, is just about everywhere. She thinks that Anna should stay at home to bake, iron, and procreate, while I do the whole hunter-gatherer thing in a stuffy suburban office somewhere. Every day that Anna and I continue along the perverted path that we have chosen for ourselves, we are edging ever nearer to the abyss of some ill-defined catastrophe. Consequently Theresa always looks at us with a mixture of wrinkle-nosed disapproval and wide-eyed compassion.

The most irritating manifestation of Theresa's flaw-lessness is the never-ending supply of home-baked deli-cacies that she brings to every family gathering. Her unstoppable culinary industry means that throughout our stays we are assailed by an onslaught of jellies, jams and marmalades, gateaux and galettes, clafoutis and crum-bles, pies, pastries and puddings, bread, biscuits, brownies and buns, muffins and madeleines, cupcakes, cheesecakes and shortcakes, tortes and tarts, pavlovas, baklavas and latkes, quiches and scones, florentines and fudge. All of this prodigious domestic output is, of course, primarily designed to reprimand Anna and me for our dissolute lifestyle. It's not exactly subtle. She might as well just bludgeon us over the head with a bag of her home-made macaroons.

'Look,' I say, before Theresa has a chance to warm up and really get going, 'I think I might get our stuff in from the car.' Before she can object, I escape.

I carry our bags up to Anna's childhood bedroom, where we always sleep. We have two suitcases and two large bags of presents. With a sigh I dump them on the floor. I imagine the look on Anna's face when she opens her Christmas present. A shiver of terrified anticipation passes through me.

'Hello, Matthew.'

I jump. 'Jesus, Hector, you nearly gave me a heart attack.'

Hector is sitting in the corner of the room, partially hidden behind the wardrobe. 'Sorry,' he says, pushing his glasses up his nose.

'What are you doing in here?' I say, delighted to see him.

Hector is Alistair and Theresa's eldest son. He is ten and a half, going on thirty-five. He is terrifyingly intelligent, a true prodigy, but rather than being obnoxiously precocious, Hector is one of the most considerate and kind people I know. I like him very much. He hauls a huge book into view. 'Just reading this.'

'What is it?'

Hector sniffs. 'It's a slightly shoddy translation of *À la Recherche*.' He pauses. 'How are you, anyway?' he asks, closing the book. He doesn't move towards me; he is too old to want a hug any more. I am too young to feel able to ask for one.

'I'm OK, I suppose.'

'Only OK?'

'Well.' I pause. 'You know, struggling on.' In fact I am vacillating between despair and fatalistic elation. One moment I find myself relishing tomorrow's showdown beneath the Christmas tree, the next I am too miserable to speak.

Hector gazes at me. 'Tough times?'

I nod. 'Tough times.'

He blinks. '*The road up and the road down are one and the same.*'

'Yeah.' I grin. 'Thanks. I'll bear that in mind.'

'Heraclitus said that,' says Hector shyly.

'Heraclitus?'

'The Greek philosopher.'

'Oh, *that* Heraclitus. Now I'm with you. Come on, let's go downstairs and join the party.'

By the time we sit down for supper, Edmund and Lavinia have gone to bed. I am sitting opposite Hector. Anna is on my right, Alistair on my left. We are having mushroom risotto, followed, inevitably, by some of Theresa's home-made chocolate loaf. I am just reaching for my fork when there is a pointed cough from next to me.

'I thought it might be nice if we said grace this evening,' says Alistair.

David Given looks hungrily at his risotto. 'All right,' he sighs. 'But keep it quick, eh, Alistair?'

Alistair closes his eyes. 'Hi, Lord,' he begins. There is a muted sigh from Elizabeth. 'This is just to say thanks for granting us another Christmas with the whole family together. We'd like to say thanks for our health and happiness. Thanks especially for this *wonderful* food.' Alistair cautiously opens an eye to see if Elizabeth thaws at all. She does not. He presses on hurriedly. 'Thanks for Anna's promotion to partnership. Thanks for our three wonderful kids, and please bless Anna and Matthew with children of their own some day soon.'

'Amen,' interjects Theresa piously.

'OK, I think that's it,' concludes Alistair, a shade informally.

'God, Alistair,' says Anna. 'That was so *undignified*. It sounds as if you're giving an acceptance speech at the Oscars, not communing with the Almighty. Whatever happened to all the thees and thines?'

Alistair looks unruffled. 'Youth, Anna,' he replies calmly. 'Youth is the key. Youth is the future.'

'Do you really think so? It's embarrassing.' This is one of the things I have always liked about Anna. She is quite happy to adopt unfashionable positions for the sake of a good argument. 'And thanks very much for the concern and everything,' she continues, 'but I don't think that we need you to pray for us on the baby front just yet.'

Bang on cue, Theresa leaps in. 'All we think —'

Anna spins around to face her. 'I don't give a toss *what* you think. It's none of your business.' She takes a big mouthful of wine. She has been drinking more or less constantly since we arrived, and is now, I realise, quite drunk.

There is an edgy pause. I turn to my brother-in-law. 'Looking forward to your sermon tomorrow, Al.'

Alistair smiles genially. 'Oh good. I think people will enjoy it. It might be a little bit different to what the good people of Surrey are used to hearing on Christmas morning.'

Elizabeth obviously doesn't want her evening spoiled by thinking about Alistair's sermon, and interjects quickly. 'Well, it certainly *is* good news about your partnership, Anna, isn't it?'

Anna eyes her mother sullenly. 'I suppose so.'

Elizabeth glances at her husband. 'We were *so* proud of you, darling. Weren't we, David?'

David nods. 'Oh, yes. Very proud. Good girl.'

I wonder what her parents would say if they knew the lengths Anna has gone to in order to secure her promotion. Sleeping with the boss shows admirable single-mindedness of purpose. I can feel the edges of my vision blur with aggression. 'I've got something to celebrate too,' I say. Everyone looks at me blankly. 'My book has just been published,' I remind them. There is a heavy silence around the table, except for an adenoidal snort of derision from Noon. 'I take it none of you have read it, then,' I say sourly.

'I have,' pipes up Hector.

I stare at my nephew. 'Hector? You *have*? Really?'

Hector nods. 'Yes. I thought it was interesting.'

'You did?' I beam at him.

'In fact there was something I wanted to ask you about it.'

I sit back in my chair, delighted. 'Fire away,' I say. I glance around the table. This young boy has put all these adults to shame!

'It's about the scene with Ivo and the prostitute,' says Hector.

'*Prostitute?*' shrieks Theresa.

'*Ivo?*' chokes David.

'What have you been poisoning my son's mind with?' barks Theresa, her hackles rippling with menace.

'Er, look, Hector, maybe we should talk about this once –'

'It's about the nipple clamps,' says Hector. The table subsides into a stunned silence.

'Nipple clamps?' whispers Elizabeth breathlessly.

Noon makes an unintelligible guttural sound.

'I mean,' continues Hector, oblivious to the electric atmosphere he has created, 'what does a nipple clamp actually *do*?'

There is a long pause. 'Well,' I say cautiously. 'It clamps your nipple.'

Hector nods. 'And I suppose my question, really, is *why* would you want to do that? What purpose does it serve?'

This is not the place for an explanation of the profound psychological malaise which drives a man like Ivo to pay strangers to inflict pain on him by way of nipple clamps (and other assorted devices). 'Well, they're really just, um, ornamental,' I stammer.

'Ornamental?' says Hector thoughtfully. 'Well, I suppose that would explain it.' He pauses. 'No accounting for taste,' he remarks, straight-faced. At this the rest of the table explodes into gales of nervous laughter, with the exception of Theresa and Noon, who are both shooting me murderous looks.

'Well said, Hector,' says David. 'No accounting for taste, that's for sure.'

'This risotto is *delicious*, Elizabeth,' grovels Alistair.

David puts down his fork. 'No,' he says, staring at the ceiling. 'No accounting for taste at all. I mean,' he muses, 'we live in a democracy, don't we?'

Too late, we suddenly realise that David is winding himself to deliver one of his seasonal political diatribes. We all begin to speak at once.

'David –'

'Listen, Dad –'

'Grandpa –'

David ignores us all. He's off. 'And since we live in a *democracy*, that means that we all have to live with the majority will of the electorate, however duped and misguided that electorate might be.' He glares down the table at us.

'That reminds me of a funny story one of my clients told me –'

'It's so – *mushroomy*. How do you do it?'

David presses on. 'That, of course, is why we have to sit back and watch as that emasculated faggot Blair slowly brings this country to its knees. And the tragedy is that people have nobody but themselves to blame. A splendid argument for restricting the right to vote to those people who are intelligent enough to exercise that right responsibly.'

Hector's eyebrows are jumping as he listens to his grandfather. The rest of us know better than to try and interrupt when David is in this sort of mood.

'Blair is so completely *spineless*,' he continues. 'He's a slave to the media and their wretched opinion polls. It's all spin, spin, spin. He doesn't have a single policy or political belief worthy of the name, except for this lily-livered obsession with political correctness. Now you have to pussyfoot around in case you end up offending someone. And what's the result? You can no longer call a spade a spade.' David shakes his head angrily. 'It's all Blair's fault. *He's* the nigger in the woodpile.'

There is an awkward silence.

'Are these *oyster* mushrooms?' asks Alistair.

'Shut up, Al,' suggests Anna.

Hector raises his hand as if he is at school. 'Grandpa?' he says.

David looks down the table at him. 'Yes, Hector?'

'What you were saying just now? About the right to vote?'

Out of the corner of my eye I see Theresa start to make frantic gestures in an attempt to shut her son up. Hector is looking directly at his grandfather and therefore, quite deliberately, fails to see her.

David smiles. 'Yes? What about it?'

'Well, do you really believe that you should disenfranchise the majority of people who are eligible to vote?' Hector looks worried. 'Isn't that going to trigger a regression to the plutocratic hegemony of the last century?'

'Hector —' says Theresa.

'I mean, Lenin talked about democracy being a state which recognises the subordination of the minority to the majority, which he considered to be socially divisive, as it effectively set one sector of society up against another. But the sort of oligarchy that you're proposing is even *more* iniquitous, as it would cause the subordination of the *majority* to the *minority*, and that would never —'

'*Hector.*'

Elizabeth interrupts forcefully. Hector subsides into his chair, looking agitated. I glance towards David, whose face has been growing darker while his grandson has been speaking.

'Grandpa was only speaking metaphorically,' begins Elizabeth.

Hector and David both frown.

'Metaphorically how?' asks Hector.

Elizabeth glances at her husband. 'When Grandpa talks about restricting the right to vote to those people who are intelligent enough to exercise that right responsibly, he doesn't mean it literally.'

David stares at his wife. 'I don't?' he asks.

'No,' confirms Elizabeth. 'You don't.'

There is a pause.

'Right,' says David acidly.

Hector frowns. 'What was the metaphor, Grandpa?'

'Ah. Well. What was the metaphor. Indeed. Good question.' David gives his wife a sardonic look.

'The *metaphor*, Hector, was that when Grandpa said that only intelligent people should have the right to vote, he was trying to convey the idea that people ought to take their responsibility to vote more seriously. Nowadays people are too easily influenced by the media. It's important to think the issues through for oneself.'

David harrumphs unhappily from the other end of the table.

'Well, Granny, that's really more hyperbole than metaphor,' says Hector politely.

Elizabeth's mouth almost disappears in irritation.

'He's right, you know,' I interject. 'As a writer –'

'Shut up, Matthew,' hisses Anna in my ear.

I shut up.

A couple of hours later, Alistair, Theresa, and Given *mère* and *père* have gone off to church for midnight mass. Noon has gone to bed, as has Hector, obviously still concerned about his grandfather's unconstitutional ramblings. Anna has fallen asleep on the sofa in the sitting room. I go upstairs and take the Christmas presents out of our bags.

I weigh Anna's present in my hand. Beneath the festive wrapping paper is the largest, most thickly veined vibrator that I was able to find during an afternoon's trawl through

Soho's seedy sex emporia. A monstrous plastic penis to do service in the place of my resolutely flaccid member seems like a suitably symbolic gift for Anna this holiday season. It is grotesque; fourteen inches long, it has three speeds and requires four huge batteries to run it. Even lying silently in its box, it emanates an aura of barely suppressed menace. It looks more like a riot stick than a sex toy.

After my failure to unearth any solid evidence of Anna's affair with Graham, I am resorting to another tactic: I am going to *shame* Anna into confessing. We shall see if she still denies everything after she has opened the vibrator in front of her whole family. They will all be curious to know why her husband should give her such a thing, and I await her explanation with interest.

At the bottom of the second bag of presents is a rectangular Tupperware box which I do not recognise. Inside are six or seven biscuits, each dotted with tiny chunks of chocolate. The biscuits are roughly hewn, obviously home-made. I shake my head in bewilderment. Where did Anna get these from? They look delicious. I take the box downstairs with the Christmas presents.

I put Anna's biscuits in the kitchen, and go through to the sitting room, where Anna is still asleep on the sofa. I carefully arrange our presents, including Anna's long, narrow box, amongst the other gaudily wrapped gifts beneath the Christmas tree.

The time bomb deposited, I creep over to the sofa and watch my wife sleep. Her legs are tucked up under her, and she is hugging a cushion tightly to her chest. She looks so beautiful, so peaceful, so incapable of causing harm, that for a moment I feel my resolve threatening to disintegrate. I glance towards the Christmas tree.

Suddenly Anna opens her eyes. She looks at me as if I have two heads. 'What time is it?' she asks groggily.

'After midnight. Merry Christmas.' I kiss the side of her head.

'I feel like shit,' she tells me.

'Come on,' I reply, gently tugging her upright. 'Bed.'

Thwock!

Edmund's boot connects with my head.

I struggle to prop myself up on my elbows. 'For God's sake, Edmund. Why won't you ever leave me alone? *Ow*. Jesus.' I sink back into my pillow, and Edmund weighs in with his fists, pummelling my head. I manage to palm him off, and deposit him on the other side of the bed, which is empty. He sits back and looks at me, and farts wetly. My forehead throbs where he kicked me. I peer around the bedroom. Anna is crouched over our bags.

'Hello,' I say. 'Merry Christmas. What time is it?'

'Fuck, fuck, *fuck*,' mutters Anna.

I sit up. 'Anna? What's wrong?'

Anna turns to look at me. 'Oh, Jesus. Look at you!'

'What?'

'Your eye. You look like a panda. What a shiner.' She is grimly amused.

I climb out of bed and look at myself in the mirror. A dramatic scallop of aubergine glistens beneath my right eye, where Edmund thumped me on our arrival yesterday. I groan. 'Thanks, Edmund. That'll look perfect in church.'

Edmund rolls over and sticks his head into Anna's pillow with a happy sigh.

'Have you lost something?' I ask Anna.

'You haven't seen a white plastic box, by any chance? I'm sure I put it in here.'

'A Tupperware box? With biscuits in it?'

Anna's face floods with relief. 'Where is it?'

I yawn. 'Downstairs.'

Anna freezes. 'What?'

'I took it downstairs last night. Very nice of you to –'

Anna grips my arm. '*Are you serious?*' she hisses.

I stare at her. 'Is there a problem?'

She springs to her feet. 'Fuck. *Fuck!* Yes, Matthew, there *is* a problem.' She looks at me. 'Those biscuits were strictly for our consumption only.'

'That's a little selfish, isn't it? They looked delic –'

'They were *hash* cookies, you idiot.'

We stare at each other for a moment.

'They were supposed to be a *surprise*,' says Anna. 'I thought we could have a nibble later on when things got unbearable downstairs.'

'So those biscuits –'

'– contain large chunks of cannabis, yes, that's right. Come on.'

'I'm sorry,' I say. 'I didn't realise –'

'Forget it,' snaps Anna, already halfway down the corridor. I stumble after her, adjusting my pyjamas as I go.

When we arrive in the kitchen, Elizabeth, Theresa, and Alistair are standing around the Aga. They look up as we walk in. Seeing my black eye, all three of them immediately dissolve into fits of uncontrollable giggles.

Anna turns to me. 'Too late,' she says icily.

'What happened to *you*?' snorts Theresa.

'What a beauty,' says Elizabeth, pointing at me before bursting into another convulsion of giggles. 'Oh, God,' she gasps. 'I have to pee.'

'Good morning, everyone,' says Anna coolly. 'Merry Christmas.' The Tupperware box is open on the kitchen table. 'I see you found my home-made biscuits,' remarks Anna dryly.

'Mmm, they were *delicious*,' says Theresa. 'Well done, you. You must give me the recipe.'

'I don't think so,' replies Anna. 'Are there any left?'

Elizabeth shakes her head. 'We ate the lot. Sorry. Couldn't resist them.'

Anna goes pale. 'Just the three of you?'

Alistair nods. 'They were lovely.' He pauses. 'Although I do feel a bit odd.'

Lavinia walks into the kitchen, beaming at us. 'Look what I got in my stocking!' she exclaims. She brandishes a doll.

I bend down towards her. 'Let me see.'

'What happened to your eye?' asks my niece.

'That's where Edmund punched me last night,' I explain.

At this Theresa, Al, and Elizabeth dissolve into hysterics again. Lavinia looks at her parents and grandmother curiously. 'Why are they laughing so much?' she asks.

'Tell me about your new doll, sweetheart,' I suggest.

'It's a Domestic Goddess Barbie,' says Lavinia proudly. 'She's got her own apron and everything.'

'Wow,' I say. Theresa's political agenda has struck again.

'She's got her own pots and pans, too. She's the best cook *ever*.'

'Perhaps she can help with Christmas dinner, then,' I say.

Lavinia's eyes shine in excitement. 'Oh, *yes*,' she breathes. 'She'd like that.'

I stand up. 'What are we going to do about this lot?' I ask Anna, who is looking grimly at the trio of giggling grown-ups.

'I don't know.' Anna looks at her watch. 'We're going to need to put the turkey in soon. And Alistair is never going to be able to take this morning's service. Look at him.' Our brother-in-law is bouncing around the room with his hands tucked up under his chin, puckering up his mouth to show his two front teeth. He is, I think, pretending to be a rabbit.

'Right, this is what we'll do,' says Anna, taking charge. 'I'll make some strong black coffee, and try and sober them up. You're the poultry expert, Matthew. Can you see what you can do with the turkey?'

I gulp. 'Right.'

Theresa wobbles towards us. 'Hello, you chaps.' Her eye-balls seem to be rotating quite independently of each other.

'Oh, Christ,' says Anna. 'Houston, we have a problem.'

Anthony is for Christmas dinner.

Elizabeth always buys the Given Christmas turkey from a nearby organic farm. On the basis that a happy turkey is a tasty turkey, the farm specialises in five-star butchery, deluxe slaughter. Each bird is named, has its own pen in which to eat and run around, and is generally treated like royalty right up until the point when it is rudely murdered. All of this comes at a wallet-melting price, of course, but Elizabeth knows the value of a good dinner-party anecdote when she sees one.

Anthony is almost too big to fit into the Givens' oven. While Anna plies her mother and sister and Alistair with coffee, I am left in the kitchen to wrestle with the monstrous bird. He sits in an enormous roasting dish, pinkly magnificent, as I study Elizabeth's cookery books, trying to work out how long I need to cook him for. I calculate that he needs to be in the oven for at least five and a half hours, and immediately begin to panic. At this rate we won't be eating until halfway through the afternoon. I leave Anthony on the kitchen table while the oven heats up, and go and see how my stoned in-laws are getting on.

In the sitting room, Theresa is splayed out on the sofa, gazing unblinkingly at the ceiling, an O of frazzled amazement playing on her lips. Alistair is earnestly talking to Anna, his lips wet with excited spittle. Elizabeth has passed out in an armchair.

'Everything all right in here?' I ask.

Anna looks at me sardonically. 'Oh, yes, we're having a jolly old time. Aren't we, Al?'

Alistair looks up. '*Fantastic*,' he answers eagerly.

Anna and I exchange glances. 'What are we going to *do*?' she asks plaintively, pointing at her brother-in-law. 'He's hopeless.' She pauses. 'They're all hopeless.'

Noon hobbles into the sitting room. She stops and looks at Theresa, Al and Elizabeth. 'What's wrong with this lot?' she demands.

'We don't know, Noon,' says Anna carefully. 'I don't think they're terribly well.'

'Not terribly well?' squawks Noon. 'Look at them, Anna. They're off their faces.'

'Sorry?'

'They're *stoned*, you silly girl. Drugs. And I bet I know

253

who's responsible for this,' she continues, delivering a venomous look in my direction.

'I have to go and put the turkey in,' I say awkwardly.

'Oh, that's right, run away,' shrieks Noon at my retreating back.

I do precisely that.

Back in the kitchen, Lavinia is standing on a chair, inspecting Anthony the turkey.

'Hello, Matthew,' she says.

'Is everything all right, Lavinia?'

My niece nods. 'He's big, isn't he?' She climbs down from the chair.

'Pretty big,' I agree. The oven has now reached the correct temperature. I carefully pick up the roasting tray and put Anthony in. A thought occurs to me. 'Have you seen Edmund lately?'

Lavinia shakes her head. 'Not for ages.'

I listen. The house sounds eerily quiet. A pang of anxiety flashes through me. In our hurry to recover Anna's hash cookies, we left Edmund alone in our bedroom. I quickly climb the stairs.

Hector is sitting cross-legged on our bed, still unmade following our earlier hasty exit, reading aloud from his huge edition of Proust. Edmund is asleep, calmly sucking his thumb, his head in his brother's lap.

'Hector. Thank heavens.'

'Hello, Matthew. What happened to your eye?'

I ignore this. 'Is everything all right?'

Hector shrugs. 'Fine. Edmund likes it when I read out loud to him.'

At this Edmund opens one eye and looks at me incuriously while he continues to suck rhythmically on his thumb.

After a moment he goes placidly back to sleep. Silently I praise the soporific qualities of Proust. It has always had the same effect on me.

Back in the kitchen, my mind turns reluctantly to the vast array of vegetables and other sundries that need to be prepared before lunch. Suddenly an acrid whiff floats under my nose. I peer through the darkened glass of the oven door. Anthony seems fine. Perhaps I imagined it. This is *paranoia de cuisine* – I'm suffering from the culinary equivalent of stage fright. It's one thing to prepare a couple of chicken breasts each evening; quite another to cook a vast creature like Anthony for your extended, and hypercritical, family. I need to relax. I stand at the sink and begin to peel potatoes.

A few minutes later, the unpleasant smell wafts up my nostrils again, stronger this time. I open the oven door, and a cloud of black smoke billows out into my face. There is now a definite odour of charred *something*.

'What's that funny smell?' asks Lavinia, who has appeared by the kitchen door.

'I'm not sure,' I reply. 'Something's burning.' I put on oven mitts and carefully pull the roasting tray out of the oven.

'Shall I get Nigella now?' asks Lavinia as I carry Anthony over to the kitchen table for further examination.

'Who?' I mutter.

'Nigella. My Domestic Goddess Barbie.'

'If you must,' I reply, still trying to work out where the burning smell is coming from.

'Will you help me, Matthew?'

I put the roasting tray down. 'I will, Lavinia, but I really have to sort this out first.'

'But she's there.'

'Where?'

'*There.*' Lavinia is pointing at the roasting tray.

I turn the dish around. In the bottom of the tray lie the fat-spattered remains of Lavinia's doll. The flesh-coloured plastic has begun to melt.

I spin around, aghast. 'Lavinia! Did you *know* the doll was in there?'

She nods calmly, not tall enough to see the carnage. 'I put her in the tray. It was *your* idea that she could help with the cooking. And she *is* the best cook in the world.'

I blink in disbelief. When I agreed to look after the turkey I hadn't thought to consider the destructive effects of a five-year-old's over-active imagination. The doll is obviously doomed, but I may still be able to save Anthony. The principal difficulty is Lavinia, who is standing patiently next to me, awaiting news.

'Can I have Nigella back now?' she asks.

'Ah, well, you see, Lavinia, there might be a bit of a –'

'*Please.*'

I take a deep breath. 'Actually, sweetheart, there's been a slight accident.'

My niece frowns. 'An accident?'

I gingerly lift the doll out of the tray. Its melted skin is sticky to the touch. My thumb leaves a ghoulish indent on its right shoulder. Nigella's face is an indistinguishable mash of hillocks and bumps. She's Reconstructive Plastic Surgery Barbie. Her hair has been vaporised. She is now bald. I hold the doll up for Lavinia to see.

'I'm afraid it was too hot for her in the oven. She's melted.'

Lavinia's lip wobbles, and then she begins to scream.

'Don't worry, Lavinia, we'll be able to get you another –'

I am drowned out by shrill hysteria. Lavinia has an impressive set of lungs on her. She may be a quiet little girl most of the time, but she can generate quite a bit of noise when she tries. She throws her head back and lets rip with the loudest bawl imaginable.

I remain rooted to the spot, holding Roasted Nigella Barbie out in front of me. Thirty seconds later, Anna rushes into the kitchen, followed by Noon, hobbling along behind. Lavinia ignores them both, and continues to wail.

'What in Hell's name is *that*?' demands Anna.

I swallow. 'It's Lavinia's new doll.'

'Oh God,' breathes Anna.

'What have you *done*?' yells Noon, advancing towards me, brandishing her tiny fist.

Anna raises a placatory hand, wincing as she does so at the volume of Lavinia's yells. For the first time it occurs to me that she must be quite hungover from all the wine she drank last night. 'Matthew,' she says as steadily as she can. 'What exactly has happened here?' She bends down and picks Lavinia up.

'Look, it's pretty simple, really. Lavinia put Nigella – that's the name of the doll – into the roasting dish when I wasn't looking. She wanted to keep Anthony – that's the name of the turkey – company.'

Anna and Noon look at me as if I am quite mad.

I try again. 'Lavinia put the doll in the tray behind the turkey. I didn't see it, and just whacked the whole lot in the oven. It was only when I smelled burning that I realised there was something wrong.'

At this point David appears in his dressing gown, obviously put out.

'What in God's name is going on?' he demands. 'Who's screaming?'

Anna explains what has happened. David shoots me a look of unspeakable loathing.

'I was just trying to help,' I say lamely.

'Where are the others?' asks David gruffly.

'Ah. Well. Good question,' begins Anna carefully.

'They're *stoned*,' interrupts Noon with relish.

Anna shoots her grandmother a reproachful look.

My father-in-law rubs his eyes. 'What?'

'They're lying in the sitting room,' explains Noon excitedly. 'They're all completely lashed.'

'What? *Who* are?'

'Elizabeth, Theresa, and Alistair.' Noon turns towards me, and raises a triumphant finger towards me as she delivers the *coup de grâce*. 'And it's all *his fault*,' she cackles.

'Elizabeth has taken *drugs*?' gasps David, appalled. He has already forgotten about his granddaughter. 'Why? How? I don't understand.'

'It's all his fault,' repeats Noon, pointing at me.

'Anna, will you please tell me what on earth has been going on?' David isn't really a morning person. I can tell that this is not how he likes to start his day. 'What is all this about *drugs*?'

Bang on cue, Alistair arrives in the kitchen. He grins affably at his angry father-in-law. 'Hey, Dave. Morning.' He collapses into a fit of giggles.

David's face goes a little redder. I can hear the air whistling through the dense thickets of nasal hair that sprout tuftily from his nostrils.

'Alistair,' says Anna gently. 'We've had a bit of an accident with Lavinia's new doll.' Lavinia is snuffling into Anna's sweater; her tears have subsided somewhat. I hold up the congealing plastic remains of Nigella the Domestic Goddess Barbie. Alistair looks at the deformed mass of beige limbs for a few moments with a frown on his face. Then, as the dim light of understanding slowly dawns somewhere in the depths of Alistair's brain, we all watch in horror as a wide smile appears across his face.

'I get it,' he says, nodding slowly, beaming at us.

'No,' says Anna. 'There really has been —'

Alistair points at Nigella, and slumps against the fridge. Lavinia stops crying to watch her father, who has begun to shake with silent laughter.

Not unreasonably, she bursts into tears again.

'Oh, this is intolerable,' snaps David, glaring at Alistair in disgust. I am quietly delighted. Despite Noon's best efforts, David has forgotten which of his sons-in-law he should be angry with. 'There's no way you can possibly take a church service in this state,' he growls.

Alistair waves his hand carelessly. 'Sure I can. Piece of piss.'

David draws himself up with as much dignity as he can in his rather ratty dressing gown. 'I'm off to find my wife,' he announces. He sweeps out of the kitchen, leaving us waiting in edgy silence.

Alistair slumps into a chair and lays his head down on the kitchen table. His eyes are shut. 'Woaah,' he murmurs.

'What's wrong with Daddy?' asks Lavinia between sobs.

'Nothing,' says Anna briskly, kissing the top of her head. 'He's a bit tired, that's all. Why don't we go and find those brothers of yours?'

Lavinia brightens. 'All right.' Anna carries her out of the kitchen, shooting me an unreadable look as she goes.

I walk over to the bin and drop the doll into it. 'We can always get her another one,' I say. Noon rolls her eyes malevolently, but before she can say anything Elizabeth appears at the kitchen door, her face flushed.

'I'm starving,' she announces. 'Is there any nosh?'

This is fabulous. My mother-in-law has the munchies.

For the first time in decades, the Givens do not go to church on Christmas Day. Realising that Alistair cannot be allowed anywhere near the church in his state, David telephones the vicar at St Mary's and regretfully announces that Alistair has come down with a virulent bout of gastroenteritis, and so is not able to help officiate with the service that morning, after all. David then decides, given the equally incoherent state of Elizabeth and Theresa, that it is best if we all stay away, rather than turning up with severely depleted forces.

As for my inaugural Christmas dinner, I don't exactly cover myself in glory. Anthony seems unharmed by the accident with Lavinia's doll, but I am terrified of undercooking him. I don't want to cause a genuine case of gastroenteritis to accompany Alistair's fictitious bout, and so I spend ages crouched in front of the oven, armed with an array of pokers, prodders and thermometers, wondering whether Anthony is ready to eat.

It is after three o'clock when I finally decide to risk it. As I begin to carve Anthony up, the flesh flakes away from the carcass like huge pieces of dandruff. The meat is dry, over-cooked, and utterly tasteless.

By the time we sit down to eat, Lavinia has just about recovered from the trauma of seeing Nigella the Domestic

Goddess Barbie transmogrify from beautiful, pan-wielding brunette to extra from *Night of the Living Dead*. As she clambers up on to her chair at the dinner table, though, rather than giving me her usual big smile, she looks away from me. It is the worst moment of the day. So far.

The meal is well below par, both gastronomically and in terms of seasonal jollity. Theresa, Alistair, and Elizabeth take small sips of water throughout the meal, wincing as they do so. David stares down the table with a black look on his face. He is furious that we have missed the Queen's broadcast, and the children are fractious because the present-opening ceremony has been delayed until their parents and grandmother are back on the same planet as the rest of us. We chew on our leathery pieces of turkey in silence. The meal is only rescued by Theresa's Christmas pudding, accompanied by her irritatingly delicious home-made cinnamon ice cream.

Noon, of course, is revelling in all this. In her eyes, blame for the drugs, the annihilation of Lavinia's new doll, and the awful food, can all be lain squarely at my door. She is exultant.

Personally, I think it's all a bit unfair.

After coffee, we file obediently into the sitting room to begin the present-giving ceremony. We arrange ourselves into small groups. Anna and I sit next to each other. Noon sits next to us, and David and Elizabeth (who is still looking rather green) are on the large sofa opposite. The children are no longer able to contain their excitement. Edmund kicks me hard on the shin.

The distribution of Christmas presents is usually

tightly marshalled by Elizabeth, but this afternoon she is in no state to boss people about. Instead Anna claps her hands together. She points to the tree and leans over towards Lavinia. 'Lavinia, darling, why don't you give that one to Granny?' And so the process begins. As the presents are unwrapped and inspected, I keep my eye on Anna's gift, ready to jump in if anyone should hand it to her too early.

As usual, I have been in charge of buying presents for Anna's family, and, as usual, the gifts I have chosen for the children have been selected to provoke the greatest look of horror on Theresa's face. I have bought Lavinia a pink fairy dress with lots of frilly lace and ribbons. She adores it, and insists on putting it on immediately.

'You look *lovely*, darling,' says Theresa unconvincingly, as Lavinia twirls ecstatically around the sitting room.

'We could stick you on top of the tree if the angel falls off,' says Anna.

Lavinia giggles.

Theresa looks a little sick at the sight of her daughter resplendent in lurid pink, but when Edmund tears the wrapping off his present and delightedly shows off the drum I have bought him, she suddenly looks very ill indeed.

'A *drum*.' She reels. 'How very considerate of you, Matthew.' I grin at her affably. Edmund locates the drumsticks and begins to bash merry hell out of his new toy.

'Golly,' says Anna after a few moments.

'Quite loud, isn't it?' I shout.

'It is, quite,' agrees Hector.

'Here, Edmund.' Elizabeth makes a visible movement for the first time in half an hour. She sits up and smiles thinly at her grandson. With a grin, Edmund marches over to her and proudly shows her his drum. 'That's lovely,' she says, before bending down and snatching it away from him.

'*Mum*,' chides Anna.

'Thank Christ,' mutters David.

'You can play with it later,' says Elizabeth. 'Once you get home.'

Edmund stands in front of his grandmother, and with a bloodcurdling yell he begins to clatter her with his drumsticks. Elizabeth shrieks, unsure how to defend herself. After a moment, Alistair picks up his screaming son and carries him out of reach of his grandmother. Edmund is furious. Elizabeth looks shaken.

'Sorry about that,' mumbles Alistair. Edmund is bawling loudly.

I settle back in my chair, enjoying myself immensely. I couldn't have hoped for such spectacular results.

'Here, Matthew,' says Theresa, leaning across towards me. 'This is for you.' She hands me what is obviously a record, wrapped up in green paper.

I smile. 'Thanks, Theresa.'

She waves a hand. 'You may have it already. I just saw it, and took a punt. I don't know anything about this sort of stuff.'

I tear off the paper, and am left holding a brown cardboard sleeve with no markings on it. Curious, I slide the record out on to my hand, and then my world stops for a few moments.

The white label in the centre of the record is blank, except for the words, scribbled in pencil, 'Duke Ellington Solo Piano – August 1967'.

August 1967 was the month that Duke recorded his

tribute album to Billy Strayhorn. *Solo Piano*? Could this be what I think it is? My head starts to spin.

'Is it OK?' asks Theresa. 'I know you like his stuff, but I've got no –'

'Where did you *find* this?' I am struggling to stay in my seat. I want to give her a huge hug and waltz her around the room.

Theresa shrugs. 'A second-hand record shop in Winchester. I just went in and asked if they had any Duke Ellington records. The shop assistant gave me this. Said it had just come in the week before. It was all they had.' She pauses, uncertain. 'Do you like it?'

'*Like* it? It's perfect. *Perfect*.' I sit back in wonderment.

'Well done, sis,' remarks Anna, smiling, squeezing my arm as she does so. 'You've just eclipsed my present by about a million light years, though.'

'Well, good,' says Theresa, rather bemused.

I sit staring stupidly at my present, wondering whether this can really be the missing recording I have dreamt of for so long. My heart soars with thrilled excitement. I longingly eye the stereo which sits in the corner of the room, but decide to wait. I want to savour the moment when I first hear this; I want to be able to immerse myself in the music with nothing to distract me.

My elation is marred, although only slightly, when a few minutes later Elizabeth gives Theresa a copy of *Virgin on Mergin'*.

'Oh, wonderful,' gushes Theresa. 'I adore her.'

'*Him*,' I correct.

'Oh, that's right. Him. Isn't that extraordinary? How do you think he manages to get so inside the female characters' heads? It's uncanny.'

'Obviously the man's a genius,' says Alistair in that sincere way of his that makes me want to thump him.

We are nearing the end of the presents. Finally I hand Anna her box. She grins at me. 'Thanks, sweetheart.' She puts it down, and reaches behind her. 'This is for you.' She hands me a small package.

'Great,' I say, not even looking at it. 'Thank you.'

Anna grins. A look of happy intrigue plays on her lips as she carefully runs her fingernail underneath the tape at one end of the box. She looks up at me. 'Aren't you going to open yours?'

I nod, and begin to pull at the paper distractedly.

Edmund quietly goes around the back of the sofa where his grandparents are sitting and pulls his drum off the table.

Anna puts the wrapped box to her ear, and rattles it. She grins, shaking her head. My heart starts to go faster. Soon everyone will know.

Edmund has now found his drumsticks, and begins hitting the drum again, twice as loudly as before. 'Right, buster,' says Theresa, climbing out of her chair. 'I'll take *that*, thank you.' Theresa snatches Edmund's drum from him. Another shrill yell of anger erupts from his throat.

I pull the rest of the paper off my present. I am left holding a small black box.

Then Anna unwraps her present, and screams. As her hands fly to her mouth, the box tips off her lap. The lid flies open, and the huge plastic penis falls out. It rolls to a stop in the middle of the floor.

There is silence as the whole family looks at Anna's present.

'What's that?' asks Lavinia with interest.

Slowly Anna raises her eyes towards me. They are wide

with confusion and fear. 'Matthew,' she whispers. 'What's going on?'

Noon, Theresa and Alistair stare dumbly at the vibrator, all unable to speak. Elizabeth lets out a small moan.

'I think you'd better explain yourself –' splutters David furiously. Anna waves at him to be quiet, and he subsides back into the sofa.

'What's this about?' whispers Anna, staring at me. She shakes her head. 'How could you *do* this?' One tear begins its lonely fall down her cheek.

I look at her, and then at the rest of her family. I have rehearsed my lines a thousand times, but as I speak them, they sound all wrong. 'You *know* what this is about, Anna,' I say, trying to keep my voice level. 'I think you have something that you need to tell everyone, don't you?'

Suddenly Anna's face goes white with fury. She straightens her back and wipes her tear away with a brusque sweep of her hand. 'No,' she replies coldly. 'I don't.'

Now it is my turn to stare at her in disbelief. Surely she's not *still* going to deny everything?

Edmund, apoplectic at having lost his drum yet again, storms into the middle of the room and picks up the vibrator before anybody can stop him. Then he is running towards me, brandishing it above his head. We all watch, paralysed, as he brings it down on top of my precious new Ellington record. There is the sound of splintering acetate as the flimsy cardboard cover crumples beneath the force of Edmund's blow. He continues to smash the plastic penis against the record with all his might. Finally Theresa picks her son up and quickly removes it from his tiny fists without saying a word.

I am staring at Anna. 'What do you –'

'I want you to leave, now,' she says quietly. 'I want you out of this house in the next ten minutes.' Without looking at me, she stands up and walks out of the room.

There is a dreadful silence.

'You had better go,' says David grimly.

I am still holding Anna's present. I open the box. Inside lie two familiar silver cufflinks.

PART THREE

PART THREE

When I was young, a framed piece of embroidery sat on the wall of my parents' kitchen in Hertfordshire, just above the kettle. Amidst garlands of roses and perfectly square houses with red triangular roofs, chunky letters of sky-blue cotton bellowed: 'GOOD MORNING! TODAY IS THE START OF THE REST OF YOUR LIFE!'

I haul myself out of bed and plant both feet in a pool of vomit that I deposited on the floor at some point during the night. I blink at my now dirty feet. 'GOOD MORNING!' bellows the puddle of sour puke. 'TODAY IS THE START OF THE REST OF YOUR LIFE!'

I get back into bed.

Ten minutes later, when I can no longer bear the sensation of vomit slithering around my toes, I clamber reluctantly out of bed and go into the bathroom. I wipe my feet, and wearily begin to brush my teeth, inspecting myself in the cracked, dirty mirror. My pink-tinged eyes are sunk into ghoulish hollows. My skin is the colour of uncooked rice, except for the cold sore that loiters malignantly on my upper lip.

I may look dreadful, but I don't actually feel too bad: I no longer notice my hangovers. My brain broke off diplomatic relations with the rest of my body about a week ago. Anyway, alcohol poisoning is just one way of feeling like shit, and I have enough alternatives at my disposal right now.

I haven't seen Anna for four weeks.

They have been the worst four weeks of my life.

I pass the fortification of cardboard boxes in the middle of the sitting room, and walk into the kitchen. The cold tap drips gangrenously into an unwashed milk bottle. I switch on the kettle and open the dwarf fridge; the light inside remains resolutely off. I peer in dispiritedly. There is such a rich variety of lurgy festering on the fridge's walls that if lightning were to strike it, evolution would begin all over again. There is no milk.

The battle-worn Formica counter top is riddled with craters gouged out by angry kitchen implements. A takeaway pizza box sits near the rusting electric hob. I lift its lid. Inside there is an abandoned crust, a lonely arc of dried-out dough, flecked with cold melted cheese. I pop it into my mouth and chew thoughtfully while the kettle splutters to a boil. Next to the pizza box is an empty bottle of vodka. Three cartons of cranberry juice lie on the floor near the bin. So. Last night it was sea breezes.

The last evening that I can actually remember, that didn't dissolve into a sorry fuzz of inebriated oblivion, was about three weeks ago. Since then I have drunk myself into a miserable stupor every night. For the first few evenings I drank wine, until I realised that this was a very slow and expensive way to get blind drunk. Experimentation followed: gin made me weepy, whisky made me hysterical, and vodka made me fall over. I stuck with vodka. I have managed to wipe my memory banks of every sorry, tortured moment of my evenings alone. All there is behind me is a grey haze of unhappiness.

I finally manage to swallow the pizza crust. Breakfast over with, I walk into the sitting room with my milkless tea. I light a cigarette, and inhale deeply, staring dully at the wall of unpacked boxes in front of me.

Home sweet home.

I have left our lovely flat in Camden. Now I am installed in a bijou one-bedroom shit-hole beyond the back of the back of beyond, in Stratford, that drab, suburban hell of choked traffic jams and single-decker Hopper buses. This is, in theory, East London, but the nearest large conurbation might as well be Vladivostok. I nearly live in bloody *Essex*, for God's sake. My new flat is about half a mile away from Stratford Shopping Centre, a squalid aggregation of drab chain stores and discount shops, where slow-shuffling pensioners forage for bargains beneath the glare of white neon, and cabals of bored youths lean against walls, cupping smokes behind their fists. This is the slow death of Zone 5. London's siren call – real, proper London – torments me from afar. The sense of isolation is slowly crushing my spirit.

If all this wasn't enough, my bastard estate agent forgot to mention that the neighbouring shit-hole to my shit-hole is occupied by thirty or so insomniac Kurdish refugees. Since I moved in there has been a non-stop, twenty-four-hour party going on. Musical entertainment generally seems to consist of the diabolical caterwauling of castrated goats, underpinned by a chorus of raucous fax machines. The wall between the flats is the approximate thickness of rice paper. Only the alcohol allows me to sleep through the unholy racket.

I flick ash on to the carpet. My typewriter sits untouched on the floor. Cold January rain lashes the windows. On the arm of the sofa lies last night's attempt at a reconciliatory *billet doux* to Anna. I have lost count of how many letters I have written. I settle back into the sofa and begin to read. Halfway down the second page, my handwriting becomes illegible. This is probably just as well: at around the same juncture, the vodka finally won its mismatched battle with my self-respect and I began begging Anna wretchedly to forgive me.

I ball the letter up and throw it at the wastepaper basket. It hits the side of the bin and bounces on to the carpet. With a sigh, I haul myself off the sofa and drop the ball of paper into the basket to join my other letters – all unsent.

I have royally fucked things up.

I was wrong, all wrong.

It's the cruellest of ironies that, of all people, it should have been *Graham's* cufflinks that Anna had liked so much that she decided to give me a pair for Christmas. That's why they were hidden in her underwear drawer: they were for me, all along. When Anna went off to Paris, she simply hid them somewhere better so that I wouldn't find them. It was just unfortunate that Graham happened to be wearing his own pair on the evening we met in the restaurant, which made me jump to so many wrong conclusions. Bad bloody luck.

I worked all this out on the drive back from Surrey to London on Christmas Day. Anna had refused to see me before I left. None of her family would look me in the eye. I packed my bags as quickly as I could and escaped.

I spent the next two days fretfully pacing up and down the flat, slowly realising the enormity of my mistake. I didn't dare go out in case Anna telephoned, but I couldn't summon up the courage to ring her parents' house. Finally, Theresa called. Anna, she said, didn't want to speak to me. She wanted me to move out of the flat, at once.

Out of the flat? I choked.

Yes, until things were resolved. Right now Anna needed space, Theresa said, her voice dripping with excited compassion, and she needed time. The best thing I could do was to give her both.

Numbly, stupidly, I agreed. I reasoned that if I wanted Anna to forgive me, I had little choice but to do whatever she wanted. I began to look for short-term rentals. After three days of inspecting a succession of damp-infested, cockroach-overrun hell-holes, I was shown around my present home. It was, by some distance, the worst flat I had visited, but as I stood in the gloomy kitchen, I realised that there was no point worrying too much about where I was going to stay. This would only be a temporary arrangement, after all. Besides, without Anna I wasn't going to be happy *anywhere*. I abruptly decided to stop wasting my time, and asked to sign the papers.

So here I am. All I can do now is protest my innocence from the wrong end of the A11, and wait for Anna to forgive me. I must be patient, penitent, and understanding. Since Christmas Day we have only spoken to each other once, when she telephoned to ask me to remove my record collection from the flat. The conversation lasted for less than a minute. She had replaced the receiver before I could launch into my overwrought hymn of contrition. The records now lie in the cardboard boxes in front of me. I haven't bothered to unpack them, as Anna refused to let me take the record player.

I shower and climb into yesterday's clothes, and light another cigarette. I have started to smoke a lot more now. I can't really afford it, but it somehow feels right, this rather pedestrian method of self-immolation. If I really wanted to do the whole martyr-for-Love thing properly, I could always go and skip blindfolded amongst the rush-hour traffic in the Stratford one-way system, but forty a day will do for starters.

Then I remember with a dull jolt that it's Saturday morning, and my fragile, perpetually teetering equilibrium is threatened once again.

Our weekends were always sacred.

All those blissful days together that I took for granted at the time now seem more precious than life itself. Right now I would give anything for just a few hours of that familiar contentment.

Our weekends were always heralded by a lazy bout of lovemaking. We would slowly make that delicious journey from sleep to arousal, gently caressing each other awake. Saturday morning sex was a relaxed, considerate affair. There were never any eye-popping gymnastics, nothing too ambitious or exotic. We simply took our sweet time.

Then I would go out for the newspaper while Anna

enjoyed one of her marathon baths, soaking away the strains and worries of the week just gone. A large pot of steaming coffee, tottering stacks of hot toast and expensive marmalade from Fortnum and Mason, and we would spend the rest of the morning sitting at the kitchen table, the radio on quietly in the background, reading the paper. Anna always read the news and finance sections first, while I buried myself in the sport and culture supplements, scoffing humourlessly at the book reviews. From time to time we would read things out loud to each other. In between we sat in contented silence. After lunch, we got on with our lives: during the football season I would leave for Highbury, and Anna would meander around the markets and sneak off to Tower Records to buy her weekly dose of crap pop. But nothing came between us and our mornings.

We had a different routine for Sundays. Once a month or so, we would catch the Tube to Leicester Square and wander through the deserted streets of Soho, wading through the accumulated rubbish of the night before as the area slowly woke up around us. Then we would go to the Golden Dragon on Gerrard Street for dim sum at eleven o'clock. We were usually the only western people in the place; I used to look at the surrounding tables, bursting with large, squalling Chinese families, smugly convinced that this was the genuine dim sum experience – as if its authenticity mattered more than the food. Afterwards, we would cross Shaftesbury Avenue to the Curzon Soho for an art-house matinée that Anna had chosen. As we settled back into our chairs, happily replete, I would always congratulate myself on how clever we were, to have got everything so *right*. This was what weekends were for, after all — the urbane selection of all the right items from London's cultural smorgasbord. I felt so damn *pleased* with myself; I was living the sort of life that I had always believed I deserved, and I was living it with the girl of my dreams. I just wished that there could have been someone there to bear admiring witness to the sophistication of it all.

Our weekends were jewels, sparkling brilliantly amidst the lonely drudgery of the rest of my week. I cherished them, hoarded their delights. I thought they would go on for ever.

I hear the rusty flap of the letter box creak open. There is a soft thud as a small volley of letters lands on the hallway carpet. Every morning I still hope for a letter from Anna. I bend down to inspect the post as a sub-arctic wind whistles beneath the inch-wide gap beneath the front door.

Suddenly I see the expansive whorls of Anna's hand-writing. The world shifts down into looping slow-motion for a moment until I realise that she has just forwarded on a letter to me. I open the envelope. It is a Christmas card from my parents, wishing us both a happy holiday season, with apologies for the slight delay. It's only a month, and a lifetime, too late.

I feel very alone.

There are two other letters. One is addressed to someone I do not know, presumably a former inmate. The other has my name neatly typed in the middle of a heavy, cream envelope, which bears the unmistakable whiff of officialdom. I drop them both unopened on to the small mound of similar letters lying on the carpet by the front door, and return to the sitting room with my parents' Christmas card, which I place in solitary splendour on the grubby windowsill.

On top of one of the boxes in the sitting room sits a plastic bag. It contains the shattered fragments of the record that Edmund smashed on Christmas Day with his avenging swipes of Anna's vibrator. *Was* this Ellington's long-lost Strayhorn elegy? I'll never know now: I'm doomed to an eternity of helpless conjecture. Curiously, though, I'm feeling quite sanguine about the prospect.

All my life, my eyes have drifted beyond the present. I was always planning the next step, eagerly anticipating developments still to come. I was never satisfied with what I had, too busy eyeing the next excitement coming over the horizon. When I was given my first saxophone I immediately wanted to play like Charlie Parker. As soon as I got my first car, I wanted a newer, faster one. Nothing was ever good enough; everything could be improved upon. My headlong rush into the future blinded me to more immediate pleasures: listening to my Duke Ellington records, my enjoyment was muted by my dreams of the one album that I *didn't* have.

Perhaps – just perhaps – that recording lies next to me now. But over the past few weeks I've begun to understand that I've been missing the point. The myth of the lost Ellington recording has distracted me from the music that I already possess. The *real* treasure has been here all along. It's the sound of the band in full, glorious flight that gives me the irresistible buzz of excitement, that high-octane blast of crazy joy. I *know* the bliss of Paul Gonsalves's tenor solo, all twenty-seven delirious choruses of it, at the 1956 Newport Jazz Festival. I *know* the sat-isfaction of a tightly-syncopated horn section blasting melodies into the stratosphere. That is what's important. I look at the brittle fragments of the smashed record. Who needs another piece of vinyl, a few more notes? I have enough.

Without a record player, the only music I've heard in the last month has come from my own saxophone. Each night I have been practising assiduously before I begin my descent to the bottom of a new vodka bottle. The quartet's gig at the wine bar in Clerkenwell is next week. The prospect shines like a beacon through my days and nights, the one bright feature on an otherwise dark horizon. I live for our Tuesday night rehearsals and the chance to chase away my grim reality with music. I am determined to relish my moment in front of an audience. I shall cover myself in irrelevant glory. I want to live someone else's life for a while.

And so I dream my dream:

The band are swinging hard now. Look at the sax player! See how he twists and bends, squeezing notes out of his horn. The spotlight fixes him in its eye; behind him, his long shadow dances. The crowd is cheering as the players cut loose. This is what it's all about: the wailing sax, the grooving piano, the thumping drums, the driving bass. Four men, a roomful of sound.

Jazz, baby, jazz.

I smoke two more cigarettes on the sofa, my mind a dull trough of willed nothingness, reluctant to consider the day ahead. Through the wall, fifteen or so Kurds begin a heated argument, and then spontaneously break into rousing song.

Finally, I put on my coat and open the front door. It's time for me to go to work.

Yes, work.

On a Saturday.

I have to eat, you know.

'Thank you.'

'That's £6.99, please.'

'Can I give you this?'

'Certainly.'

The card is swiped.

'Is this as good as everyone says it is?'

'Well, that's really a matter of opinion. Sign there for me, please.'

'Have you read it?'

'Uh, yes. Yes, I have.'

'What did *you* think of it?'

I pause. 'I thought it was *wonderful*.'

'Great.'

I pick up the book and put it in a bag. 'Well,' I say, 'I hope you enjoy it.'

An unseeing smile. 'Thanks.' The customer turns to go. A thin hiss escapes my lips as I slump against the cash register.

'There,' says Dawn, who is standing right behind me. 'That wasn't so hard, now, was it?'

I turn away, gagging on the bilious waves of resentment rising up within me.

'Remember,' says Dawn, 'our job is to sell books.'

I sigh. 'Yes.'

'Our job is *not* to slag off authors we don't like and abuse customers whose taste happens to differ from our own.'

'OK,' I say, looking at my shoes. 'Message understood.'

'We love *all* books, remember? Even that one.' She points at the colossal piles of *Virgin on Mergin'* that take up most of the front of the shop. '*Especially* that one, in fact. Your job is to shift the stock. Particularly here, and particularly today.'

'Right,' I mutter. This evening, Bernadette Brannigan, now unmasked and roundly fêted as Alan Rossiter, is coming into our bookshop to give his first ever reading. Consequently, there are people everywhere. In one corner a camera crew is shooting a location report. Tonight's reading has attracted unprecedented media attention for a literary event. Of course it has. *Virgin on Mergin'* was already top of the best seller lists when news of the author's true identity broke, but now the sales figures are record-breakingly stratospheric. The publishers are scarcely able to keep up with demand, both for the new book and for Bernadette Brannigan's entire backlist. I am getting an idea what it must have been like working in a record shop during Beatlemania: in last week's paperback fiction charts, spots one to six were all filled by the *Virgin* novels. (Number seven, depressingly, was the latest cloth-cap-and-clogs saga by Candida Divine.)

In the past month, Alan Rossiter has been interviewed by every talk show host in the country, and has been profiled at length in every newspaper. He has already appeared on *Desert Island Discs*, and has even had a twelve-page colour spread in *OK!* magazine showing off his dreadful mock-Tudor home in Swindon. He has become the most talked-about man in Britain. Everywhere I turn I am confronted by his smug smile. And it is all my fault.

It is unspeakably depressing.

Unfortunately Dawn (who is manager of the fiction department, even though she has quite obviously never read a decent book in her life, and had never even *heard* of me until I applied for a job here) overheard me speaking to a customer who had come up to the till with *all six* Bernadette Brannigan novels under his arm. All I did was to suggest somewhere where he could shove his books, rather than the usual carrier bag. Dawn, who obviously fancies me something rotten, gave me a formal reprimand, and now every time someone approaches the desk bearing a *Virgin* novel (about every other customer at the moment), I am pushed forward to ring the sale through. She has also rearranged staffing rotas so that I will be working tonight when the great man comes into the shop. I had planned to be long gone, tucked up cosily in my flat, ready to lay siege to a new bottle of vodka. However, after my official warning, I have little choice but to work tonight if I want to keep my job. Which I do, as I have to find some way of paying the rent. And vodka doesn't come cheap, even the larynx-eroding stuff that I buy. I look miserably through the window at the motionless traffic on Charing Cross Road. Just around the corner is the Curzon Soho. Since I began working here, I have not dared to take the three-minute walk to see what's showing, terrified of my memories.

Returning to full-time employment has proved to be something of a shock to the system. Perhaps *returning* to full-time employment is a tad disingenuous – apart from my ill-fated foray into the world of advertising, the last full-time job I had was in a bakery in Potters Bar during university holidays, which funded a summer's InterRailing around Europe with Anna. (While I was skilfully operating a machine which lightly coated doughnuts with sugar, Anna did a student placement in a law firm, and was involved in the largest hostile corporate takeover of the decade.) The humdrum, quotidian concerns of the workplace are wearisome; they chip slowly but resolutely away at one's soul. I can feel my creative spirit being stifled by the pettifogging straitjacket of corporate boddery. And this is a *bookshop*, for God's sake. I thought people who worked in bookshops were supposed to be passionate about books. They're not. All they're passionate about here is making sure that nobody takes an extra five minutes for their tea break.

Of course, my position is not made any easier by the fact that I am a published author. I can sense the jealousy that this provokes – understandable in the circumstances, I suppose, as most people who work here probably harbour dreams of being a writer one day. Consequently, many of my colleagues have been somewhat frosty towards me. I have done my best to put people at ease and to show them that I'm the same as the next man, but it doesn't always seem to work. I suppose I would feel anxious, too, if I found myself standing next to Alexander Solzhenitsyn every day. Only Dawn seems resolutely unimpressed by my literary status, but my instinct tells me that her consistently aggressive attitude towards me is her way of letting me know that she finds me attractive. (Not, I should add, that I am remotely interested. I'm a married man, after all. And Dawn is an ugly cow. Not to mention an utter bitch.)

I should not be here. I should be slaving away over my typewriter, not working in this arid, soulless place with its bright lights, bland Scandinavian flooring, and gurgling cappuccino machine. Maybe Neville has a point, after all. There *is* more to books than this crass commercialism. Heaven help us if there isn't.

But despite all the drawbacks, there is one good reason why I want to keep this particular job. It is sitting on the corner of the large table at the front of the shop. Ever since it arrived last week, I have hardly taken my eyes off the shop's single copy of *Licked*, an island of integrity in that monstrous sea of brightly coloured, over-hyped dross. (Three days into the job, I surreptitiously telephoned the wholesale suppliers and ordered a copy of the book. A neatly wrapped package soon arrived in the post. It was so *easy*. So why haven't any other bookshops bothered to do it?) Now at least I can ensure that my book finally gets the attention that it deserves, and this makes the myriad hardships and humiliations of employment easier to bear. After a careful study of the flow of customers, I have placed *Licked* in the most conspicuous position in the shop. So far only one person – a middle-aged, intelligent-looking lady – has actually picked it up. As she read the back cover, I could see her brow furrow in intrigued curiosity. I watched, holding my breath. Eventually she put the book back down on the table, shaking her head in wry admiration, and moved on. I felt crushed, rejected, and humiliated. The woman had taken a long, hard look at what I had to offer, and had finally said no thank you. (Mind you, a few minutes later she approached the till brandishing a Jeffrey

Archer paperback. This gave me some comfort: she obviously wasn't as clever as she looked.)

By seven o'clock, the shop is deserted. The store manager decided to close early when it became apparent that thousands of people were loitering in the hope of catching a glimpse of Bernadette Brannigan. When we asked everyone to leave, they simply recongregated on the pavement outside the shop. Since then the crowd has swelled as other curious passers-by have joined the throng. They eventually spilled on to the road, causing cars to grind to a bad-tempered standstill. Rather than trying to shift such large numbers of people, the police diverted traffic along Shaftesbury Avenue.

In view of all the excitement, the shop has hired two huge bouncers, their fake bow ties dwarfed by tree-trunk necks. Immediately behind a hastily erected cordon of thick gold rope stands a scrabbling posse of paparazzi. There are also five outside broadcast television units. The glare from their lighting equipment casts ethereal pools of light over the front of the shop. I sigh. This is ridiculous. It's more like a film premier than a book reading. I try and not think about my trip to Preston last year.

Finally, the audience starts to arrive. At the door, the bouncers inspect invitations. One by one, the sea of chairs that I carefully arranged this afternoon is filled up. The audience bustles with self-importance. Dawn tells me that they are principally journalists, critics, and some of the great and good of the publishing industry. A low murmur of excited conversation hums through the room. I think I spot Hanif Kureishi and Alan Bennett. Each guest takes a glass of Pinot Grigio from my tray without looking at me.

By the time every seat is filled, the tension has risen considerably. Suddenly there is a roar of excitement from the crowd outside, and a ferocious blaze of flash bulbs. Moments later, Alan Rossiter walks into the shop, closely followed by Sean and another man, who – I assume from the expensive cut of his suit – is Bernadette Brannigan's publisher.

Alan Rossiter himself is a singularly unimpressive figure. He is in his mid-forties, and has greying hair which is receding badly. He is wearing faded jeans and scuffed shoes, an unironed shirt and a brown corduroy jacket. This affectation annoys me intensely. It's as if he wasn't *expecting* this. As he steps into the shop, the audience turns around, stands up, and bursts into applause. Rossiter acknowledges them, pretending to look bewildered at all the attention.

The store manager now steps forward, and fawningly introduces himself to the newly arrived trio. He then introduces Dawn, who actually *curtsies*, the silly cow. The group approaches my tray for refreshment. As he takes a glass of wine, Sean winks at me cheerfully.

The party walks to the front of the room, accompanied by increasingly ecstatic applause. The man in the expensive suit waves at the audience to sit down. An expectant silence settles. The man clears his throat, and makes a few introductory remarks of such mesmerising fatuousness that there can be no doubt that he is indeed the publisher. He finally turns and gestures towards Alan Rossiter. The crowd erupts again. I pour myself a glass of wine and gulp most of it down in one needful swallow. As the cheering continues, Sean pats Alan Rossiter supportively on the back and makes his way back past the audience, towards me.

'Matt,' he says as he approaches. 'How're you doing?'

I grimace. 'OK.'

'Job going well?'

'Oh yes. Loving every moment of it, Sean.'

The irony passes Sean by. 'Like a duck to water? Great. Can I have another one of those?' He points to the glasses of wine on the tray.

'Help yourself. This is quite a show, isn't it?'

Sean nods. 'They've pulled out all the stops. They wanted to come out with all guns blazing.' He sips his wine. Alan Rossiter has begun to read from *Virgin on Mergin'*. The room has descended into a reverent silence. Sean lowers his voice. 'Listen, Matt, I just wanted to say thank you.'

I frown. 'What for?'

'For your part in all this. We couldn't have done it without you.'

I stare at him. 'What are you talking about?' I whisper.

Sean rolls his eyes. 'You know.' He winks. 'None of this would have happened without a certain *leak* to the newspapers.'

My head begins to spin.

'I always knew I could rely on you,' continues Sean, turning to watch his client read. He takes another sip of wine. 'And your, ah, little indiscretion is very much appreciated. It was important that the story came from an outside source, so nobody could accuse us of deliberately manipulating the media.' He taps his nose. 'Which, of course, we would never dream of doing.'

'How do you know it was me?' I ask weakly.

'Had to be,' replies Sean. 'You were the only person I told.'

The audience erupts into sycophantic hysterics at something Alan Rossiter has just read. 'Oh,' I say quietly.

'And obviously it's had the desired effect,' continues Sean, gesturing in front of him. 'Sales of the last book were a little disappointing.'

'Disappointing?' I repeat dully.

Sean nods. 'Only one and a half million. So we thought the time had come to do a bit of dirty washing in public, make a clean breast of it, you know, and see if we couldn't give the figures a bit of a boost.' He nudges me. 'To tell you the truth, I didn't think it would be quite as successful as this.'

'No,' I agree numbly.

'Anyway, thanks a million.' Sean smiles.

'Well, er, of course, you're welcome,' I stammer. Sean nods and turns back towards Alan Rossiter. I pour myself some more wine, my mind racing. Sean *knew* I would be too jealous to be able to keep the news to myself. He has played my neuroses like a virtuoso. That's why Alan Rossiter didn't look particularly surprised when the journalist from the *Sun* confronted him on his doorstep. He was *expecting* it. This whole thing has all been carefully engineered, and my mean-spirited envy has been the pivotal cog in the plan's wheel. I feel simultaneously mortified and furious that Sean should have exploited me like this. And now he is pretending that it was all tacitly agreed in advance, that I was in on the plan from the start. Is he *trying* to make me feel even worse than I already do?

Sean turns back to me. 'Alan wants to meet you afterwards to thank you personally,' he whispers.

I start. 'Oh, no, that really won't be —'

Sean slaps me on the back. 'Don't be silly,' he reassures me. 'Of course he would. He's very grateful to you. We all are. You deserve it.'

Deserve it? Deserve what? The humiliation of being exposed as a petulant tittle-tattle? Well, perhaps Sean is right. Maybe I *do* deserve it. Shame floods through me. 'All right, then,' I mutter. 'If you like.'

'Excellent,' says Sean. 'I know he'll be delighted.'

There is another long laugh from the audience.

The standing ovation goes on for eight and a half minutes. I know, because I time it. Immediately afterwards, half of the audience come towards me on the hunt for more wine, and the other half flock around the author.

I step through the milling crowds, filling glasses as I go. Suddenly I see Sean striding towards me. Two steps behind him is his famous client. 'Matt,' says Sean, as I turn to escape. 'I'd like you to meet the man of the moment.'

I turn to face them both. Alan Rossiter steps forward, smiling. 'Good to meet you, finally, er, Matt,' he says, glancing quickly at my laminated name tag.

'Hello.' I shake his hand.

'Sean's explained your part in all of this,' Alan Rossiter continues, 'and I just wanted to thank you myself. We couldn't have done it without you.'

Jesus, don't remind me.

I eye Sean questioningly, wondering exactly what he has said. 'Well,' I say awkwardly, 'you're welcome. Mr Rossiter.'

He laughs. 'Please. *Alan.*'

'Alan.' I grin stupidly. 'OK.' There is a pause. 'I'm a big fan of yours,' I say, rather to my surprise.

'Really? Thanks. It's always good to get the approval of one's fellow writers.'

'Oh, well, I'd hardly call myself –'

'Sean tells me that you have a book out at the moment as well.'

'Yes. Yes, that's right,' I reply. 'I do.'

He spreads out his hands. 'Do they have any in stock? I'd love to get a copy.'

I stare at him. 'You would?'

'Absolutely. Would that be all right?'

'Of course,' I splutter. 'I think I saw one about here earlier.' I casually pick up the shop's single copy of *Licked* and show it to him. 'Here we are.' Alan Rossiter inspects it politely, and reads the back cover.

'Well,' he says after a moment. 'I shall look forward to reading it *immensely*. Need to know what the competition is doing, eh?' He looks at me, and winks. 'I'm a voracious reader, you know.'

'Oh, yes,' I gabble. 'Me too. *Voracious*.'

'Would you be kind enough to sign it for me?'

'Certainly.' I beam at him. I think for a moment and then scribble a brief dedication in carefully messy handwriting – I do this every day of the week! – before signing my name with a flourish. I am conscious of several people watching me, and I feel my cheeks redden.

'That's wonderful,' says Alan Rossiter as I hand the book back to him. He doesn't open it to read what I have written. 'Thank you very much. Who do I pay?'

I look around in confusion. All the tills were shut long ago. 'Look, don't worry,' I say. 'Just take it. My treat.'

'Oh, great. Well, thanks a lot.' There is a small pause. 'I suppose I'd better go and mingle,' he says, rolling his eyes. 'You know how it is. People to talk to.' He looks for all the world as if there's nothing he'd rather do than stay chatting with me, two belletrists together discussing writerly things, but, alas, his hands are tied. He shrugs. 'Anyway, best of luck, Mark. See you soon.'

'OK. Thank you. Bye.'

'And thanks again for this.' He waves my novel at me. 'And for, you know, that other thing.' He winks at me again. Just our little secret, him and me.

'Really,' I mumble, 'think nothing of it.'

Alan Rossiter leaves, directed away by Sean's hand in the middle of his back. I watch him go, the grin frozen on to my face. Just as they pass out of sight, Alan Rossiter hands my book to Sean.

To Bernadette / Alan (!)

I hope you enjoy this humble offering as much as I have relished your own bewitching miracles of our craft. Long may your literary schitzophrenia continue!

With best wishes
Your friend
Matthew Moore
(Matt)

The week after my encounter with Alan Rossiter in the bookshop follows much the same pattern as before. I drift through the working day, selling lorryloads of *Virgin* books under the watchful eye of Dawn, and spend my evenings achieving a state of dribbling inebriation in the discomfort of my own home, anxiously waiting for a conciliatory word from Anna to land on my damp-ridden doormat. None arrives.

I also spend the week berating myself for misspelling 'schizophrenia' in my dedication to Alan Rossiter. How incredibly stupid of me. I got his address off Sean and dashed off (at the eleventh attempt) a brief postcard, pretending that I had done it on purpose – part of a sophisticated (but undefined) author's joke. So far he hasn't written back.

I miss Anna terribly. Loneliness threatens to swallow me whole. Every evening, as the viscous horizon inside the vodka bottle sinks slowly towards the table top, I curse my stupidity in a lachrymose haze and plan my campaign to win Anna back, hatching increasingly elaborate plans to effect an operatic reconciliation. Of course, nothing ever comes of these alcohol-fuelled schemes. Each morning, hungover indolence settles upon me once again. I wallow in my pit of miserable inertia, unable to help myself. The tally of unsent letters grows daily.

The only thing that keeps me going during this benighted time is the prospect of our jazz gig in Clerkenwell. When the appointed day finally arrives, the hours drag past even more slowly than usual. That evening, as I walk towards Stratford station, saxophone case slung rakishly over my shoulder, I notice people glance at me. Look, they think, there goes a musician. As they continue their dreary walk home, I imagine them quietly wishing that they were musicians too, off to a gig of their own. The envy of strangers chases me down the street, cheering me considerably.

I catch the Tube into town and emerge at Old Street station. As I approach the venue, I am stretched taut by fluttering nerves, but I try to look bored. It doesn't do for jazzmen to appear too excited. I arrive at the address that Gavin has given me. The place is called Bar Bar Black Sheep.

Inside, it takes my eyes a few moments to adjust to the almost total lack of light. Finally I am able to make out a long bar which stretches down one side of the room. Cleverly angled spotlights create small pools of light along its length. Behind the bar is a long mirror, which enables customers (or at least customers who have been eating their carrots) to admire themselves while they drink. Vases of lilies are dotted along the bar's black marble surface. It's redolent of a funky funeral parlour.

'Matt! Over here!' I can just make out Gavin on the other side of the room, talking to another man. I walk over to them. Gavin is beaming. 'Matt, this is my friend Vivian-

André, the owner. Vivian-André, this is Matt Moore, our saxophonist.'

Vivian-André has the limpest handshake I have ever experienced. His palm is cool and clammy. It's rather like squeezing a ball of refrigerated sausage meat. 'Hi, Matt,' he says. 'Super to meet you.'

'And you.' I look around. 'Nice place.'

'*Thank* you. We like it. Did you see our back-lit latex wall?' He points over my shoulder. I turn around. The wall behind me is a shimmering expanse of black.

'Wow,' I say carefully.

'It was designed for us by Per Umlaut,' enthuses Vivian-André.

'Per Umlaut?' I ask, worried.

'You know, the Norwegian interior designer,' says Gavin pointedly.

'He's a personal friend of ours,' boasts Vivian-André.

'Oh, *that* Per Umlaut,' I say weakly.

'We just *love* Per,' gushes Vivian-André, clasping his hands together ardently. '*Such* wonderful work. And we're *really* looking forward to hearing you play later.'

'Thanks,' I say.

'Great place, isn't it, Matt?' says Gavin, brown-nosing hopelessly.

'Yeah. Cool. And I like the name.'

'That?' Vivian-André waves dismissively. 'That'll change.'

'Oh?'

He nods. 'Every week.'

'Won't that be a bit confusing for the customers?'

'Not really. We'll always call it something bar related. You know. Bar-itone. Bar-ometer. Bar-oque. Bar-racuda.'

'Bar-biturate,' suggests Gavin eagerly.

Vivian-André nods. 'Once everyone's got the hang of it we'll abandon all that, and just call it "Bar". We want to appropriate the generic term for ourselves.' He bows his head modestly.

'Like Sellotape,' I suggest. 'Or Durex.'

'Will you excuse me?' says Vivian-André suddenly. 'I need to see the chef about his pan-fried macadamia nuts.' He walks off without another word, his back stiff.

'Isn't he cool?' breathes Gavin, awestruck.

'Jesus, Gavin, the man is a moron. How pretentious.' I look around me. 'This place is ridiculous.'

'But it's one of the most stylistically innovative bars in London,' insists Gavin querulously.

Suddenly I realise why Gavin is drooling over Vivian-André. Of course: he's opened a *bar*. The ultimate ambition of readers of *Bloke* magazine everywhere. I spot something on the lapel of Gavin's Armani jacket.

'What's that badge you're wearing, Gav?'

He glances down. 'This? Oh, nothing.'

'No, come on. Tell me. I recognise it.' Gavin's badge says, in discreet silver type, 'Hødelfütt'.

Gavin snorts. 'You? Recognise it? Don't think so.'

'Yes I do. I've seen adverts for it.' Jean-Philippe Durand's perfect jaw-line floats into my head. 'I couldn't work out what it was an advert *for*.'

Gavin grins at me smugly. 'Well, of course you couldn't. That's because nobody knows yet.'

'What do you mean?'

'At the moment, right, Hødelfütt is just a concept.'

'OK. What's the concept?'

'Well, that's it. The *concept* is that it's just a concept. See?'

'No.'

Gavin sighs. 'Look. These guys are right at the cutting edge.'

'The cutting edge of what?'

He hesitates, infinitesimally. 'Of high concept retailing. They've created this, this *thing*, yeah, which everybody wants, but nobody knows what it is.'

'The whole bloke in a café thing.'

'*Exactly*. But they haven't yet announced what it is they're going to be selling.'

I point at his badge. 'So what's that?'

'Ah, well.' Gavin grins proudly. 'That shows I've already ordered one.'

'One what?'

'One of whatever it is that Hødelfütt is going to be.'

I am struggling to keep up. 'But you don't know —'

'No, I don't know what it is. At least not yet.'

I look at Gavin suspiciously, wondering whether he's deliberately trying to fuck with my head. There is a shout from behind us.

'Ahoy there!' yells Ron from across the room, lugging his bass drum towards us. 'Christ, this place is all right, isn't it? *Très* swank.'

A pained look passes over Gavin's face.

'Where's the totty?' asks Ron, looking around him. The bar is almost empty at the moment, unless everyone is hiding in the shadows.

'Early days yet, Ron,' I assure him. 'They'll be here, don't worry.'

A few minutes later, Ron has carried the rest of his drum kit into the bar and we toast each other with bottles of Korean monk-trodden beer. As we drink, Abdullah appears, his legs almost buckling beneath the weight of his double bass. 'Evening all,' he says as he approaches. He puts down his case with evident relief. 'Everyone well?'

We shrug and grunt like the expressive creative types that we are.

'I meant to ask you guys,' I say. 'Have any of you had a chance to buy my book yet?'

Gavin and Ron snort with laughter.

'Fuck off,' says Ron. 'A book? As in, a *book*?'

'That's right,' I say.

'Yeah, *right*.' Ron laughs some more. 'Fuck *off*,' he says again through his guffaws.

Abdullah looks at me. 'You've written a book?' he says, interested.

'You didn't know?'

He shakes his head.

'But Abdullah, I'm a writer. That's what I *do*.'

'Oh, are you?' he says. 'Cool.'

I stare at him. 'What did you think I did for a living?'

He shrugs his long body. 'Never really thought about it.'

'Right, well, now that you know, do you think you might buy a copy?' I ask.

'What's it about?'

Why is everyone so interested in what my damn book is *about*? 'Well,' I start. 'It's a fable for modern –'

'Is it science fiction?' asks Abdullah.

'Certainly not,' I reply coldly.

'In that case I don't think I'll bother,' he says cheerfully. 'That's really my thing, you see.'

'Surely you don't *just* read science fiction?'

He nods. 'Pretty much. Ursula LeGuin, mainly. I've read her books hundreds of times. They're brilliant. In *The*

Left Hand of Darkness, right, there's this planet —'

'Never mind.' I put up my hands in self-defence. There's only so far I'm willing to go to persuade someone to buy my book, and a discussion of Ursula LeGuin is way out there, miles — light years, to coin *le mot juste* — beyond the proverbial pale.

'Still, that's very cool that you're a writer,' says Abdullah. 'Well done.'

'Yeah,' I say grumpily. 'Thanks very much.'

'What's it like?' asks Gavin, swigging his beer.

'What do you mean?'

'Being a published writer. Because you're sort of public property, now, aren't you? You know, you've written your book, and now it's, like, out there, for anyone in the whole world to read.'

I shrug. 'Can't say I've ever really thought about it,' I lie.

'Maybe there are lots of famous people who have read your book,' says Abdullah.

'Maybe,' I say cautiously.

'Perhaps, I don't know, Madonna thinks you're the greatest writer who's ever lived,' he continues.

There is a pause as the four of us consider this (to my mind improbable) scenario.

'By the same token, there may be other people who think that you should be shot,' says Ron cheerfully.

'Hmm,' I agree. 'More likely.'

'Doesn't that worry you?' asks Gavin. 'That some loony might hate your books and decide that the world would be a better place without you in it?'

'Well, we're all at risk, if you think about it,' says Ron. 'I mean, here we are, about to get up on stage to play in front of a group of complete strangers. Who knows what sort of madmen are out there.' He gestures towards the shadows. 'We're exposing ourselves to every fucked-up psycho who happens to wander in tonight.'

'It's a cheery thought,' says Gavin. 'Thanks, Ron.'

I pull a face. 'I'd better not play any bum notes, then.'

'Chance would be a fine thing,' cracks Gavin. I playfully punch his arm, slightly harder than is necessary.

A while later, we are set up and ready to begin. At our last rehearsal, we agreed the set list that we are going to play. It is a mixture of standards and original compositions by Gavin. We have decided not to announce any of the songs. There are several reasons for this. Firstly, and most fundamentally, we can't agree who should do the announcing. Secondly, not talking to the audience is quite cool, in a sort of misanthropic, Miles Davis kind of way. Thirdly, nobody actually *wants* to stand up and announce songs with titles like 'Urban Machinations – the Plight of the Zeitgeist'.

We stand huddled around Ron's drum kit, watching the crowd in front of us. Ron and I smoke non-stop, both to calm our nerves and because that is what jazz musicians are supposed to do. I scan the audience, looking for Dawn. This afternoon I told her about the gig, and beneath her transparent veneer of indifference, she was obviously itching to come, so I invited her along. She hasn't appeared, but suddenly I spot Neville and Patricia in the semi-darkness. At least, I spot Neville. Patricia, dressed in black, is almost completely invisible against Per Umlaut's back-lit latex wall.

'Hi guys,' I say, strolling over to them. 'This is a nice surprise.'

Neville looks up at me. 'Hi, Matthew. Thought we'd come and lend a bit of moral support.' He grins. Next to him Patricia smiles widely. Her teeth shine in the darkness, perfect flashes of brilliant, luminiferous white. 'And of course I wanted to check that you weren't going to mention the book,' adds Neville.

'The book?'

'You know, give yourself a bit of free publicity.' Neville looks serious.

'Don't worry, Neville. No cheap plugs this evening.'

'Glad to hear it. Otherwise, though, sales of *Licked* are going well.'

'Really?' I say, suddenly excited. 'Do you have figures?'

Neville nods. We peer at each other through the gloom for a moment.

'What are they?' I ask politely.

'By my reckoning, so far you've sold twelve.'

'*Twelve*?' I choke.

'Which is pretty respectable, if you ask me, for a first time novelist.'

'Twelve?' I persist. 'As in, *twelve*?'

Neville looks at me oddly. 'That's right.'

'Not, you know, twelve hundred, or twelve thousand?'

Neville chortles.

'Twelve copies, then,' I conclude sadly. 'In total.'

'Mind you,' says Neville, 'we could still get some returns. You never know.'

It occurs to me that Hector and Alan Rossiter both have copies of the book. How many novelists, I wonder, can claim to know one sixth of their entire readership? 'Well,'

I say, devastated, 'you seem quite pleased.'

Neville shrugs. 'Yeah, pleased enough. Twelve isn't bad at all.' He points behind me. 'I think your colleagues need you back over there,' he says. I turn. Gavin is beckoning to me.

'Perhaps I'll see you later,' I say.

'Good luck,' says Patricia.

'By the way, what the fuck is this?' demands Neville, brandishing a bottle of Korean beer. 'It's disgusting.'

'Ah, but it's absolutely the latest thing,' I explain. 'It might be horrible beer, Neville, but at least it's the *trendiest* horrible beer you can buy.'

'Jesus.' Neville pulls a face. I leave him muttering into the neck of his bottle, give Patricia a small smile, and head back towards the band, who are ready to start.

I pick up my saxophone and blow loosely through the mouthpiece, stretching my fingers over the keys, focusing on the music to come. Ron is behind his kit, his dark glasses now in place. He probably can't even see as far as his ride cymbal. 'Let's get jiggy with these honky motherfuckers,' he crows, twirling a drumstick.

There is no discernible change in the volume of chatter from the room in front of us, no expectant hush. I turn towards Gavin. He shrugs. I take a deep breath, and count the band into our opening tune, 'Reincarnation of a Lovebird', a Charles Mingus composition. Long winding streams of syncopated crotchets stretch over my sheet music, jumping this way and that, ready to trap the unwary. We begin hesitantly, feeling our way. I am nervous, and fluff the melodic line. My fingers feel sluggish. Some of my longer notes fall away with a sour twist. Worse, the audience *is not listening*. I nod at Gavin to take the first solo. Nerves are getting the better of me; I want this too much. Gavin puts his head down, staring fiercely at the keyboard as he tears into his improvisation.

Sixty-four bars later, and Gavin has set us back on track. His solo was simple and beautiful. When he began to play, the audience stopped talking. He has ignited a fire beneath us; we are cooking now. I launch into my solo with renewed confidence, clawing a melody out of the dizzying matrix of chords. I feel the music coalesce. A strength moves inside me, stands me squarely on the ground, and I blow. I'm no longer the paranoid author, the lonely husband, the pitiful drunk. I *am* the notes that streak out of the battered bell of my saxophone. Those trills, those impetuous eddies of notes – that's me. I am making my own progress, stepping off each precipice into the sweet, unknowable space that lies beyond the next bar. This is my music, my truth, my moment.

And maybe it's not so bad.

When we finish the piece, there is polite applause. The audience waits for us to continue. After a moment Ron carves a gentle waltz signature out of the air, and we begin to play 'Urban Machinations – the Plight of the Zeitgeist'.

Through the music, in front of me I glimpse a pair of crossed arms, a thoughtfully nodding head. As the tune's final chord hangs lingeringly in the shadows, the applause seems louder this time.

We press on.

For the next hour we scale uncharted heights. We grow in confidence with each number we play: 'Autumn Leaves', 'Scrapple from the Apple', 'Imprecation for Solitude (No 3)' (another one of Gavin's), 'Ruby My Dear', Duke's 'In a Mellotone'.

Gavin's piano wraps the band in sound. His solos are perfect, lyrical scatterings of notes or intoxicating statements of focused power and passion. His fingers fly up and down the keyboard, a purposeful blur. Ron employs his full arsenal tonight, a battery of bass drum bombs and rimcracks sharper than a sniper's bullet. He gives us a feather-light shuffle one moment and popping, multi-limbed polyrhythms the next, propelling us onwards in a shower of shimmering cymbals. The low, fat pull of Abdullah's bass steers our ship with authority, as he plucks the heavy strings with a sure hand and anchors us to the tune.

Between songs we exchange grins with each other. We are tearing up reality and presenting an alternative manifesto. If we can do *this*, then what *can't* we do? Suddenly it all seems so easy. We're kings of the universe. Our music opens up new worlds of limitless adventure and possibility. Look! Open your eyes, you can fly!

Before I know it, we are skipping through 'Groovin' High', our final tune. After the solos, we play the head once, twice, and then a third time. I turn to look enquiringly at the other three as they pull the tune back to the beginning yet again, rather than resolving to the welcoming homelands of the final chord. And I understand: they don't want this moment to end, either. We spin through the tune again, then a glance between piano and drums, a nod from the bass, and the other three drop out, leaving me to provide the epilogue, a final commentary on what we've achieved this evening. I take a deep breath, and then I'm off, blowing torrents of blues-tinged phrases, spiralling high for one last, delicious ride. I close my eyes and play out my life.

As the final breath escapes me and I lower the horn, the crowd erupts into cheers. I want to remain afloat in our sea of music, but I am tugged relentlessly ashore. Gavin is standing next to me. 'Awesome, Matt,' he whispers in my ear, smiling widely. 'Well played.'

I nod dumbly at the crowd in front of me. What am I doing here? Where have I been? I feel faint, a little nauseous.

'*Righteous*, brother,' shouts Ron from behind his drum kit.

There is much back slapping and hand shaking. Ron, mercifully, takes off his dark glasses, which means that we don't have to try and imitate the ridiculously complex ghetto handshake that he has invented. I float through the congratulations in a trance. Vivian-André appears with a tray of Korean beer. Grounded once more, suddenly I feel unequipped to handle these celebrations.

Anna is gone, gone.

What is there to celebrate?

I leave the others and dismantle my saxophone. I place its weary body back in its blue velvet bed, where it lies in the half-light, all played out. A rush of love for this creature, all rigid levers and sinuous curves, sweeps over me. Rather than closing the case and briskly clipping it shut, I leave it open on the floor, and sit down for a moment on Ron's drum stool. I light a cigarette, looking fondly at my battered, imperfect, beast of an instrument.

My reverie is disturbed by Ron, who barges up to me

in a state of high excitement. 'Mate, you've got to come and have a look at this bird.'

'Must I?'

'You must. She is fucking *gorgeous*. And she's *gagging* for it.'

'Have you talked to her yet?'

'Well.' Ron coughs. 'Not in so many words, no.'

'Ah.'

'But she's been looking at me all night. I spotted her in the crowd early on. She hasn't moved since. She's just been *staring*, you know, right at me.' He rubs his hands together gleefully.

I shake my head. 'Sorry Ron. I need a bit of time to wind down.'

'Oh, bollocks. Don't be such a tart. Come *on*. She's over by the bar. Come and have a look. But remember, I saw her first.'

I know better than to try and argue with Ron in this mood. His eyes are shining with lust and the adrenaline of triumph. I sigh, and stand up.

'Come on.' Ron directs me through the crowd. 'I reckon she must be a model.' His hand clamps down firmly on my shoulder, and we stop. 'There,' he breathes. 'By the bar. Look at that and weep. The blonde. Great legs. Nice tits. Pretty face, too. The complete package. And she looks posh. Bloody marvellous.' Ron lets out an unattractive chortle. 'What d'you reckon?'

As I stand in the middle of the overcrowded room and peer towards the bar, a heavy internal throb rolls through my head and obliterates the sound of the crowd around me with a huge, rushing crash of silence.

What the fuck is going on?

Finally I look again.

Oh, Jesus.

In front of us, looking directly at me, is my wife.

'All right, my darling,' says Ron, grabbing Anna's hand and kissing it, mock formal. 'I've had my eye on you all evening, you saucy minx.' He dribbles on to Anna's long fingers.

'Anna,' I say. 'God.'

'Hello, Matthew. I liked the set. Well played.'

'Hang on,' says Ron. 'Do you two know each other?'

'Uh, Anna, this is Ron. Ron, this is Anna.'

'Oh, that's fucking *great*,' snarls Ron. 'I suppose you think –'

'Anna's my wife,' I interrupt.

'Ah,' breathes Ron, immediately taking a step backwards. 'Right. Well, I think I'll leave you to it, then,' he says. 'Nice to, er,' he mumbles at Anna before disappearing hastily into the crowd.

'That was Ron,' I explain.

'Nice guy,' comments Anna, wiping his slobber off the back of her hand.

'Oh yes, he's a love,' I agree. What is Anna doing here? I am hurtling downwards, tailgate blazing, distress signals flaring in my wake. 'Well, this is a bit of a surprise,' I say eventually.

'You wrote the gig on this year's calendar before Christmas,' explains Anna. 'I've been staring at it every morning, and so I thought I'd come along.' She pauses. 'That's OK, isn't it?'

'God, of *course*,' I say. 'It's wonderful to see you.'

There is a small pause.

'So how are you?' she says.

I dig my hands into my pockets. 'Me? I'm *fine*.'

'Oh good.'

'You?'

Anna nods. 'I'm fine, too.'

I nod slowly. 'Great. That's great.' Even after all those nights of drunken misery and unsent letters, I am utterly unprepared for this. The arguments have been rehearsed, the rhetoric honed, but now that the moment to present my case is upon me, I am stunned into silence by the dazzling understanding of how much I have missed my wife. After the insipid monochrome of my weeks without her, life suddenly rushes up on me in fabulous technicolour. I stare at her, speechless. Perched on a bar stool, Anna looks as graceful and poised as ever. I experience that same dizzy head-rush of emotion that I felt the first time I spotted her in the college bar all those years ago.

'It's been a long time,' she says.

'It has. A long time.' Christ. I need time to *think*. I must remain dignified. Calm and rational. No hysterics. I wipe a hand across my brow, and try to think of something appropriate to say. 'Have you had your hair cut?' I ask.

Anna smiles. 'Do you like it?' She twists her head to one side.

'It suits you,' I say sadly.

'Thanks.' Anna delves into her handbag and lights a cigarette. 'To be honest, Matthew, I was expecting to hear from you before now.'

'I didn't think you wanted me to get in touch,' I say, confused.

'No, you're right. I didn't. But I rather assumed that you wouldn't be able to stop yourself.'

'Oh.' I stare at my feet. The crowd swarms around us.

'Anyway,' continues Anna, 'I appreciate the time and space you've given me. I've needed it to think everything through.'

'Oh, good,' I reply, unable to avoid an edge of bitterness. 'And have you done all the thinking you need?'

'Pretty much.' She looks at me calmly. 'We have some things to discuss.'

Yes, your honour, nods the foreman, we have reached our verdict.

I glance around. People are jostling for a place at the bar, shouting to make themselves heard. 'Look. Do you want to go somewhere a bit quieter, where we can hear ourselves think?'

Anna shakes her head. 'Here is fine. It won't take long.' Her eyes are determined, wiped free of any encumbering emotion. Beneath the Art Deco awning of her perfect eyelashes I see nothing but dark pools of dispassionate blue. A knot forms tightly in my stomach. Why did I not manage to send a single one of my letters to her? I suddenly realise that I haven't even told her that I'm *sorry*.

'Look, Anna, I didn't really get the chance to say at the time. I'm so sorry about – about the – the – you know. At Christmas. That thing. It was an awful mistake. I was wrong.'

She looks at me. 'Yes, well.'

'I suppose I thought – well, anyway. I just hope we can get over it. It was a terrible misunderstanding.'

Anna considers me thoughtfully. Suddenly she looks down at her feet. 'I brought you something,' she says.

'Yes?' I say hopefully.

'Here.' She bends down and hands me a plastic bag. I peer inside. At the bottom of the bag is the old diving mask and snorkel that I found in the bedroom cupboard a few months ago. 'I was doing a clear-out, and I found these. They're yours if you want them. Otherwise I'll just throw them out.'

'No, I'll have them,' I say. 'You never know when the next invitation for a week's snorkelling in the Bahamas may land on the doormat.' My cheerfulness sounds utterly hollow. As I am talking, Anna glances idly over my shoulder, punching a hole through my heart. With a half-smile, she hands over the plastic bag.

'Anyway,' she says, 'that's not the main reason for coming to see you.'

'No?'

She looks at me and sighs. 'Look, Matthew, I know it's probably not what you want to think about right now, but you *have* to reply to the letters.'

I start. 'Letters? What letters? I haven't had any letters. Not from you.'

Anna shakes her head. 'Not from me. From my lawyers.'

The words swarm around my head, heatedly demanding entry. 'Lawyers?' I finally stammer.

She looks away. 'About the divorce.'

My head rushes with blood.

So. Anna has not come here this evening for an orgy of forgiveness, a blissful reunion of our two lost souls. The crushing weight of despair mercilessly slams into me: she has already made up her mind.

She looks at me sadly. 'Do you know the letters I'm talking about?'

'No,' I say dully. 'That is, they may have arrived, but I haven't opened them.'

Anna sighs. 'You need to go home and read them. Get a solicitor. I'd like to get this sorted out as quickly as possible, for both of our sakes.'

As usual, Anna is moving ahead, getting on with business. She is taking what she wants, discarding what she does not. Her eyes are now fixed firmly on the future. She is like the Midnight Express streaking through the night, the unswerving track ahead lit by its ferocious beam, a vast empty blackness in its wake. I am to be jettisoned into the darkness behind, suddenly superfluous to requirements.

Is this really happening? Could this be another one of her little jokes, another casually inflicted punishment? I shake myself out of my stupefaction. 'Look, Anna, what's the rush? Don't you think it's a bit early to start talking about divorce? We don't want to do anything hasty, do we?'

Anna blinks slowly. 'Hasty?'

I nod desperately. 'This is too important to do anything without thinking it through properly.'

There is a ghastly pause.

'What do you think I've been *doing* for the last few weeks?' asks Anna.

'Well, I'm sure that if –'

'I've done little *else*, except think this through. Do you think I've just been carrying on as usual? Is that it? Do you think that I've just rolled up my sleeves and got on with life? Well, you're wrong, Matthew. I've been *thinking*, I can assure you. I've been trying to make sense of all this madness. I've been trying to work out what went wrong – why I'm sleeping alone every night, how we got here. This wasn't supposed to happen to *us*. So, yes, I've been thinking. Where shall I begin? Months ago. Before your book was published. To start with, you began to look at me oddly. Did you think I didn't notice? You weren't exactly subtle about it. You used to trail me around the flat, watching every move I made. Sometimes I almost asked you what was the matter. Now I wish I had. We might have been able to stop all this nonsense before things went too far. But how could I have guessed what sort of absurd fantasies you were cooking up in that head of yours? Then, the next thing I know, after that meal with Graham and Caroline, instead of being proud of me and delighted at my promotion, you turned around and accused me of having an *affair*. You thought I'd been unfaithful to you. You thought I was capable of sleeping with somebody else. Do you have the slightest idea what it feels like when the person you love more than anyone else in the world thinks such a thing? It hurts, Matthew, more than I hope you'll ever know. And with *Graham*, of all people! And if that wasn't bad enough, then you confessed about your spying trip to Paris. And this – this I still have immense trouble with. After you'd convinced yourself that Graham and I were sleeping together, you just let us go back to the hotel. How *could* you? Are you really so completely spineless, Matthew? Or did you just want to wallow in the drama of your own despair? It wasn't really about me and Graham at all, was it? This whole thing has been about *you*. Did you hate me, or were you too busy feeling sorry for yourself to do even that? I realised then that you loved me less than I thought:

you wouldn't have been so quick to condemn me if you loved me properly, the way that I loved you. Trust is so *fundamental*. What chance did we ever really have without it? Still, I tried to forgive you. I *wanted* to forgive you. I gave you another chance, if you remember. And what did you do in return? You just carried on lying. That was all the thanks I got. You promised to forget it all, and I really hoped that things would get back to normal. Then came your impotence. That was awful. You made me feel ugly, dirty, and repulsive. I started to hate myself. I blamed *myself* for the problem, you see. I went through hell, wondering what was wrong with *me*. It was just another symptom of your jealousy, wasn't it? But rather than explain anything, you preferred to let me suffer. All this time your behaviour was becoming more and more erratic. I never knew what you were thinking. We were hardly talking. It was unbearable. Then, when I confronted you, you admitted that you were *still* jealous of Graham. That was when I finally began to understand that all your suspicions were still there, festering inside you. I realised then that I would have to deny the affair. I hated you for making me do it. I wanted you to *trust* me. After that I thought we were over the worst. Things seemed to get a little better. And then came Christmas. That shameful present. I've been asking myself why you would want to humiliate me by giving me that, that *thing*, to open in front of my family. I tried to fathom why you would ever want to hurt me so badly. You still didn't believe me, did you? And you wanted to hurt me. You wanted *revenge*.'

I shake my head. 'I didn't want to hurt you. It wasn't revenge; I wanted you to *confess*. I wanted you to admit what had been going on. I thought it was the only way that we would ever be able to get back to normal. The way I saw it, until you confessed you weren't even giving me a chance to *forgive* you.'

Anna looks at me. 'You really thought I'd been lying to you all that time?'

'Yes. But look at it from my point of –'

She holds up her hand. 'No, Matthew. I won't. Why should I? You wouldn't look at it from mine, would you?' I remain silent. 'Do you want me to continue?'

'There's more?'

'Oh yes, Matthew. There's more.' Anna lights another cigarette. 'When I got back to work after the Christmas holidays, Graham told me that he and Caroline were getting a divorce.'

I stare at Anna, shocked. 'What are you saying? Now that Graham's a free agent, you're considering –'

'This has got nothing to do with *Graham*, Matthew.'

'No?'

She shakes her head slowly. 'It's to do with Caroline.'

The world stops revolving for a moment.

'Caroline?'

'Graham's wife. Remember her?'

'Ye-es,' I reply cautiously. 'We met that night –'

'– at the restaurant, yes, that's right.' There is a pause. 'I finally discovered what her hysterical performance that evening was about.'

I swallow. 'Oh?'

She nods. 'Apparently, rather like you, poor old Caroline had got it into her head that Graham and I were having an affair. Quite a coincidence, really – except that I gather she's been accusing him of sleeping with his female colleagues for years. Anyway, she got quite obsessed about it. She was completely unbalanced, apparently. At least, that's the only way Graham could explain her behaviour.'

'Her —?'

'It seems that Graham and Caroline's Christmas Day wasn't much better than ours.' Anna pulls hard on her cigarette without looking at me. 'Caroline had far too much to drink, as usual. Graham finally lost his temper and told her to go to bed. That was when she turned round and told him – this was in front of the whole family, mind you – that *she* was having an affair.'

A block of ice smashes into my chest, scattering a million shards of bitter chill straight through me. 'An *affair?*'

'Of course, I told Graham that you would never do such a thing.'

My hand flies up to my chest. 'Me? What did she —'

'She told Graham that the two of you kissed that night in the restaurant. Downstairs, by the loos. She claimed that she'd propositioned you and that you had responded, with some enthusiasm. It was only because you were interrupted that you didn't fuck each other's brains out on the spot.' I stare at Anna, appalled. 'I told Graham that it was pure fantasy. I said that you would never do that. You may have many faults, Matthew, but infidelity isn't one of them.'

An age. 'Thank you for not thinking the worst of me,' I finally mumble.

'Then I started to wonder why Caroline would invent such a silly, vicious little story in the first place.'

I am too terrified to speak.

Anna turns to extinguish her cigarette in the ashtray on the bar next to her. 'It's pretty obvious, when you think about it: she wanted to hurt Graham. She wanted *revenge*.

And that pulled me up short. Revenge again, you see. Then I remembered that both of you *were* away from the table for quite a while that night. And I started to wonder whether there were enough coincidences to make me doubt you.'

There is a pause.

'And were there?' I ask.

She gazes around the room coolly before settling her eyes back upon me. 'Yes.'

I swallow dryly. 'Meaning?'

'Meaning that suddenly I didn't know whether Caroline was telling the truth or not. Meaning that I no longer knew for sure that you *wouldn't* do such a thing.'

I make a decision. If I have to lie to save my marriage, then lie I will. 'Anna, you have to believe me, there's absolutely no truth —'

She interrupts me with a brisk shake of her head. 'You don't understand, Matthew. Whether or not you groped and slobbered over each other that night is irrelevant now. The important thing is that all of a sudden, after thirteen years, I didn't know what to think. Can't you see? I lost my faith in you.'

'But —'

'I don't trust you any more, Matthew. I *can't* trust you. I'll never know what's going through your head.' Anna pauses. 'You didn't trust me. Then you lied and lied. And now *I* can't trust *you*.'

'But I didn't —'

'It doesn't *matter*, Matthew. When I realised that I couldn't be certain of you, I knew it was too late to try and salvage things. I'm sorry.'

I look at my wife, devastated.

'Now, do you really want to discuss this some more, and drag us both through it all again? I've done my thinking, Matthew. I've reached my decision. There's nothing more to say.' A pearl of a tear escapes through Anna's lashes. It glistens, proud and resolute, high on her cheek. 'What happened to you?' She looks searchingly into my eyes. 'Where did you go? Where's the bright, funny, ambitious man I fell in love with?'

A lump comes to my throat. Where did I go?

We look at each other for an age, strangers again. It's suddenly as if our time together never happened. The sensation makes me feel dead inside.

What kind of hell have I put her through?

'Can I ask you a question?' I say after a moment.

Anna looks at me warily. 'Go on.'

'Do you remember the day of the launch party? You said you had to go shopping for something to wear.'

She nods. 'I remember.'

I take a deep breath. 'I followed you to the cinema on Haverstock Hill.'

Anna looks startled. 'For God's sake, Matthew —'

'You went to watch *Citizen Kane*,' I interrupt. 'And when you came home you pretended that you had been shopping, after all.'

'Yes.' Dry-eyed and defiant, now.

I shrug. 'Why did you lie to me?'

'You were driving me *mad*, Matthew. You were so nervous about the party you couldn't sit in one place for more than five minutes. I just needed to get away for the afternoon. I knew that if I told you that I was going to the cinema, you would have wanted to come too. I'm sorry I lied to you, but it was for your own benefit. I didn't want to upset you before your party.' She pauses. 'All this time you've been thinking about that and never said anything?'

I look at Anna, pained. How could I have been so stupid, so paranoid? 'There were other things,' I say.

'Things? What sort of things?'

'I don't know. You seemed more distracted. You were getting home later and later.'

'Matthew, I was *working*. I knew I was being considered for partnership and I had to put in the hours. Good grief. I thought you would have at least understood *that*.'

'Then there was Ravel.'

Anna frowns. 'Ravel?'

'The violin trio.'

'What about it? It was the soundtrack to some French film I watched on the TV one evening while you were at your rehearsal. I loved the music, and so I bought the CD.' She pauses. 'Surely you didn't think –'

'I don't know what I thought. It was just different from the usual stuff you buy.'

'And?'

'That's it. It was *different*.'

Anna looks at me. 'You didn't ever want me to change, is that it?'

'No, it's not that. I just didn't –' I stop. Yes, it was that. It was exactly that. I didn't ever want her to change.

Anna looks at me, her eyes full of sorrow. 'Oh, Matthew. What have you done?'

There is a pause.

'Surely we can –'

'You've ruined everything.'

I look at my beautiful wife, and I know that she is right.

'We had it all,' she says softly. 'Look at us now.'

There is nothing left for me to say.

Anna shuts her eyes for a moment. When she opens them again, the regret has been blinked away. 'You need to read the letters and get a solicitor,' she says, businesslike again.

'What if I refuse to co-operate? What if I want to stay married?'

'You can't,' Anna replies. 'There's unilateral divorce these days. I don't need your consent. I can divorce you whether you like it or not.' She pauses. 'But let's not go down that route, please. It won't achieve anything. Except make us both unhappy.'

Unhappy?

Anna – careful, rational, sensible Anna – has thought this through, considered all the angles, and she has decided that she no longer wants to be married to me.

'But, Anna,' I say, 'I *love* you. Madly.'

She blinks slowly, and another small tear spills on to her cheek. 'I'm sorry, Matthew. It's over.'

I am hollow, scraped out inside.

There is a pause.

'I'd better go,' says Anna.

'Stay for another drink,' I say. I can't bear to let her leave right now. Not just yet.

She shakes her head. 'I don't think so.' A pause. 'You'll go and see a lawyer?'

Our eyes meet and hold each other's gaze.

Finally, I say, 'I promise.'

Anna hops nimbly off the bar stool. 'We'll keep in touch,' she says.

I look at this beautiful woman, for so long the axis around which my life has revolved, about to disappear out of my orbit for ever. 'Anna, wait.' I grab her hand as she turns to go. Her gaze rests warily on me. She has done what she needed to do; now she wants to leave this mess behind her. Give me one last chance, I want to shout. I've learned my lesson. I'll change. I love you. I *love* you.

How can you walk away from someone who loves you as much as I do?

A sudden, sad calmness settles on me.

'Take care of yourself,' I say. I let go of her hand.

Anna looks at me. 'You too.'

She turns and makes her way towards the exit through the mass of bodies. People instinctively make way for her as she approaches. Her back is straight and erect, elegant in Italian silk. She doesn't turn around. She pushes open the door and steps out of my life without a backward glance.

I will not run after her. Me and my dignity stand by the bar, brothers in arms, watching her go.

The resilience of the human spirit is extraordinary. Some scientists have attributed mankind's dominance in the natural world to the fortuitous genetic accident which gave us that miraculously skewed fifth digit, the opposable thumb, but it is our bloody-mindedness that really distinguishes us from the rest of the animal kingdom. Without it, Scott would have fled home from the Antarctic to nurse his frostbitten toes, Watson and Crick would have given up on the double helix structure of DNA, and I would never have made it through the rest of the evening. Although I concede that my thumb did make it easier to hold my beer bottle.

So – here I am. Still here, and still going, despite everything. Anna has walked calmly, definitively, out of my life, and I am left at the bar, still breathing and sentient. Now I just have to struggle through the mess that remains. I think: I'm thirty-three years old. What in fuck's name am I supposed to *do* for the next forty-odd years?

If only Anna had a bit more dramatic flair: there could have been an angry confrontation, a flash of burnished metal, a deafening blast . . . the weeping widow gives herself up to the police, and the husband goes out in a blaze of glory, spared the bother of having to live the rest of his life without her. The trumpeter Lee Morgan was shot dead by his girlfriend in a New York jazz club while he was still on the band stand. He might have had his solo cut short, but what a way to go. No time for regrets or recriminations. Bang.

But no. I'm still here, and there is no respectful pause of mourning, no minute's silence. Around me people jostle and shout and squeeze. Another couple splits up: big deal. Nothing new. I look at the faces around me. They shine with excitement, full of hope.

Gavin comes up to me. 'Matt,' he exclaims, 'there you are.'

'Here I am.'

'What are you doing?'

'I was – talking to someone.' I pause. 'She's gone now.'

Gavin puts an arm around my shoulder. It's the first time anyone has touched me for weeks, and the warmth of human contact makes me want to hug him back, cling on to him and never let go. 'Come on,' he says. 'Come and have a drink. We're celebrating.'

I stare at the plastic bag that Anna gave me. 'I don't know, Gav. I'm knackered. I think I might shoot off home.' Part of me wants to stay. Perhaps if I drink enough I'll be able to obliterate Anna from my thoughts once again. There will, after all, be plenty of time to consider all this when I wake up tomorrow. And the next day. And the next.

'Come *on*. One drink.' Gavin leans towards me. 'Vivian-André has asked us to come back and play here every month. A regular gig! Can you believe it?'

Somehow, I manage a grin. 'I was obviously mistaken, then. The man has exquisite taste after all.'

'What do you say, then? One drink before you go?'

Among the quartet there is great excitement at Vivian-André's offer. Each of us is uncharacteristically bashful, heaping extravagant praise on the others. Such is the nature of success: suddenly we can afford to be generous with our compliments, piling on top of each other in an orgy of mutual admiration. At next Tuesday's rehearsal, of course, we will revert to the usual bickering and complaining, but this evening we are above all that.

Finally I make my excuses and leave. At this time of night, the Central Line is almost deserted. I sit slumped in the litter-strewn carriage, and stare at my reflection in the window opposite. I look the same as I did when I travelled into town earlier this evening – same suit, same saxophone, same tired face. There is nothing to suggest that in between trips my life has been irreversibly blown apart. That's because I'm bravely holding myself together: my brain is fighting a valiant rearguard action against the truth. What happened back there – that was some other guy. My denial is complete, my defences entrenched. I am looking the other way:

Dawn never made it in the end well probably a bit shy I suppose I was only trying to be friendly I do hope she hasn't got the wrong end of the stick and thought that something else was afoot honestly typical female good to see Patricia again though God she really is gorgeous what the fuck is she doing with Neville? twelve copies twelve miserable sodding copies after all that effort three and a half years of my life wasted just so that twelve people or a few more I suppose if they lent it to friends could read my bloody book although perhaps I should look on the bright side twelve copies is better than none at all but talk about suffering for your art I guess Neville's right there are more important things than sales figures try telling that to Sean and Alan Rossiter mind you now that I think about it Poppy Flipflop is really quite a sophisticated paradigm of the unreliable narrator I wish Mum and Dad were here

Finally, in exhausted self-defence, I allow my brain to go blank.

Back in the flat, I walk into the sitting room and switch on the light. The bare light bulb, hanging lopsidedly on its frayed piece of flex, brashly illuminates the room. I sit down heavily on the sofa.

I will stop running now.

I turn, finally, towards Anna. Reluctantly I lower my defences, crank down the drawbridge, and allow her words to storm through.

I'm sorry, Matthew. It's over.

I bury my head in my hands and begin to cry.

Anna is gone. She wants no more of me. I have driven her away. All of that inescapable chest-tightening fear has finally done me in. Our marriage has been the victim of a terrible self-fulfilling prophecy.

I was given too much time to think, too much time to wallow in the excesses of my hyperactive imagination. The empty tedium of my days was the perfect terrain on which the acorn of my suspicion could take root and prosper. Nourished by my indolence, it grew into a mammoth, impregnable oak of jealousy, bearing the most poisonous fruit. I have been toppled by my own monstrous solipsism, hoodwinked by the belief that everything revolves around *me*. Why was I so quick to assume the worst? Why was I so blind to alternative, more innocent hypotheses? *I* am the one who has veered catastrophically off the path of marital harmony. *I* am the one who has struck the bum notes, created the discord. I leapt in delirious despair to all the wrong conclusions. I was judge, jury, and prosecuting counsel rolled into one hysterical whole, and never gave Anna the chance to defend herself until it was too late. She never stood a chance. *We* never stood a chance.

The tears that I cry are a sorry cocktail of self-pity and sadness. I almost wish Anna *had* had an affair with Graham. At least then there would have been a point to all this misery.

I replay our last conversation in my head. I hadn't been able to admit what had really happened with Caroline, even when there was nothing left to lose. And I never did confess that all I had to show for the last eighteen months was a solitary sentence. I always wanted Anna to think the best of me, even if the best wasn't actually true.

Unutterable loneliness sweeps over me. My brain bravely tries to put a positive spin on things. Look at it this way, it tells me: now you're *free*. Just imagine all those girls out there – Patricia, the girl in the bookshop in Preston, Virginie the Eurostar waitress. All those supermodels with PhDs. Now I can pursue them with impunity; I can reinvent myself as a roguish sophisticate, a literary hunk. I shall be utterly irresistible. I shall fuck my way out of trouble.

Then I am hit by the bleak realisation that I don't *want* to screw an army of beautiful women. All I want is my wife back. The manifold glories of monogamy suddenly threaten to overwhelm me – the closeness, the reassuring predictability, the easy familiarity, the constant, unspoken warmth. I glance at my wedding ring. I used to wear it with such pride: Yes, I wanted to tell the world, I'm sorted. I've got all that good stuff.

All gone.

I don't know how long my crying jag lasts. The next time I look up from my fists, it is two o'clock in the morning. A weariness has settled in my bones. My heaving sobs have left me brittle with exhaustion, but I know that I won't sleep. The truth snaps remorselessly at my heels. My marriage is over. There is no escape, no easy oblivion for me, not tonight.

I will stop running now.

I walk to the front door and inspect the pile of unopened correspondence on the carpet. I extract the neatly typed envelopes which I ignored when they first dropped through the letterbox. There are three of them. Apprehensively I open the letter with the earliest postmark.

Dear Sir

Our Client: Ms Anna Given

We have been consulted by your wife, Ms Anna Given, with regard to the difficulties that have arisen in your marriage. Our client has reached the conclusion that the marriage has broken down irretrievably and that there is no prospect of a reconciliation. In the circumstances we have been instructed to issue proceedings for a divorce based on

the grounds of your unreasonable behaviour, which will be
served on you in due course. We are willing to provide a
copy of the draft particulars setting out the grounds of
unreasonable behaviour for your consideration and
approval prior to issue in the hope that many of the issues
between you and our client can be dealt with by way of
agreement.

It will also be necessary to resolve financial matters
between you and in particular to establish a suitable and
mutually agreed division of the communal assets. In this
regard, you will both be required to provide financial dis-
closure which can take place on a voluntary basis provided
you are willing to co-operate and deal with it promptly.

We suggest that you seek independent legal advice and
look forward to hearing from you or your solicitor within
seven days of the date of this letter.

Yours faithfully

KEOWN & CO, SOLICITORS

I reread the letter, twice. All of our years together have
been distilled into a series of leaden stock phrases pulled
off the computer by some faceless stranger in a suit. All
of that happiness extinguished by a few blandly formulaic
sentences. Our marriage is no more than another legal
conundrum to be sorted out.

I numbly open the other two letters. The second is
couched in the same, drably formal language, its tone
more aggressive, demanding to know why no response
had been received to the first letter. The third letter,
which arrived last Saturday, consists of two paragraphs of
snarling invective, spitting threats if I do not respond

immediately, promising unspecified misery if I continue to impede due legal process.

Whoever wrote these letters has misunderstood: due legal process means nothing to me now. These threats are empty. Anna is all I want, all I ever wanted. Without her, I have nothing to lose. This pompous legal bullshit doesn't scare me. What can be worse than what has already happened?

I think about what Anna told me in the bar. If I resist the divorce and make them drag me kicking and snarling to court, I will look pathetic and desperate, and I will still lose. I sigh. It's time to admit defeat. If I am to lose Anna, I should at least try and claw back some dignity and self-respect: I shall concede with as much grace as possible.

I pick up the first letter again. I wonder what 'a suitable and mutually agreed division of the communal assets' means. I don't want to squabble about who gets to keep the dinner service; our marriage deserves a better legacy than that. Perhaps Anna is expecting me to try and squeeze as much money out of her as possible.

And suddenly I see my way out of this mess: she should have everything.

Let her keep the accumulated trophies of our life together. After all, she paid for them. The only thing I will ask for is the record player. If I can listen to my Duke Ellington records, that will be enough. Besides, if I'm going to make a fresh start, I don't want to be surrounded by reminders of a past that I cannot go back to. My memories will haunt me enough as it is. What I need to salvage from our marriage isn't a coffee pot, or assorted items of furniture, but the strength to stand on my own feet and move forward alone. Anna was right. I *had* lost my self-respect, I had no belief in *me*. Anna – beautiful, intelligent, gorgeous Anna – loved *me*. She *loved* me. Above all else, I must preserve that thought, cherish it, nurture it, protect it from the destructive rampage of 'due legal process'.

The decision fills me with white terror.

I put the letters down and look around the cramped, cluttered sitting room. This is no longer a temporary place to lay my head. The road back to Camden has been irrevocably cut off.

This is now my home.

Bang on cue, a blast of electronic noise begins to thud through the wall from the Kurds next door, as loud and proud as any official pageant of welcome. It is half past two in the morning. I cast my eyes around the room. Perhaps this place could be all right. A coat of paint, maybe a small rug to hide that stain on the carpet where I knocked over my third bottle of cheap red wine a few weeks ago. Once the boxes are unpacked there might even be enough room for a table to put my typewriter on.

I light a cigarette and begin to open the boxes on the floor in front of me. After ten minutes of searching I find the most recent draft of my solitary opening sentence. Behind it nestles the embryonic manifesto for CARP. I read the paragraph again, and, for the first time, I am not suffused with breathless admiration. A writer's work should hold a mirror up to his thoughts, his dreams, his soul. How can I say that of what I have written? Frankly, I find Goran and Illic rather boring – Eastern Europeans or not. I consider the sheet of paper for a few moments more, and then tear it down the middle.

I'm a writer. That's what I do. So I should write. I need to make a fresh start, but this time I'll write about things that matter to *me*. I sit back on the sofa and stare at the ceiling.

I have always yearned for a life that fitted me better than my own. Life, real *life*, seemed elusive, shimmering tantalisingly on the horizon. I have skulked along, wilfully detached, telling myself that the main show hadn't yet begun. I gazed loftily down upon events, wondering when things would finally start in earnest. Now, tucked up alone in this cold, tiny flat, it's time to stop waiting for something better to come along: there will be no miraculous metamorphosis into a parallel universe. I'm marooned in East London, and this is my life.

I open the plastic bag at my feet, and pull out the mask and snorkel that Anna brought with her tonight. The mask is covered in dust. I go into the bathroom and wash it clean in the sink. I lower the mask over my eyes and put the snorkel's mouthpiece between my lips, biting down on the black rubber nodules. The alien figure in the bathroom mirror peers back at me, inscrutable. The room fills with the sound of my breath as it rasps up and down the plastic tube. I turn the bath taps on. Through the mask I watch the water slowly fill up the bath.

I've spent too long trying to rein everything in. I've wasted my energy trying in vain to exert control – to hold on to things, places, memories. I've mired myself in a morass of petty concerns and impossible hopes. I need to let the past slip away. I must wait for the future to come to me. It's time to start living in the present.

When the bath is full, I turn off the taps and step out of my clothes, keeping the mask and snorkel in place. I climb into the tub and gingerly lie down on my stomach. After a moment I lower my head beneath the surface. The warm water closes over my head and fills my ears. Submerged in my aquatic cocoon, the Kurds' music is no more than a muffled echo. The world retreats, and I am left floating in my own insulated universe. The weight of past disappointments lifts lightly from my shoulders; Anna, Graham, and the rest of them shimmer and vanish into the distance. There's nobody here but me.

I stare at the plug, a boy again. I twist my head to the left and then to the right, considering how the light is caught through the water.

I begin to swim away.

AUTHOR'S NOTE

The editorial process for this novel – the haul from submitted draft manuscript to final bound book – has been long and challenging, but also rewarding. I'm very grateful to Jennifer Parr, my editor at HarperCollins, for her patience and good humour throughout. She has gently prodded me in all the right directions with her inimitable intelligence and grace; the book is incalculably better as a result. Thanks, too, to Tony Mulliken and Vivienne Pattison and all the team at Midas Public Relations for their help and enthusiasm, to my agent, Bruce Hunter, to Lisa Darnell, to Freddie Ljunberg and Robert Pires, to Martin Hibbert for the website, and to Simone Katzenberg for all the coffee, chat and free legal advice. A raised glass to my good friend Louis Barfe, *bon viveur*, drummer of finesse, and walking encyclopaedia of jazz arcana, for Ellington-related advice and ideas. Finally, and most of all, my thanks and love to my wife, Christina, for her unfailing good humour and astute advice, and for all her patience, support and love, without which this book would never have been written. But I owe her my deepest thanks for Hallam, our beautiful blue-eyed boy, whose laugh fills our home with sunshine.

Working it Out

Alex George

Johnathan Burlip – a man with a redundant 'h', a legal career that's on the skids and an unfortunate way with animals

Tormented by his soon-to-be-ex-girlfriend, his dysfunctional family and petulant colleagues, things get even worse for Johnathan when he loses his fat-cat corporate job and finds himself struggling to survive in a dodgy legal practice in North London. There he is introduced to psychotic Spanish restaurateurs, well-manicured mobsters, and star legal exhibit, *Eddie* the tarantula.

Johnathan's PC parents are desperate for him to be gay, whilst Johnathan is desperate to go out with the unpredictable and alluring *Kibby*.

Morty, the heroic hamster, meanwhile, is desperately trying to keep himself afloat in a toilet bowl. When life repeatedly kicks you in the groin, you can either go down screaming, or work out what's happening and take action . . .

0 00 651332 8

Man and Wife

Tony Parsons

The unforgettable sequel to *Man and Boy*

Man and Wife is a novel about love and marriage – about why we fall in love and why we marry; about why we stay and why we go.

Harry Silver is a man coming to terms with a divorce and a new marriage. He has to juggle with time and relationships, with his wife and his ex-wife, his son and his stepdaughter, his own work and his wife's fast-growing career.

Meanwhile his mother, who stood so steadfastly by his father until he died, is not getting any younger or stronger herself.

In fact, everything in Harry's life seems complicated. And when he meets a woman in a million, it gets even more so . . .

Man and Wife stands on its own as a brilliant novel about families in the new century, written with all the humour, passion and superb storytelling that have made Tony Parsons a favourite author in over thirty countries.

Anthony Giardina

The Country of Marriage

'Welcome to the psyche of the married man. Through the eyes of the passive adulterer, the contented father, the guilty cheater and the cuckold, this strange and honest set of portraits affords insight into the masculine desire to act without making decisions or taking responsibility.'

SALLY FELDMAN, *Good Housekeeping*

'Here's a rare thing: a man writing about men and their marriages. And though these are regular, middle-aged Americans – medics, firemen, academics, with their wives, neighbours, kids and affairs – they're among the most gripping fictional characters I've ever encountered. Imagine all those monosyllabic guys in the books and movies of the past decade suddenly turning around and explaining themselves. Quite how Giardina makes domestic drama seem so urgent and thrilling is a mystery, but every story in this classic collection is a page-turner.'

JULIE MYERSON, *Mail on Sunday*

'Giardina's stories offer no lists of things to do to improve your marriage overnight. They simply describe what being inside a marriage is like, with elegant and often painful accuracy. His prose is full of insights which will make men nod in rueful recognition.'   BRANDON ROBSHAW, *Independent*

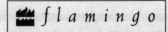